THE UNINVITED GUEST

By Jean Filewych

◆ FriesenPress

One Printers Way
Altona, MB R0G 0B0
Canada

www.friesenpress.com

Copyright © 2024 by Jean Filewych
First Edition — 2024

All rights reserved.

This is a work of fiction inspired by the author's own experiences. The characters, events, and timeline within this novel have been shaped for narrative purposes. Some organizations, medical facilities, and other locations are represented within the novel in accord with the author's experiences.

No part of this publication may be reproduced in any form, or by any means, electronic or mechanical, including photocopying, recording, or any information browsing, storage, or retrieval system, without permission in writing from FriesenPress.

ISBN
978-1-03-919572-1 (Hardcover)
978-1-03-919571-4 (Paperback)
978-1-03-919573-8 (eBook)

1. FICTION, FAMILY LIFE

Distributed to the trade by The Ingram Book Company

This novel is inspired by my late husband, Len Filewych, who lived a lifetime of grace and courage. This book is dedicated to the granddaughters that he never got to meet: Donatella and Alessandra.

Chapter 1: The Clarion Call
1992

"So, it's not all in my head?" Paul Fletcher asks the man sitting across the desk from him.

"Not at all," Carol hears the doctor tell her husband. Dr. Wilby's white coat sharply contrasts his red thick head of hair. It unnerves Carol that there are no family photos on his desk. Not a one.

The doctor continues. "The spinal tap confirms that you have multiple sclerosis." The neurologist holds up a small chart and points to the lowest bar with his sharpie. "But this black bar is where you *want* to be, the less severe form of this disease called relapsing-remitting multiple sclerosis, MS for short."

Carol peeks at the two bars above the black one. The top one is red, meaning danger she supposes.

He continues. "MS is an autoimmune disease, a fancy way of saying that your immune system is attacking your body, scarring the myelin sheath that covers your nerves." Dr. Wilby's tone gets conversational. "Think of myelin as the plastic covering on an old electrical cord that's getting hardened. Because your myelin is being scarred, Paul, there's a disruption in the electrical impulses being sent to your brain, a kind of short circuiting so that messages can't get through. That's what's causing your present symptoms."

Instant relief is visible on Paul's face. He pulls out a small paper from inside the breast pocket of his suit jacket, unfolds it, and reads aloud. "Blurry vision all morning. Off balance after lunch. Left leg dragging today. Pins and needles feeling in my legs and arms. Numb left cheek." Symptoms he's obviously documented for some time—something he's kept secret from his demure wife.

Carol listens—spellbound—at her husband's clandestine list, her wifely-role-hat slightly askew.

"You self-diagnosed yourself, Paul... just didn't know what name to give it," says the neurologist.

Paul looks up from his notes and begins telling the doctor about the time at work when a customer thought he was drunk because he was wobbling on his cane in the showroom. He couldn't even escort the customer outdoors to inspect a car on the lot, he tells the doctor.

Next, Paul delves into a lengthy explanation of something that had occurred at least a year ago now. "I was lying in the bathtub, and I couldn't stand up. It took fifteen minutes—over fifteen minutes—for my legs to work before I could get out of the water...."

"Not surprising," says Dr. Wilby. "Hot water brings out the symptoms of MS. It's called an *exacerbation.*" Previously, Paul had shared his bathtub incident with a doctor who worked at the Medicentre a few miles from their house. That doctor had told Paul to shower rather than bathe then. You'd think he'd have known about exacerbations.

"Remember, Paul," Dr. Wilby continues, "you have relapsing-remitting MS so you could go into remission at any time, and for a good long time, years even." The doctor smiles at them. "Some lifestyle changes are what I see for your foreseeable future, manageable ones besides the cane you're occasionally using now, I mean."

Is the neurologist trying too hard not to frighten us? Carol thinks as the doctor brings the appointment to its end.

The bathtub incident had become a source of humour for Paul's twisted family when he had shared his frightening experience with them. And no one had even wondered where he was for that length of time because they all knew that he was never one to sit around: pruning this or putting a first coat on that, washing a car, fixing a gate, volunteering at the local extended care centre, being a ball coach or a cub leader or a church council member.

Being held captive in a bathtub was the first *clarion call*—telling, if one were listening—that this was a manifestation of something *serious*. And they all missed it.

After the doctor visit, Paul and Carol go out for dinner as previously planned. But it's not the conversation Carol expected to have with her husband.

"I thought I was losing it, but something is actually wrong with me. I'm not imagining it." Paul sounds almost triumphant, certainly vindicated. As she listens, Carol fingers the silver bracelet Paul had bought her on their fifteenth wedding anniversary, six years ago now. They've picked out a charm for the bracelet every year since, often on their family holiday. She wonders if it brought them any good luck today, any at all.

Eventually the couple discuss how and with whom to share the diagnosis. They know that their daughter Heather—the only one of their three children still living at home—is at a volleyball practice at the university, but she won't be out late because she has an early morning class. And it won't be too late to call their twin sons either. Glen and his wife Tracy in Calgary; Nate and Julie in Vancouver.

Heather sits in their living room crying softly as her parents tell her of Dr. Wilby's diagnosis. Paul and Carol wait for the barrage of questions, but they never come. Her bedtime hug tells it all though—their daughter clings to them both as if she might be leaving and won't see them for a long, long time.

The phone call to Glen is essentially one-sided. An awkward silence is made more so over speakerphone. They can hear their daughter-in-law Tracy in the background and Glen ends the call by assuring his parents that she's listened in on the news.

The Vancouver call is not silent. Nate asks question after question. *Is this doctor a specialist? Are they going to get a second opinion? How old is this guy? What's the treatment? When do you see him again?* The latter is the only question that they answer. Carol reminds Nate to share the news with their daughter-in-law Julie who's not home at present.

And so, the couple survive day one. Diagnosis day. *Should we shorten it to D-Day?* thinks Carol as she crawls into bed beside her relieved husband. Her relief comes in another form. *At least it's not cancer,* she thinks before drifting off.

Carol makes an early morning call to her best friend Barb who just happens to be Paul's brother's wife. Barb is a travel agent, almost impossible to get a hold of during the day for personal calls. Barb needs to know the situation *tout de suite* because she's scheduled to pick Carol up for book club at 6:30 that very evening. Barb seems struck mute. John takes over the phone and asks to speak to his brother. Paul doesn't say much. John is obviously playing his big brother role to a tee—probably offering possible solutions to Paul's diagnosis—the counsellor role being big in the lives of these brothers. Carol is curious as to what exactly those suggestions might be today.

By day's end, the entire extended family know the news. For the next while, they huddle. It's what families do. Sarah,

The Uninvited Guest

Carol's mother, although tiny in stature has shoulders broad enough to carry the weight of this diagnosis. She focuses on her three grandchildren, the grandmother role central to her life as an extension of years being a single mom. Angie, Carol's little sister who is a dead lookalike for her (but a much sweeter version) seems most concerned about Carol. And Paul's brother John swoops in with advice every chance he gets.

Whenever the topic of the diagnosis comes up in the next weeks, Carol chimes in that Paul might finally get to work a bit less and have more time to develop new hobbies—see, not all bad news. Besides, Carol had just landed the speech therapist job of a lifetime mere months ago. She's trying to control the narrative in the story that she tells herself. Isn't it a kind of fate that after being a stay-at-home mom for most of her married life, she's venturing out into a career in speech therapy just as Paul is getting somewhat close to the time he could work part-time or retire? Paul had been her best cheerleader throughout these past four years of university studies as an adult student. And now, it's a role reversal of sorts—her turn to support Paul, she tells each of her family members in turn, albeit a bit untimely she must admit.

Carol's pep talks play right into her penchant for role-playing too. It feels exciting to anticipate a new role but she's not sure how MS fits in this newest story, nor can she quite put her finger on what to call her new role.

A niggling memory supplants her self-pep-talk: the twenty-year-old version of herself was in hospital giving birth to twins. Coincidently, Paul had ended up in the same hospital because he'd had, without apparent cause, lost the sight in his left eye. Upon his return to work, Carol had taken the follow-up call from a neurologist on that long-ago day.

The doctor had relayed the good news. "The inflammation in your husband's left eye has cleared up completely," Carol remembers him saying.

When the young wife had asked the cause of the sight loss, the doctor described it as one of those anomalies that sometimes happens and then just goes away. Carol does remember how relieved she felt when the doctor added, "Probably nothing to worry about."

Today, Carol feels a rush of gratitude to the doctor of her youth, whose name she doesn't recall. She believes in her heart of hearts, he made a calculated decision to spare this young husband and wife with newborn twin boys in tow from all the ghastly possibilities related to an inflammation of the optic nerve, giving them a reprieve of sorts.

What a blessed gift of time he bestowed upon this family, inadvertently or not. Years to add a wee baby girl to complete their family clan; years to grow into a solid, comfortable marriage, headed up by a man with a storied career in a car dealership whose natural business acumen was second only to his integrity. Best of all, Paul had years and years of the enjoyment of raising three children.

The doctor's reprieve had another effect though: it gave Carol ample time to develop into a serial worrier. Hers was not the garden-variety anxiety that most mothers feel from time to time—it was the debilitating kind which convinced her that the jealous gods might snatch her brood away from her at any moment. She trotted all three of her children to the pediatrician for all ailments—perceived or otherwise. She guarded them as they crossed the street. She held their hands to prevent falls on stairs. She was sore afraid.

She never shared her recurring nightmare with a soul, afraid to give it oxygen: in her night terror, a bear would come between her and one of the children as they threw rocks at a river's edge. She would wake—her heart pounding.

But her primordial fears were even more complicated: her mom, Sarah, had been widowed when Carol was five and her sister Angie, three. While juggling the raising of her two daughters and a job, Sarah was often distracted. Carol was determined that she would not repeat history. She would be an *undistracted stay-at-home mom,* her role distilled to three words: keep them safe.

As the children got older, she let down her guard—was unaware that the neurologist's reprieve was winding down.

But it wasn't the children, after all: it was Paul.

Paul has MS. Relapsing. Remitting. Multiple sclerosis.

Hiding in plain sight.

Chapter 2: Saving Her Marriage
1992

Paul puts off filing for his disability insurance.

As Carol folds towels in the bathroom one evening, she overhears him say to Heather, "The doctor said that I could still go into remission."

He delivers a different variation to Carol. "Sure, I'm having trouble with mobility... but not enough to call it a disability."

Eventually, Paul calls his insurance company only to learn how the insurance world operates. His plan to delegate the running of his car dealership to his co-owner George—to work part-time essentially—is a no go. In order to qualify for the benefit, Paul must choose between disabled (their word, not his) or employed. He chooses to forgo the benefit and work part-time.

Paul's body makes a different decision for him within six weeks: he simply cannot manage running the large Edmonton Chevrolet dealership. With or without a cane. Fatigue, dizziness, numbness, buckling knees, as well as his unsteady gait dictate the obvious to him.

Carol's glossed-over version of his transition from work to having more time for hobbies, turns out to be just that: glossed-over.

The Uninvited Guest

Good thing Paul is skillful at filling out forms: those for disability are extensive. Good thing too, that he kept a running list of his symptoms over time. These symptoms must be clearly described, dated, and verified by the doctor.

His business partner, George, having watched Paul struggle at work is not surprised to find himself brokering a deal for the sale of the dealership. But there's a twist, George soon finds out.

When Carol hears Paul's plan for the dealership sale, it sounds like a thought experiment.

"What if I offer George the opportunity to buy out my half of the dealership in installments, over... say, five years?" Carol holds her tongue for a change. "If during that time my MS goes into remission, I could sell for him—not run the business but sell cars—which is what I love best about the business anyway. We could build that option into the sales contract."

Carol cannot wait to hear George's reaction to the notion.

"He agreed," Paul tells her the very next evening.

She's relieved. And sad. And confused.

Her mother telephones to see how the dealership sale is progressing. It is Sarah who helps unravel Paul's surprise solution.

"I can see how Paul would like to have his finger in the pie for as long as possible, to know that what he's built over the years will survive," says Sarah.

Carol figures out the rest by herself in church. She's always been able to do some of her best thinking during Father Francis' homilies. Since Paul's diagnosis she's been grappling with her rollercoaster faith; today, the grappling switches to her husband's idea of not giving up his dealership completely.

Paul will still have hope. Even a faint hope of working again, is better than none.

Carol gets it now. She and her husband are clinging to the doctor's word—remission—each, in their own way.

So, Paul adds a faint hope clause to his new life and to the sales contract of the dealership. George is fully on board.

And so it comes to pass, in the late spring of 1993, after meetings with lawyers and everyone having signed on the dotted line that Paul leaves his office, most of his possessions packed away in boxes and stacked in the dealership storage room. He leaves with hope.

His sole key to the dealership he ran for years is to that storage room, the others having been turned over to George.

A staff member telephones Carol regarding Paul's send-off party. Carol is muddled as to what to call it. The staff eventually settle on Paul's Open House, as good a moniker as any, Carol supposes. During the event, the advertising manager, Betty, takes Carol aside.

"I can't believe Paul has to retire so young." Carol notices Betty fighting back tears as she speaks.

***

Paul begins to align himself to his post-career reality. He cleans. He cooks. Things he never got to do as a busy businessman. He is determined to master the washing machine and dryer.

"I haven't washed clothes since I was at college in Calgary," he reminds Carol.

She says one day, in not so quiet desperation: "Don't carry the laundry basket down the stairs… throw the clothes down to the basement so you'll have two hands for your cane and the railing."

But Carol seems to be worrying for nothing. Paul likes doing laundry. As well, he feels a bit stronger. Both wife and daughter listen to his concern that he may have pulled the ripcord on work too soon.

"Think I'll call George, let him know I'm better and can come in and sell a couple of days a week."

Then, things fall apart.

The very next day Paul cannot get out of bed. In a panic, Heather goes out and buys a wheelchair at a consignment store. "Just in case," is how she justifies the purchase to her mother.

"How did you get it home?" Carol asks.

"Bruce. My friend from school." Her daughter suddenly sounds self-conscious. "Bruce sometimes drops me off at the Claireview LRT after class, but today he drove me home and helped me unload the chair in the garage."

Hmm, a new name in her daughter's life, muses Carol.

When Paul gets going again, he tells Heather that he doesn't need the chair, but he does take Carol up on her suggestion to throw the clothes down the steps in a laundry bag instead of trying to navigate the twelve-step journey to the dungeon basement. When Paul vacuums, it turns into an extreme sport of sorts: the vacuum wand holding him up. The shopping cart in a grocery store acts in a similar fashion. And the day comes all too soon when even his right leg on the gas and brake in the car is suspect.

But it's not only his legs.

"My hands feel like wood. I can't even push a dumb grocery cart anymore," Paul expresses with a self-loathing Carol has never heard before.

As Paul struggles to unpack the groceries he's brought home, she hangs up his jacket. She takes his keys out of his pocket and comes across a handful of Paul's business cards, bringing her to the brink. The cards flutter from her hand and scatter on the hallway linoleum.

15

One day Carol comes home to find Paul cooking a steak perched atop one of their rec room bar stools set in front of the stove. Carol comes up from behind—startling him—to snap a picture. Proof that he's figuring out the solution to cooking dinner.

It's taking Carol longer to figure things out.

It isn't until the new year, her dutiful-wife-genes in overdrive, that she scours to find the pamphlet that Dr. Wilby had handed her on the day of Paul's diagnosis. She finds it stuffed in her bedside table drawer and reads the line that had previously caught her attention: *The collateral damage of living with MS is marital stress.*

Of course, she must act. To save her marriage.

One evening, while Paul files a few bank statements, Carol mentions her plan. "I've been thinking," she begins cleverly, "it might be nice for us to have some quality alone time."

"For sure," Paul answers readily.

"We always talk about how we need more exercise. Now that you have more time, we should join a Tai Chi class." She chooses her next words carefully. "Just the two of us and... and Tai Chi is a soft exercise that would be easy for both of us." Carol deliberately omits that the classes are specifically designed for persons with MS.

"I like the sound of the *two* of us," Paul tells his wife.

That's as much blessing as Carol needs to sign them up for Saturday classes at the MS Society.

On the day of the class, he doesn't even suggest that he drive. However, the couple can't agree on whether to bring the secondhand wheelchair sitting idly in the garage.

"I still can't figure out why Heather bought that thing in the first place," Paul says, his ire rising. "It doesn't make much sense going to an exercise class if I can't walk in on my own steam."

The Uninvited Guest

Carol crosses her legs and sits up straighter. "If you use the chair, you'll have more energy for the class." Paul frowns, seemingly unconvinced. "At least we know the MS Society is barrier-free, so maybe it's a place to try out the chair without anyone watching," Carol adds.

Paul relents. Driving to the MS Society with the wheelchair folded in the trunk of their car, Carol steals a glance at Paul, just so darn pleased with herself. She thanks Dr. Wilby in her head.

The tall slim instructor meets them, clipboard in hand, at a desk just inside the double doors of the foyer. She is both friendly and efficient, ticking off names. All participants at the class have MS or are the spouses of... brothers of... friends of, and so on. But not all have arrived in wheelchairs, as has Paul.

Sophie gathers them in the gym to begin the class. Paul leaves the wheelchair and stands with the group. The instructor's voice floats above the crowd. She pauses slightly between commands. "Plant your right foot in front of the other, as if you're taking a small step. Lift your arms shoulder high, if possible... now stretch your right arm forward."

Carol is smug. She's the petite wife, stretching impressively, next to her tall handsome husband. Sophie addresses the group. "Looking good, looking good."

Carol finds the movements rejuvenating. If their new life journey involves this elegant exercise, things are not that bad. Okay, so they're in the slightly run-down MS Society building, not some fancy schmancy spa, but think of all the benefits of this outing. She glances toward Paul but is surprised to find him no longer beside her. *Where is he?* She sees him sitting down... back in the wheelchair.

Guess he needs a little rest, she imagines.

Carol is left trying to reach her Zen state all on her own.

Back in the car, Carol chatters about how much she enjoyed the class. "Wasn't the instructor patient? And everyone so friendly?" She gesticulates wildly. "The time flew by... and next time maybe we should stop for a coffee, like a Saturday afternoon date."

"I hated it," Paul blurts out. "My balance was awful. I was dizzy. I felt like I was going to fall the whole time."

They don't return. Never learn another Tai Chi move. Never hear the instructor's mellifluous voice again. Never stop for coffee, after all.

Even with Tai Chi officially a no go, Carol forges on. She switches from exercise to support groups. Once more, she phones the MS Society. She marks the next meeting on the calendar and, lo and behold, the couple find themselves at the Society again, sitting in a haphazard circle comprised of six wheelchairs interspersed with folding chairs. That dreary Thursday evening, they are informed that Paul is a statistical anomaly. MS is a woman's disease: three to four women get the disease for every man.

Carol sits in her folding chair as a crying boy perched on his dad's lap stretches out his arms to a woman in a wheelchair beside them. She also bears witness to the sight of another woman whose arm dangles grotesquely (it slipped off the wheelchair armrest moments before) and her partner places it back where it belongs.

The lamentation from the youngest-looking woman in the group is haunting. "I don't think we could ever manage a baby right now," she says, glancing at her young husband.

Carol pushes Paul to the car and his chair feels a thousand pounds heavy. Once seated in the front seat, Paul places his numb left hand on her arm and declares, "Carol, that can't happen again. Ever."

Paul's right. They can't go back to the support group.

The Uninvited Guest

Carol can't believe what she did. She paraded people down a catwalk before Paul's eyes—all the terrifying sights and sounds of the varying stages of MS—that are probably now seared into his memory.

Carol makes a solemn vow that day: if Paul wants to avoid all things MS for the rest of his life, so be it. That is not how everyone would do this journey but it's Paul's journey and that's how he wants to do it.

Carol tries to make amends.

"Maybe we could hook up with John and Barb and go to a movie," she says to Paul one evening shortly thereafter, "or take Heather for dinner."

Paul nods. "Either one sounds good to me."

Occasionally, Carol can't help but wonder how the rest of the MS gang is doing down at the centre.

The women in chairs. The kids. Their husbands. Wives. Mothers. She wonders only in her head though. Never once giving voice to the thought.

Chapter 3: The Keys to the Castle
1993

Carol spends September testing her assigned students. She's much more familiar with the diagnostic tools and timeline of her duties, now that she's in her second year as the SLP (speech language pathologist). It's also helpful that she's at the same school, where everyone calls her by her first name. It took some getting used to, but she loves that for the first time in her adult life, she's not Paul's wife or Heather, Glen, or Nate's mom. She's Carol. It's exhilarating. She's added some art prints to her office this year, featuring inspirational sayings that her students noticed and commented on immediately. She loves the energy of junior high students.

From day one of working, Carol was determined not to be pulled into her home-life worries: she's instituted a firm rule that once she's left the house, she must park her worries about home—at home. Only after work as she nears home does Carol allow herself to think of Paul and what awaits her. But today, she's most worried about her daughter: Heather seems stressed *all the time*. She loves everything about university, so that's not it.

Carol shares her work rule with her daughter one day as Heather hangs her book bag in the back porch, but Heather doesn't comment. Carol can't decide whether her daughter thinks it's a cruel solution to a cruel problem or simply knows that compartmentalizing to that degree is beyond her.

Carol's two sons are slightly removed from the Fletcher adjustments, living in different cities, getting their information second-hand; it's even more complex because the versions of the stories they get differ dramatically, depending on whom they are talking to.

"We're managing just fine," Carol says to her son in Calgary. "No need to worry… we're fine."

To Nate, in Vancouver, she delivers her "we're okay" assessment with more fervor, determined not to worry this young man who is by nature given to anxiety. It's not only her marriage that needs saving.

Carol's suspicion is that Heather gives her brothers the real goods, *falling* and *unsafe*, most likely the two predominant words of those late-night sibling conversations.

Later in the school year, it all comes to a head.

"When I got home from school, Dad was lying on the sidewalk next to the tulip bed." Heather pauses.

"Oh no," Carol says.

"He looked pretty calm, considering."

Carol can imagine Paul using this new vantage point as an opportunity to admire his handiwork up close, perhaps remembering an earlier spring in his life planting those very tulip bulbs.

"I ran across the alley to get Bob. He helped me get Dad to his feet."

"I'm so glad Bob was home," Carol answers.

"Dad seemed embarrassed and kept thanking Bob."

The severity of the situation and its implications are not lost on Carol as her daughter winds down her story.

Next day, Carol watches as her determined daughter hauls in the second-hand wheelchair from the garage—drawing a line in the sand, as only a daughter can do—and says, "Either you use this thing, Dad, or I'm not going to school."

So, Paul is forced to trade legs for wheels.

A few weeks later, not a one of their family figures out exactly how it comes to be that Paul's fraternity, the Knights of Columbus, show up on a Saturday morning offering to build a wheelchair ramp. They enter the house briefly to talk to Paul, but mostly they need to measure the width of his chair. They show up prepared: before long the men are hammering and nailing unpainted plywood to create a steep walkway with rails from the front steps of their house to the sidewalk.

Carol passes the front door wheelchair ramp every morning on the way to work and it never fails to startle her.

While it's true that Heather's solution of her dad wheeling himself around the house is safer, Carol soon realizes that it's not the energy saver that they had both hoped it would be. Once the pedals are off the chair, his weak legs need to do all the work especially on days that his hands and arms are too weak to roll the chair.

"If only my hands worked better," Paul laments, "I could work an electric chair."

One Saturday morning Carol notices firsthand Paul's challenges. She thinks back to the barrier-free bathrooms she's seen and suddenly understands why there's empty space rather than cabinets beneath the countertops. Their bathroom is long and narrow so there's no way the pedals on the wheelchair can be left on. Paul sits, sidled up to the sink—at a right angle—his stocking-feet on the floor. He bends sideways awkwardly reaching for the taps. Forget about looking into the mirror as he sits in his chair, even for a man as tall as Paul. He uses a hand mirror for shaving but can barely manage holding it and his electric shaver. It's as if danger is written all over him. Buckling legs. Fumbling hands. Shaving blind. He can't win.

Paul needs more than a wheelchair to make this work, thinks Carol. *We must make some changes around here. If we can just hold on until summer.*

***

A watershed moment occurs even before summer.

By now, the well-established dynamic is that Paul is home alone, all day long. He manages a nifty side transfer from wheelchair to bed every afternoon to rest. Surprisingly—or perhaps not, considering Paul's fascination with all things on wheels—he's good at the transfer.

More surprising is that he's the one tired all the time now, whereas in the entirety of their married lives together, it was Carol in constant need of a nap. She remembers taking every opportunity—unlike the other stay-at-home moms she hung out with—to crash on their living room couch when her twins were napping. Of course, two babies napping at the same time was a thing to behold, resulting in a call to Paul at work to boast of her triumph.

But on this watershed day, no one is boasting. This is how it went down, according to the rendition Paul relates to his wife and daughter once they're both home.

"The doorbell rang when I was in bed, but I knew I couldn't get to the door in time, so I let it ring. It rang twice more." He continues, "A couple of minutes later, I heard clomping up the stairs from the basement and someone opening the back door."

"Are you saying that one guy opened the back door for another guy?" asks Heather, sounding horrified.

"Yup," Paul says, "then in seconds I heard footsteps in the hall. I looked up at two men... well actually, they looked like teenagers, standing in the bedroom doorway."

Carol is envisioning the culprits as they stood in their doorway—suspended in time—and imagines their surprise when they realized that someone was at home, in bed.

"Before I could think straight, the teens were out the front door. Gone."

Their neighbour Dale fills in the rest of the story when he drops in after dinner, explaining that he witnessed two teenagers catapult out the Fletchers' front door as he was driving by the house. Dale stopped and entered the open front door to check on Paul.

Being the good neighbour that he is, thinks Carol.

"Maybe I should have driven right into those lowlifes, would've served them right," Dale says, looking directly at Paul seated before him in his wheelchair.

Carol and Heather take Dale downstairs to see the broken bedroom window, the teenagers' point of entry. Paul's too tired for the trek.

Carol's mind reels. What if the invaders had spotted the wheelchair sitting next to the bed? What if they had panicked? What if they'd had a weapon? Carol vaguely remembers reading a news story a few years ago about a woman right here in Edmonton: stabbed to death in her own home while investigating a noise in the middle of the night.

Heather is crying; Carol is scared; Dale and Paul are discussing insurance claims. *Will we ever have ordinary things to be sad about again?* Carol wonders.

A moment of truth: Paul cannot be alone all day.

"So... what... now I need a babysitter?" Paul asks, when confronted with Carol and Heather's solution the day after the home invasion.

"Do you want me to quit my job in my second year to look after you?" Carol asks. She knows it's an unfair ultimatum—a Sophie's choice, for sure. Her husband has lived an entire lifetime granting his wife her heart's desire. Made it his life's work, in fact.

When his brother John stops by later that day, he frames the ultimatum more generously. "It's good you figured out that Carol and Heather need a little help since your diagnosis."

In the end, Paul makes only one demand of the homecare agency that Carol contacts for some daytime help. "I don't want a woman hanging around here seeing me like this," he says. "Tell them to send a man."

So, they send one. A young man.

Carol was never territorial about her home, not even her kitchen—heck, especially her kitchen—and has no trouble turning over her husband and their home to the man named Darryl who enters their lives. Darryl's shift will begin at seven in the morning and end at noon, weekdays.

Carol knows in the marrow of her bones from having lived with Paul for over two decades that Paul's adaptive skills are superb—and these last months have corroborated her belief. So, unless Darryl is an axe-murderer, Paul will be fine.

But he's not fine when the topic of the house key comes up.

"Why don't we just pass out keys to the whole damn neighbourhood?" Paul says, agitated.

His career has been cut short, his identity of being the sole supporter of their family gone, his car replaced with a wheelchair, he's about to lose his privacy and beloved solitude because of a failing body, and he's fretting about a key to the back door.

And by the way, which one of these losses would the neurologist consider 'manageable' lifestyle changes?

As Carol walks Darryl down their hall early next morning, he's chattering.

"It took me two buses to get to your house. The number five took me as far as the Coliseum stop. The number seventy got me here." He does not have to tell them that he's from Newfoundland; his accent gives it away. "The second bus was late. Almost ten minutes late."

Carol assigns Darryl's chatter to nerves, not yet realizing how chatty a fellow he is.

Darryl is dressed in a pinstripe button-down shirt and beige cotton pants that barely reach his ankles. Not the usual uniform of t-shirt and blue jeans of his generation. *Not even sneakers*, thinks Carol. It seems he dressed up for his first day of work but could do nothing to tame his curly dirty blond hair. He looks awfully young. And vulnerable somehow, but Carol's not certain why she thinks so.

Paul's dependency on Darryl develops rather quickly. *The readiness is all*, is what Carol makes of it.

She's not privy to Paul handing over control to Darryl, bit by bit, for tasks that the rest of the able-bodied masses take for granted. But she's witnessed her husband struggle enough times—to pour milk over his cereal or fill a glass with juice or uncap his toothpaste tube—that she can easily imagine Darryl's morning routine taking shape.

Darryl's affable Newfoundland ways seem to put Paul at ease. Even the unmentionables—like zipping up pants or undoing buttons or tucking in a shirt, or horror of horrors, transferring Paul from wheelchair seat to toilet seat—must be going well because Carol hears nary a word about them. *Does Paul ever have protest dreams about how fast he got here?* Carol wonders.

Darryl becomes Paul's legs and arms, and Paul seems nothing but appreciative. If he feels otherwise, it doesn't show.

The Uninvited Guest

And that's all the proof Carol needs to know that she's made the right decision: working outside the home instead of caring for Paul, that is. Besides, she wants to remain his wife, not become his nurse.

***

The recent onset of renovations to make their home wheelchair-friendly are synchronized with Darryl's arrival. It's a busy house now. And noisy. Drafty too, when a window or door must be removed or relocated.

The renovations present a united purpose for Paul and Darryl. But something else brings them together: both face difficult circumstances in their lives. Paul's woes are visible; Darryl's, not so much. Paul relays his first bump in the road with Darryl to Carol that evening.

"I asked him to make a list that I could use when tradespeople and construction workers show up for instructions or with questions... but I could tell he was reluctant."

"Really?" Carol said.

Carol hears the rest of the story. Seems that Darryl fessed up to Paul that he had not finished high school. "He told me he's a terrible speller," Paul says.

And there's more. "Darryl said that when his parents divorced when he was in grade ten, he wanted to help out so he quit school and got a job. He was vague about the whereabouts of his father but said that he's in touch with his mom regularly. He's an only child too."

It's as if Darryl reawakens Paul's fatherly instincts. It's been a long time since Paul's had to instruct anyone. Darryl now has his own tutor, and he takes to it, like a duck to water.

In time, Darryl is making lists for the construction workers, moving from single words to short sentences. Paul has his student refer to the dictionary often, being patient as Darryl hones his spelling skills.

One morning when Carol is at home with a cold, she enters the kitchen to find Darryl seated at their kitchen table. He looks up from a small notebook and says, "Oh, I thought you'd already left for work."

Carol spies Darryl covertly slipping a paperback dictionary into the open backpack at his feet.

Seems like Darryl is taking his tutelage with Paul a step further– all on his own.

In short shrift, Darryl is the one holding the phone speaking to tradesmen, referring to the list he'd written at Paul's request. The backyard workers come to rely on him too, often bypassing Paul to ask him questions.

The family display a wonderful photo of Darryl, sitting atop a backhoe in their backyard (a worker's idea, apparently) just moments before the machine is about to break ground to dig an elevator shaft. These are heady days.

Darryl's literacy lessons take a turn one morning, creating some high drama. For one reason or another, Carol is more frantic than usual in her preparation to get out the door. As she is leaving, she apologizes to Darryl for having been so erratic that morning.

Later, Heather shares with Carol what she overheard at breakfast before leaving for university: "Darryl mentioned to Dad that you were sure *erotic* when you left for work."

Carol raises her eyebrows.

Heather chuckles as she tells her mom how the discussion ended. "Dad tried to correct Darryl and said that he might mean to say that you were *erratic*. But Darryl doubled down, repeating that you were sure *erotic* this morning, Mom."

"I think the mistake had more to do with pronunciation than word usage," Carol says, matching her daughter's chuckling.

Paul being Paul, he extends his literacy lessons to include the large globe that stands strategically at his right hand in the sitting room.

"What does a globe have to do with the renovations?" Carol asks Paul playfully. She answers her own question: "Nothing."

"Well, I was thinking that Darryl is a young man and when he gets his car, he might want to take a holiday or two." Paul grins. "He's already pointed out the small town near St. John's that he's from."

The family see right through Paul: he's still curious about where cities and capitals are located, the distances between cities and where he might go next. He can't help himself.

Watching the two men with explorers' hearts poring over the globe is Carol's guilty pleasure. It does not matter that these journeys will never happen. It's a geography lesson for the ages.

Carol cannot hide her Cheshire cat grin.

Chapter 4: Gold, Frankincense, and Myrrh
1994

Months later when most of the renos are complete, Heather gives her Grandma Sarah and Aunt Angie the full tour, including the state-of-the-art newly installed Shindler elevator. Heather explains that it stops at three levels: the backyard, living, and basement. It was Paul's idea that the elevator descends to the rec room, which automatically necessitated the digging of a shaft below ground to grant basement access. The consensus between Carol and her children was that it was well worth the extra cost.

Paul sits in his lift chair in the sitting room, awaiting the completion of the reno tour. The innovation of this hydraulic lift chair—their newest piece of furniture—had surprised Carol as it can lift Paul to an almost standing position.

As Heather, Sarah, and Angie exit the elevator, Carol arrives from the kitchen with the sandwich lunch she's been preparing for the whole lot of them.

"This elevator's going to make your lives a lot easier," says Angie.

The Uninvited Guest

Sarah glances at Paul adding, "And imagine the resale value this adds to your house." Carol hopes the money-whispering works.

Early in the renovations, Paul had been stewing about finances. "We're dipping into our retirement savings even with the extra dealership sales money coming in," Paul had told her as the reno costs piled up. Carol had tried to hint that these *were* Paul's retirement years, what he'd spent years saving for. She had never envisioned having to replace the word retirement with *handicapped*.

It's satisfying to claim their house back from tradespeople and workers. Besides, everyone agrees that the renovations are impressive.

In addition to the amazing elevator, other accommodations were made. Paul's bathroom now sits discreetly off the sitting area, behind a nifty space-saving sliding pocket door. In this spacious addition, the wheelchair is easily sidled up to the toilet plus the barrier-free shower and sink allow Paul much more independence.

The centre of gravity in their home shifts from the kitchen and dining area to the new sitting room. What was once a small bedroom that housed twin boys in bunk beds is now two and a half times its original size. An arch replaces the once standard doorway, widened and built on an angle at the end of the hallway for easier wheelchair access, giving this otherwise modest bungalow a grand doorway. The addition is on the west side of the house: hence, it gets dubbed the *West Wing*. The nickname sticks and causes many a raised eyebrow when Carol welcomes visitors to the West Wing.

But it's the outdoor changes that delight Paul most. A new elevated deck looks out on the plum tree Paul planted long ago. A custom-sized set of patio doors allow a full view of the new deck and yard, now maintained by their homecare worker and their daughter. The renovation crew dismantled the wooden ramp that the Knights of Columbus fraternity had kindly erected, then poured new sidewalks the entire length of their lot, more than wide enough to accommodate Paul's wheelchair. The wider walks and the installation of the elevator allow Paul to reclaim his front yard.

For Paul, to be able to enjoy the outdoors again—even through windows—softens the blow of the laundry list of unpleasant adjustments thrust upon them, pretty much daily now. Yet, it feels like a bit of a tease to Carol. Never mind. Paul gets to be house-proud and yard-proud yet again.

The completed renovations allow Carol to more easily cast aside the obvious—how much more help Paul needs with every task. Her smugness is a better frame of mind for battle than fear.

In the meantime, the family begin to purchase other items too. The biggest is a new wheelchair.

Cancer survivors get to ring a bell to signal that they have finished treatment, a small reward to motivate them during difficult days. Could ordering a new wheelchair possibly become small compensation for diminishing mobility?

Paul peppers the Healthcare and Rehab personnel with questions when they arrive to do measurements for the chair, as this one will be built to specs for Paul's height and weight. *"Do the tires ever need replacing?"* *"Where is the wheelchair made?"* *"How much does it weigh?"* Turns out, purchasing anything with wheels brings Paul pleasure.

Carol's mind drifts to the secondhand scooter they had purchased two summers ago. Paul had taken it for an occasional spin down the back alley. Too soon though, dizziness and imbalance made it unsafe. That vehicle is now a relic gathering dust in their garage, a sombre reminder that this pox upon their house is not going away anytime soon.

The Uninvited Guest

Paul must be pushed in his new wheelchair from day one.

Pushing the chair around is the very least they can do as Paul is forced to give up one set of wheels after another. Knowing Paul's meticulous nature, they are careful not to drive the chair into a wall, or scuff its tires, or leave it muddy after an outing. Carol buys a sheepskin piece that fits over the high-tech cushion that graces the chair. She has the Healthcare and Rehab people fashion removable arm rests out of the sheepskin too. Both measures are specifically designed to guard against skin ulcers. It's all good. Or so it seems.

A pert occupational therapist arrives at their door a few weeks after the wheelchair team to do a mobility assessment. She is vehemently making a pitch: the replacement of their bed for a mechanical one. "It can be cranked up so that a patient can be easily sponge-bathed or even eat breakfast in bed. It's also ideal for transferring to a wheelchair because the height of the bed can be adjusted."

But Paul washes his face at the sink and eats at the kitchen table, Carol wants to scream. Why doesn't this woman know that or ask that? Can't she stray from the script in her head for one minute to respond to the needs of the couple in front of her?

The pert woman resumes her pitch. "The mechanical bed is important too because as mobility diminishes, changing positions wards off bedsores, and even backaches." She ends with startling information that frankly had never dawned on Carol. "Being upright as much as possible is essential to keep the body's internal organs working."

The therapist finally switches gears. She pulls out eating utensils from the bag at her feet, a spoon, a fork, and a knife—each with dense white foam slid over the handle.

"These make holding the fork or spoon easier," she says as if she's discovered a cure for MS.

"Thanks," Paul says, "I'll see how it works."

That evening he tries the fork with the foam-covered handle. He sets it down suddenly though and blurts out to Carol, "I'm so much trouble. Why don't you just... just... put me... in a home, or something?"

"Is that what you'd do with me, if I had MS?" Carol reactively shoots back at Paul, silencing him.

The evening is shattered.

But it gets worse. "Is the therapist going to ask me to stop wearing my wedding ring next?" Paul says.

"What does your wedding ring have to do with anything?" Carol asks. Though deep inside, she intuits what her husband is hinting at.

Besides, his attachment to that ring is well-documented family lore, the ring having slipped off his finger while swimming in a lake on a camping trip a decade before. Paul dove deep into the cold water, time after time, determined to retrieve it. And he did. The ring is now a testament to both his marriage and his strong lungs.

But he can't dive into the water to save their matrimonial bed: before his eyes, it's being dismantled and replaced with a cold, industrial steel one.

A huge triumph for MS.

The couple each mourn this loss in their own way. Carol, white-knuckled-hanging-on, insisting that she's okay; and Paul, well, his face tells another story. Even their three adult kids have a hard time getting used to the newest addition to their parental home, preferring a visit with their dad in his new lift chair in the sitting room.

They say time heals all things. Carol certainly hopes this truism holds.

Carol thinks some retail therapy might soften the blow: she buys expensive Egyptian cotton sheets and pillowcases in Paul's favourite colour, blue, and a luxurious geometrically-patterned quilt, blue as well. Somehow it ends up looking like a child's bed. Paul does not seem to notice the childish look, but he continues fretting.

Carol tries more damage control: she assures him that she will lie beside him daily, after work, during his rest period, and it will be easier because they can incline the bed if they want to talk.

Herein lies the rub: she's afraid to broach what she knows is really bothering her husband about the removal of their marriage bed, the intimacy it stands for. They are a shy couple who never even mustered up the courage to have *the talk* with each child as he or she hit puberty. Besides, discussions of intimacy for the handicapped, even on radio and TV, are still societal taboos, so why would it be any different for Carol and Paul?

Carol, who now reads everything related to autoimmune diseases, recently came across a newspaper article written by a young man battling ALS. He was rapidly losing ability after ability. One statement from the article stayed with her: *The first thing we have is our body and the last thing we have is our body.* It frightened Carol.

The one advantage of the hospital bed that Paul appreciates immediately is sitting in an upright position allowing him to look at a newspaper, a map, or even a gas bill propped up on his beanbag tray in front of him. Paul is no longer the savvy businessman in a suit and tie reading the journal every morning at their breakfast table. But he is still reading, his brain fully alive. The occupational therapist has redeemed herself somewhat, for the moment, at least.

The problem of where Carol sleeps, now that they no longer have a double bed, is easily solved: they buy a futon mattress. It stands upright, like a foot soldier by day, in the roll-in shower— unfurled nightly on the floor and placed parallel to Paul's hospital bed. Early-to-bed people their whole-live-long-lives-through, Paul and Carol have one less adjustment to make as he's in bed by 9:30, and she in her futon shortly thereafter.

"Lucky for me," Carol brags in her *I'm okay* voice, "I can fall asleep anywhere... just like my mom."

And she can. Even the radio that Paul listens to before falling asleep does not disturb her. And if Carol is awake late enough, she hears overseas broadcasts which she thoroughly enjoys—a much needed escape to another land. Their country's national broadcasting station, CBC, is a welcome soundtrack to their new lives.

The Fletchers follow the other advice given by the occupational therapist by installing four strategically placed floor-to-ceiling poles throughout their home: one beside Paul's toilet, one by his sitting room lift chair, one by the hospital bed, and even one in their formal living room, though he seldom gets there anymore. Carol is trying hard to make 'function over form' her new life's mantra regarding home style but every time she glances at one of the steel poles she conjures up a seedy men's club. There's no beautifying them either. Grey industrial steel.

To put things in perspective, the poles are tremendous back-saving devices for all who aid Paul with his mobility: as Paul sits in his wheelchair, he reaches up to grab the pole, then pulls and lifts himself to standing, greatly assisting with any attempted transfer.

As well, Paul seems energized every time he's standing. Not quite walking but using his legs, his body momentarily upright. Wobbly, but standing, nonetheless. This is as good as it gets.

How many more times are they going to have to move the goalposts (grey steel utility ones) in this journey?

The Uninvited Guest

The answer comes sooner than they think. One evening in February, at dinnertime, Heather lies to both her dad and mom. "I'm spending too much time on the LRT getting to and from the university."

Later in the evening, out of earshot of her dad she confesses, "Our house is like Grand Central Station run amok." She looks her mom in the eyes. "I just have to leave."

Carol's rant as she reclines on her futon-bed that night is long. Silent too. Long, silent, and frantic.

She's sick of it, all of it, including hearing the broken record of Paul's gratitude expressed every time he receives help: *Thanks for getting my breakfast, Thanks for doing my leg exercises, Thanks for getting the newspaper. Thanks for the travel brochure. Thanks for the atlas.* It's a constant reminder of all that he cannot do.

And it sounds like a Dr. Seuss book. *Thanks for that. Thanks for this. Thanks for every tiny bit.* That's what she feels like screeching on her bad days. Maybe her only daughter, her tea buddy, is sick of it too.

She hates what this disease is doing to their lives. Perhaps, if this uninvited guest had not shown up on their doorstep, Heather would not be leaving.

In late March, the couple become empty nesters.

Heather keeps insisting that her mom can drop over for tea at her new digs, any old time. And that she'll be back at the house constantly to visit and cut the grass. Carol misses seeing Heather's schoolbag hanging in the back porch or spying her sensible school shoes on the mat at the back door. Misses their evening girl chats. Misses overhearing Heather's voice on the phone in the late evenings. Probably talking to Bruce, the name popping up more and more frequently these days.

As usual, Paul finds something positive to focus on: "Our youngest is sure independent. She's growing up."

With Heather gone, Carol's after school routine with Paul has become more important to steady her, clear her head. Today though she doesn't get the solace she was hoping for. Paul is propped up, as if ready for their pre-dinner chat, but on second glance she realizes that he's staring at something on his beanbag tray. He gives her a perfunctory nod as she hangs her blazer in the closet.

Then she sees it clearly. His prized possession—his driver's license—propped up against his well-worn brown wallet on the beanbag tray.

Seeing the driver's license reminds Carol of the recurring dream Paul has had of late, clear evidence of his internalized sorrow manifesting as driving dreams.

"I can't take my foot off the gas," he'll complain while still seemingly asleep. Or "I can't put my foot on the brake." Sometimes his words harken back to a bygone era of drinking and driving. "The beer between my legs is going to spill."

Usually, Carol foggily tries to appease Paul from her futon.

"You're in bed, honey. Try to sleep," she tells him.

Other nights, Carol delivers tough love in her sternest voice.

"Paul, you're not in the car. Go back to sleep."

Upon waking one night, Carol feels inspired, goes along with the dream—heck, embraces it even.

"I've put my foot on the brake, so no need to worry."

Paul sees right through her. Always could. Even in his dreams.

"I didn't see your leg move, so how could it be on the brake?"

This man took pure unadulterated joy in the physical act of driving; no wonder he still dreams about it. The next time she's awoken from her sleep, she's going to put down the steel bar on the side of the bed, climb in, snuggle in close, adjust the mirror, rustle the road map, and ask Paul where he'd like to go. They'll go anywhere his heart desires.

The Uninvited Guest

It would be just like in their early married life, road trip after road trip, national park after national park, zoo after zoo, dam after dam. Camping spot after camping spot. Kids in tow.

Paul loved documenting their journeys. Since he couldn't drive and document simultaneously, Carol obliged: she penned details as dictated by her husband. She wrote in a small, white coil-notebook, one of many the energy company mailed to their home yearly, as advertising. But while she began these duties with enthusiasm, Carol soon tired of the task. Nevertheless, she always wrote down the gas mileage they were making as this seemed like gospel to Paul, his frugality on full display.

Once back home from a trip, Carol had no recollection of how the white coil-notebook got from glove compartment to house: it was only by the grace of God that those books still existed, their fate not falling into the hands of a too-tidy wife, exercising her right to purge.

Honestly, she could not have imagined all those years ago that the words in the white coil-notebooks that she was writing in—those seemingly puny records—would one day bring to life the many places Paul and his family had traveled to. The gas prices did matter, because they conjured up places they'd visited in bygone days; the campsite names sparked funny stories like the one about the crow trying to tug a steak off the picnic table when Paul momentarily walked away to fetch the barbecue sauce. The bridges and dams and names of mountain ranges reminded them of where the family had hiked. Paul walking. With ease. Walking.

The gods have no ordinary man on the ropes here.

Those small, coil notebooks are the gold, frankincense, and myrrh of their lives.

Jean Filewych

Mea culpa, mea culpa, mea culpa, Carol murmurs in her head as she snuggles into bed beside Paul, *why did I not take more care to capture the glinting sun dancing off the shiny, healthy bodies of my family in the swimming pool—especially Paul's—splashing and jumping up to spike the beach ball to one of our children? Why, oh why, did I not document the night sky just outside our motorhome window? Or write down every story the kids told around the evening campfire?*

Paul interrupts Carol's reverie saying, "Honey, could you please put my driver's license away?"

She leans over and tucks the driver's license neatly into its rightful place in Paul's scratched, brown leather wallet.

Naturally, he keeps it.

Chapter 5: Going to the Movies
1995

A line from Robert Frost's poem creeps into Carol's mind one late autumn evening: *Yet knowing how way leads on to way, I doubted if I should ever come back....*

She hates it but it follows her around like a catchy earworm jingle.

Maybe the poetry has to do with the reality that Paul has really become wheelchair-bound, as much as Carol doesn't want to admit it. Paul's steadfast assessment of his *dumb MS hands* is turning out to be too true. It's obvious that Paul will never sell cars again.

In a few months, it will be their third Christmas since Paul's diagnosis. Last year, he could not get out of the car easily nor could the wheelchair be easily pushed through a snowy tree lot, so he watched from inside the car as Carol and Heather picked out a tree. Carol still had principles then: it had to be a real tree. This year, she finds herself eyeing the blue and green fake ones lined up in the aisles of department stores, trying to erase her memories of snowflakes gently falling in a tree lot.

One weekend, Carol decides it's time to tidy up the basement storage room. What a mistake. She unearths the outside Christmas lights which trigger her Christmas nostalgia further. She remembers the marvelous photo of Heather, age eleven or so, perched on a stepladder three quarters of the way up, her dad threading Christmas lights to her, the clips on the front of the house barely visible above Heather's head. Paul wears his lovely beaver hat, set back on his wavy-haired head; Heather wears navy blue earmuffs. Father and daughter look Christmas-card-happy in the lightly falling snow. Carol quickly puts the lights back in their basement grave.

But she cannot stop her thoughts. The office Christmas parties are long gone. The family ritual of playing cribbage or the card game passed down by their late grandfather, gone by the wayside. Dropping cards made the games more ordeal than fun. Why, oh why, is she reliving these happy days? *Funny, Paul never brings any of this up.*

Carol finds herself sharing a week's worth of Christmas angst late one November night when she visits Heather at her apartment. "The hardest part of Christmas is watching your dad." Her breathing speeds up. "And everyone is supposed to be happy." Her voice rises in volume. "How in the world can we be happy while your dad sits there?" Carol is wailing now. "I can't stand it."

"Dad still enjoys Christmas," Heather insists. "He's our official cookie taster when we make Grandma Pearl's famous shortbread recipe." There's a longer pause. "And, we can start new traditions that work."

"The shortbread will probably make him cough. And what's with all his coughing lately?" Carol asks her daughter.

"Mom, please," sighs Heather.

On her drive back home, Carol feels defeated. She has only enough energy to feel guilty about sharing her Christmas sorrow with Heather. She wishes that they could just lose Christmas this year.

The Uninvited Guest

The church tries to save Christmas for them. A week or so before the 25th, a group from their congregational choir show up at the house with musical instruments in hand. Unheralded, dressed in red and green. But even the matching colours annoy Carol. She's obviously beyond redemption.

"Thought you could use a little Christmas cheer," says one member of the foursome standing before Paul in their sitting room. They play and sing a few carols. "Any favourite you'd like to hear?"

Paul thinks a moment and then says, "*Greensleeves.*"

They don't immediately recognize the carol.

Paul clears up the confusion. "I think it's sometimes called *What Child Is This?*"

"Of course," the lead singer says, before breaking into song once more. When the carolers leave, Paul wonders aloud if they should have offered them a drink.

"No," says Carol sharply. "They're from church, for Pete's sake." Her mood remains morose.

This year there will be no Fletcher cousins to share Grandma Pearl's homemade sausage, homemade bread, and homemade pickles. Those activities and people are but a quaint memory from their happy past. There will be no Midnight Mass either. No Boxing Day ice-fishing crew at Hanmore Lake taking delight in watching Grandpa Steve use an auger to fashion a hole in the thick ice.

But the kids and their spouses do make it home for the holidays. And they do make their yearly batch of Christmas shortbread with Paul as the official cookie tester; he coughs only once. Thankfully it does not escalate.

Also, as usual, they listen to *The Messiah* on CBC as they prepare the turkey and hear that *unto them a child is born who shall be called wonderful.* The trumpet does sound in almost every room of their home. Bing Crosby croons about a *White*

Christmas. More than once. But Paul's favourite is clear: *The Nutcracker Suite.* Paul listens to the piece throughout the year, too.

Thankfully when Carol's at work. The piece annoys her, far too whimsical for her taste.

Sombre and dark work better for her. Especially since each Christmas seems to bring a more Scrooge-like version of the holiday. One of these days, she'd like to put on a requiem—blaring it loudly—and see what they all say about that—Mozart's Requiem, for sure.

And yet, after a surprisingly uneventful Christmas Day, the family gather once more on Boxing day before they head home. Carol sees her kids and their spouses settle in at the card table for one last night of cards; she hears Paul ask Nate to push him to the end of the table so he can watch.

What fun can that be? Carol wonders to herself. *I know how much he'd rather be playing.* She takes her sadness to the kitchen and unloads the dishwasher, listening to the laughter in the next room.

After the card game, Glen calls his mom back into the room. "We have a surprise for everyone before we leave. Let's go to the movies..." He pops a video into the VCR and says, "It's called *Dad's Life.*"

"Hang on Glen. What's a movie without popcorn?" Heather quips, obviously in on the surprise. She slips into the kitchen while the family jockey for position around the television. Nate parks the wheelchair front and centre so Paul has the best view.

Carol notices Paul eying the popcorn Heather is handing around to the crowd. As she hands Darryl a small bowl that he will inevitably share with Paul, Carol worries about an inevitable coughing fit.

Glen had enlisted his sister as an assistant (unpaid, of course) and used a work video camera to show off some of the

The Uninvited Guest

film-study prowess that had recently landed him a job editing in a Calgary newsroom. Film studies was where Glen had met his wife, Tracy.

The movie begins. "This was your first home, Mom and Dad," Glen reports to the world as he stands on a sidewalk, microphone in hand.

Carol notices Heather look over and smile at her dad.

"It was 1971," Glen says, pointing to the modest four-story brick apartment building behind him. "Looks like a pretty nice place for a first apartment."

Carol jumps up and points out the exact window of their basement suite.

Next, the camera catches Glen's movements, up and down the street. "I'm doing a forensic search for the ruins of the Royalite Service Station you worked at, Dad. The one you worked at when you left Smoky Lake as a young man. Stay tuned."

Glen pauses the video, turns to the group and says, "We didn't realize until we got there that the building had been torn down. We were looking for a shadow building but didn't know it."

"I heard that it was torn down a few years ago," Paul acknowledges.

Glen presses play and Paul's last place of employment comes up on screen. It's an impressive car dealership on an expansive corner lot: new Chevrolets in various colours fan out on either side of the building.

"Here is your dealership Dad," Glen reports, standing beside a turquoise car. "Where you and George were running the whole show." He looks into the camera and winks.

The amateur filmmakers create a little slapstick comedy at their next location: the curling club that Paul played at for years. Heather zooms in on her brother who mimics Paul's unmistakable upright-square-shouldered curling delivery, right there on dry pavement, minus the broom and granite rock. "Now, who does this remind you of?"

Glen's special effects may not be tricking the eye, but they are certainly tricking the heart.

The documentarians end with a sentimental trip down the memory lane of their childhood to the elementary school they'd all attended. Heather zooms in on the small door at the side of the school that released them as little people—so many years before.

Glen continues, "This was where you picked us up, Dad." Heather does a cutaway to the bike racks. Glen points. "I remember you standing right there smoking your pipe. Then, we'd pile into the car—not a seatbelt in sight—and go home for lunch."

In that moment, Carol realizes that all this happened long before it was in vogue for fathers to do school drop-offs or pick-ups, never mind lunches. Ah, fatherhood—Paul was to the manner born.

Glen almost breaks into song for his last words. "Thanks for the memories, Dad... oh yeah, and you too, Mom."

The credits roll.

Producer: Glen Fletcher.

Camerawoman: Heather Fletcher.

Off Location Consultant: Nate Fletcher.

The End comes up on screen. Carol claps. Paul can't clap but he beams proudly.

Nate says to his siblings, "Really impressive stuff, you guys. Nice work." His wife Julie smiles and nods in agreement.

And so, Heather was right, as usual. The family is reinventing the holiday season, finding things Paul can do.

And he can certainly star in his own life.

The Uninvited Guest

Heather, Julie, and Tracy help Carol gather up the wine glasses and dessert plates. Carol reloads the dishwasher for the second time that day while Darryl readies Paul for bed.

Carol turns to her kids. "It's been nice having everyone around for Christmas... so important now," she says leaving the conversation dangling.

Once Heather has left and their out-of-town guests have gone to bed, Carol picks up the video cassette from the coffee table. Surely, Paul will want to watch it again... soon. It seems that their adult children are in the let's-make-Dad's-life-better stage.

Does this somehow fit the stages of grief Carol's read about? Are their adult kids moving any closer to the acceptance phase of their dad's disease? Is she?

Chapter 6: Papa
1996

It's a Monday in early January. Carol and a grade seven student named Wayne spend much of their time together working on the articulation of his *l* and *r* sounds. Carol is assessing whether he hears the sounds. "Can't produce what you don't hear," she tells the student's homeroom teacher who has joined her for lunch at the pale, yellow staffroom table.

"Just wish his speech difficulties had been diagnosed sooner," the classroom teacher shares with Carol. The teacher takes a right turn in their conversation. "By the way, how are things for you at home these days, Carol?"

Carol is caught off guard. She seldom mentions 'home' at school.

"I... I think we're finally getting the hang of it. It's been over three years now, so it feels kinda normal... living with MS, I mean... and all the adjustments it has brought."

She hears herself babbling but can't stop.

"Well, that's good," the teacher says when Carol finally takes a breath.

They are interrupted by an announcement over the PA system. End of conversation.

As she walks down the hall to pick up her next student, she tries to imagine what else she might have disclosed to the teacher.

By the time Carol gets home, Paul has done his own mid-afternoon side transfer—a shaky one is Carol's guess—and is now lying in his bed awaiting her arrival.

She removes her watch, placing it on the bedside table before crawling in beside Paul, lying on top of the bedding. They chat. They fill each other in on their respective days, like regular married folk might do over a kitchen table.

Carol wonders if she's losing her grip on reality: she told her co-worker, that very day, that their lives with MS were starting to feel normal. Who is she trying to kid? She's in a hospital bed. In the middle of their bedroom at four thirty in the afternoon. Chatting with her husband who uses a wheelchair, which sits lurking in a corner of this room. He cannot easily get on the toilet seat himself. Or dress himself. Or get his breakfast. And he needs a caregiver to unscrew his toothpaste. Every night, Carol sleeps on a futon on the floor parallel to the hospital bed. How is any of this normal?

And, what Carol has on her mind today is not normal either. She's been carefully working it out in her head for weeks—trying to find the right moment and the right words—to proclaim what she's come to terms with.

Paul's numb hands precipitated the decision: grabbing and holding onto the pole beside his bed is getting near impossible. And without that pole to hang on to, a side transfer without help is more than risky, it's dangerous. She had discussed this with her sister Angie who had concurred, confirming her decision to talk to Paul.

She begins gingerly, leaning into Paul's shoulder. "I know you probably don't want to hear this, but I've been thinking for some time now... well, I think we need more help... with your care."

"Yeah, I've been thinking that too," Paul replies. "Every day there's something new I need help with."

Wait a minute. *No resistance? Just like that?*

And then she realizes that Paul is ahead of her. Way ahead of the sound and the fury in her head, to quote Shakespeare. Ready to get on with life, even if it means more help.

It's the kids who need convincing, not of the extra help, but rather, of the time of the help. They cannot figure out why Carol thinks hiring someone for weekday evenings and weekends, rather than for the long afternoons Paul spends alone, makes any sense. Carol explains that getting Paul's dinner and readying him for bed swallow up her entire evening. It's exhausting. As are the Saturdays and Sundays. If Carol is to continue with a full-time career, it means getting help at the times that suit her. And, of course, Paul too, she quickly adds.

Besides, their dad will not have to give up his much beloved solitude, Carol stealthily reminds them out of Paul's earshot.

After some back and forth, and the assurance that Carol will approach Darryl about staying until 2 p.m. each weekday to get Paul into bed before he leaves, the children relent.

Darryl agrees to the two extra hours each day but is not interested in a split shift of evenings too—it will interfere with his evening classes. He has no time to work weekends either. So, the Fletchers turn to the placement agency again.

This time the agency sends a woman. In her interview Rosa says, "My husband and I came to Edmonton two years ago now. Our two daughters, Amelia and Maria, are both in school." Carol and Paul are especially glad to hear the next bit. "I was a nurse in Chile and am now working on my Canadian accreditation."

The Uninvited Guest

Rosa can work the required five evenings a week from 6 to 9 p.m., and Saturdays and Sundays from 8 a.m. to 2 p.m. Perfect. There is only one awkward moment during the transition and it's on Rosa's first day of work. She shows up in her nurse's uniform and Carol hears Paul say to his newest caregiver, "You don't have to wear a uniform... I'm not sick. I just have MS."

Their new caregiver seems to take Paul's request in stride—perhaps pondering it, perhaps not.

Rosa shows up in regular garb from that day forward. A skirt and a matching blouse that has been starched and meticulously ironed, pantyhose and all.

She's obviously comfortable in her skin. And mature. Paul's care seems like an extension of the work she did with patients in her home country, in uniform.

In no time at all, Rosa figures out how much her client loves food. To Paul's delight, whenever she prepares empanadas while cooking for her own family, she makes an extra portion which she serves to Paul during her dinnertime shift. It seems every culture has its own version of a dumpling.

Carol loves chatting with Rosa, her fascination with the immigrant story rekindled. Besides, Rosa is preparing to write the Test of English as a Foreign Language Exam (TOEFL), hence taking English as a Second Language classes, so their chats often revolve around language learning. Sometimes the stars do align.

Probably one of the best things that grows out of Rosa's presence is a routine Saturday morning shower. The shower bars are by now inadequate safety measures for Paul's shower. They take the next step: the purchase of a shockingly expensive rolling shower chair.

There sits Paul—after having been comfortably rolled into the barrier-free stall of their accessible bathroom—on his water-resistant throne lathering his hair, arms, chest, and face

51

too. Bending down to wash his own legs and feet is out of the question now, because of his imbalance. So, Rosa obliges.

Thanks to some ingenious engineer, Paul is sitting on a water-resistant doughnut-shaped seat, which reminds Carol of the poolside life preservers they used to see on holidays; the hole in the doughnut-ring allows Carol to wash and rinse her husband's private parts. It feels like the 'for better or for worse' clause of their marriage vows coming true.

It seems like eons ago that Paul had said that he wanted no woman-caregiver seeing him like this. What about two women? One with rolled up blouse sleeves and bare feet planted on the shower tiles, the other in a bathing suit (a brainwave solution Carol instituted the first day of the shower routine). *Ménage a trois* pops into Carol's head as the three of them fill the shower stall to capacity.

If Carol were a fairy godmother, she would wave her magic wand to ensure that all families on this perilous-disability-voyage had their own barrier-free bathroom, shower chair, and elevator—the works. And a Rosa working and cheerleading in their corner. It makes all the difference.

Carol hears her own singsong voice say "fresh as a daisy" upon completion of the first threesome in the shower. The words are a bittersweet memory because she'd voiced them for years while bathing each of her three toddlers. The sweetness comes from seeing Paul, water running over him, rejuvenated. It reminds Carol of a soap commercial she's seen on television where a man is standing under a waterfall, in all of nature's glory, lathering his upper body. The bitterness... well, better not to go there.

Carol just wishes that they could manage this shower more than once a week. She knows Paul will not request it; she's going to have to make it happen!

The Uninvited Guest

As effective as is this shower routine for grounding the family, another event grounds them even more.

And that is what happens to them next.

***

Their first grandchild is not born into their lives, but rather arrives as part of a package deal. Heather is presently dating the child's father, Bruce. He was the one who had helped her bring home Paul's first wheelchair. During one Sunday dinner, they meet his three-year-old daughter.

What is spectacular about the whole idea is how much Carol initially resists it. *Other families have exes, partners, stepchildren... we do not need this complication in our lives right now.*

The gods can't wait to serve up a little dose of humility to Carol.

Her dose comes in the shape of a tiny blond replica of her father. She is beautiful. Her name is Ann, and she talks constantly. At first, Carol finds the incessant chattering tiresome; she's unused to it, as all three of their children had been relatively quiet—certainly not chatty. Over time, Carol recognizes the little-girl-mind: Ann observes her way around their home, talks her way through to some meaning, verbalizing all she is wondering about along the way, reaches a conclusion, and voices it.

Paul seems to love Ann's chatting and Carol eventually arrives at a startling conclusion: the chance of Paul ever meeting a flesh and blood grandchild is slim. This might be it for him.

For them.

They open the gift.

There is nothing better than having a grandchild to cook a favourite meal for. A little person who has her very own glass at their house. And her own storybooks too.

She learns the Fletcher house rules early on. "Dogs have to stay outside at your house, right Grandma?" says Ann one day as soon as she steps into the back porch. Bruce and Heather exchange looks that give them away. For a fleeting moment, despite her apprehension of dogs and her dislike of dog hair, Carol reconsiders her house rule since Heather's dog Grape is a small beagle. But she can't bear the thought of having to move yet another goalpost.

No one tells Ann what to call Paul, but she makes up her own mind: Papa.

Whenever Ann visits, one of the first things she requests is to "sleep in Papa's bed." What she really means is that she wants to climb over the steel bar and have someone crank up the hospital bed as far as it will go, all the while hanging on to both bars with tiny hands, looking like an astronaut, minus the helmet, lifting off into outer space. Tittering. Gleefully.

It takes some getting used to Papa's coughing sprees, but before long Ann is reminding them at the dinner table—in case they've forgotten—that Papa has a disease.

A sour looking face usually accompanies this coughing event. Ann watches for his sour-face and names it as such. She thinks it looks funny. She giggles. So does Papa. And the coughing, something awful and ominous, is robbed of its potency: a child makes it so.

Ann gives Paul what he most craves: normalcy. Paul hates the pity, masked as stabbing sighs that he gets more and more often lately, even though he knows it is well intentioned. He's told Carol as much. And he sees the fear that's often reflected in the eyes of others, as if they are saying to themselves, *there, but for the grace of God, go I.*

The Uninvited Guest

Ann knows neither pity nor fear. She simply is. By living in the moment, she gives Paul permission to simply be. Carol witnesses it every time the wee one visits.

Ann asks Paul things, anything. She tells him things, nothing much yet everything all at once. She points to things and holds them up to show him, as children are wont to do. She leans on his wheelchair occasionally, slipping off its arm and bumping him, not treating him like glass at all. She watches television with him, adding a running narration just in case he isn't getting it. She plays checkers with him and makes her moves and his, too. Pretty soon, Paul realizes this and simply pretends to have an opinion on what might be a good next move. He's good at this; after all, he's been married to Carol for a long time by then.

Ann gives them someone to go to the zoo with, where they all laugh at Lucy the elephant's antics; she gives them a second chance to remember how much fun it had been to raise their own children.

As Shakespeare so aptly put it, "And that which should accompany old age, as honour, love," *and a grandchild,* Carol adds.

"Just wish I could play catch with Ann in the backyard like I did with Heather and the twins," Paul says, one Sunday evening after a family visit.

"I wish you could too," Carol adds.

"I like the time we surprised her in the grocery store though." Paul smiles. "Remember?"

"Yeah," says Carol. "I was trying to squeeze the wheelchair around a grocery cart in the aisle when Ann spied us and broke loose from her dad... probably scared the wits out of Bruce too... squealing 'Papa, Papa.'"

"Who told her to call me Papa anyway?" Paul wonders aloud.

"She decided herself."

"I like it," Paul says.

55

Jean Filewych

In the middle of the breakfast aisle in a grocery store, even though Paul was using wheels for legs and couldn't much move his hands— the word handicapped was stricken from the records. Replaced with the precious sweet ringing of the word 'Papa.'
   A child made it so.

Chapter 7: Pine Knots
1996

The luxury of having two homecare workers is the flexibility it affords them.

Carol gets to go on her girls' weekends again. Girlfriend getaways and symphony concerts are among the two things she misses most in this new version of their lives. She doesn't ever tell Paul she's keeping score and wonders if he is.

In late spring, she and her sister-in-law, Barb—her fair and foul weather friend—are off for a weekend getaway. They are headed to Barb's holiday trailer which is now permanently parked at a campground, as she and John do less and less highway travel.

Today, their travel companion is Barb's dog, Ginger, who keeps sniffing around their camp spot. Despite not being much of an outdoor person at all, as they sit around their evening campfire next to Barb's trailer, Carol is suddenly struck by how much Paul could use some of this 'outdoorsiness.' She moves her food-on-a-stick higher over the red-hot flames. "Do you know if there are any rentals at this place?"

"A dozen or so cabins, I think," says Barb. "Too bad we can't get Paul into our trailer. He has such a big chair."

Carol muses, "I wonder if the cabins have ramps."

"Only one way to find out."

The next morning after a light breakfast, the two women hike over to the campsite office, Barb in her sturdy well-worn hiking boots and Carol in the only pair of low heels she owns. They explain their needs briefly to the office folk and are given multiple keys to check out the cabins.

Evidently Barb is a member of good standing in Wilderness Village.

It's a mission. They scamper from empty cabin to empty cabin like squirrels searching for nuts. In the end, only one cabin will do: the one with the prerequisite wheelchair ramp. They scout out its interior: wider doorways, no insurmountable lip into the bathroom. Enough room for a wheelchair to roll up to the front of the toilet which has two strong bars on each side to ensure a safe transfer. It'll work. Funny, how a few years back, Carol would not have even known what rendered a cabin accessible.

"It'll give you and Paul something to look forward to," Barb says to Carol who stands at the office desk waiting to book the cabin for the upcoming August. "John and I will come to the trailer at the same time; it'll be like old times."

Carol and Barb have a long history together: the two women love reminding those at book club that they married brothers. Carol was a green girl of eighteen engaged to Paul—when Barb and John were newlyweds.

When Carol shares the Wilderness Village date with Paul once she's back home, his eyes light up. Barb was right: he has something to look forward to.

Spring turns into summer and soon it's August. Their planning and packing are extensive. The negotiation about which homecare worker will accompany them on their camping adventure resolves itself: Rosa cannot easily leave her husband and daughters overnight, even in summer. Darryl seems thrilled to be asked on the trip.

The sheepskin—don't forget the sheepskin for the bed, Carol thinks, remembering the doctor's warning of bedsores being the devil to cure.

And the foam-foot-form, she adds to the list in her head. *For Paul's feet*. This new addition to their lives is as weird looking as it sounds: a carved-out space in a foam block for two feet to rest, to avoid drop-foot, the doctor had explained. Carol had not even noticed that Paul's feet were flopping over as he spent more and more time in bed or sitting in his lift chair.

What does Darryl need to sponge bath Paul? Carol asks herself. The growing inventory reminds her of over-flowing-diaper-bag-days. *Never thought I'd be doing that again*, she thinks, batting the thought away as quickly as it appears.

The Fletchers arrive at Cabin #9 under clamorous thunder. Darryl does yeoman's service getting the wheelchair out of the trunk quickly, before an efficient transfer of Paul from front passenger seat to wheelchair. Darryl pushes the chair up the ramp seconds before a loud hailstorm bears down on them. A few drops render Paul damp, but they avoid the worst of it.

Even though it's early evening, Darryl transfers Paul to bed: mostly, to get him off his buttocks after the long drive and secondly, to warm him, given the slight dampness of his clothes. Paul is spellbound, not by his new surroundings, nor even by the pelting sounds overhead on the metal roof, but by the cabin ceiling. It's cedar.

"Beautiful knots," Paul says.

"Uh huh," Darryl answers, looking around to see what Paul is talking about, before spying the ceiling overhead.

Paul continues gazing upwards.

The cedar evokes another remembrance in Carol: their early camping days when the family would arrive at a campground, each member delegated to one of the tasks of setting up camp. Including chopping wood, for their evening fires.

Paul used it as an excuse: he loved chopping wood. But he chopped so much wood that, statistically speaking, they would have had to tend a roaring fire every minute of their stay, including overnight, to even come close to using it all.

"How in God's name are we going to use that much wood?" queried Carol back in the day, hands on her hips.

Paul's response was always the same. "It would be nice to leave some wood for the next family who show up here."

If anyone out there ever drove to a campsite along the Oregon Coast, or in California, Idaho, Michigan, Washington, British Columbia, Alberta, Saskatchewan, Manitoba, Quebec, or Ontario (especially in the vicinity of the Great Lakes) and came upon scads and scads of chopped and neatly piled wood, well maybe, just maybe—it was Paul who chopped it.

Barb calls through the screen door, bringing Carol back from the woodpiles of long ago to the present. Barb leaves her dripping umbrella on the stoop. "Paul, would you and your gang like to join us at our trailer tomorrow for lunch?"

"Love to," Carol answers for the three of them.

Next day, the rain stops. Off they go, using the trail between cabins and campsites. But it's hard going. Essentially, they're on rutty clay sprinkled with gravel. Not even remotely meant for a wheelchair. Not a moment too soon, the washboard ride is over. Paul's jangled body tilts to the left. Darryl shifts him upright.

They eat outdoors, delicious burgers that John charcoal barbecues, served on sourdough buns slathered with mayonnaise, fingertips away from trees reaching far into the big blue Alberta sky. The trailer door slams every time Barb or John retrieves something, a joyous summer sound.

The Uninvited Guest

Ginger wags her tail and makes happy barks, a soundtrack to their picnic.

They are reveling in the outdoors when Barb says, "Want a game of crib, Paul... like the good old days?"

Carol holds her breath. *But Paul can't hold cards.* Sure enough, he keeps dropping them. At first, Paul asks Darryl to peg his points on the crib board but finally he tells his brother that they'll have to finish the game later. The spell is broken.

"Remember to be at our cabin by six... we'll make a fire tonight," Carol says to Barb and John. "Glen should be here from Calgary by then."

The trio head off in the direction of the paved road instead of the bumpy gravel trail amid the tall trees, having learned the hard way that the scenic route is worth giving up for a sensible surface.

Glen builds a fire soon after arriving at their site. He keeps it on the small side realizing that getting a wheelchair close enough for his father to be warm, but not too close, is a dilemma.

Glen, John, and Darryl become the volunteer fire brigade, sans fire gear, watching for and warding off all errant sparks coming Paul's way. Paul is bundled up. Evenings in late August in Alberta can be cool. They kibitz. Share a drink. Darryl and John take turns holding and handing Paul his rum and coke. Mostly, holding it.

Later in the evening, Barb pops Jiffy popcorn in its shiny tinfoil container over the grate on the fire, breaking the silence with scraping sounds before the kernels begin to explode.

They do not tell any ghost stories, who knows why.

Eventually, Carol cajoles that it's time to go indoors. "I'm getting cold. And if we stay here any longer, we'll have to eat again."

61

"And I have to head back to Calgary tomorrow," Glen says. "Early."

"Not yet," utters Paul firmly, looking up at the night sky.

They stop worrying about being cold or eating again or Glen's long drive home or the impassable gravelly trail or the sting of the aborted afternoon crib game. They put aside the worry of Paul getting bedsores as a result of being in a wheelchair too long... they sit and sit under the silver slit of a moon in God's good earth and stare at the red licks of flame against a star-studded sky.

Only one thing would make the evening perfect: if Paul could rise from his wheelchair, unassisted, get the axe with its long red peeling-handle from the trunk of their car, walk briskly over to the woodpile, some fifteen feet away, and chop... scads and scads of firewood, for the next family who visit this camping spot.

Carol feels a tightness in the pit of her stomach.

Paul's son and brother would surely pitch in to stack the wood; heck, they would all happily pile the wood with him, for as long and as high as he wished.

Carol *would not* put her hands on her hips, nor say a word— of that, she is certain.

Chapter 8: The Joystick Club
1996

A few days after their Wilderness Village getaway, Paul asks Carol to write a list. "Call it, *Things I Can Still Do.*" Carol guesses its impetus: the unfinished crib game with his brother John.

Paul dictates, Carol writes, their *modus operandi* from days of old on their road trips.

1. shave (*with much difficulty,* thinks Carol)
2. turn newspaper pages (*not really,* Carol *almost* says)
3. change TV channels when I'm not too weak
4. brush my teeth after someone unscrews the toothpaste tube
5. comb my hair, but only the sides and front
6. hold the phone (*not really,* thinks Carol again)
7. sign my name (*unrecognizably* is what Carol should write, but doesn't have the heart to)

As Carol plays scrivener, the scratch of her fine-nibbed pen on paper makes her remember the detailed baby books she had kept for all three of their newborns—two blue and one pink, in strict accordance with the gender colour-code of the seventies. She had filled the books with her children's first words and the details of their first steps and even their inoculation dates. She had affixed months and years to the backs of school pictures. And, of course, pasted the classic Christmas photos of a nervous or happy child perched atop the knee of a fake-bearded Santa in every baby book. The milestones of growing up.

Who is there to document our lasts? Carol wonders. *Is that what Paul is having her do?*

Carol looks down and scans the list. It takes her breath away as she recalls how mammoth each task has become. She remembers the time Paul hurled the remote control across the sitting room. It landed on the floor, the batteries falling out, making a heck of a clatter. Uncharacteristically, he had shown his frustration and it had frightened Carol.

Paul's raw courage takes all her husband's energy and concentration, and, yes, all his might. He is not going gently into that good night.

The list haunts Carol almost as much as the chance encounter they have at church, a month later.

Their Sunday Mass attendance of late has become sporadic, simply requiring too much planning. It's always pleasant when they get there, as there are many precious relics stored in the confines of that spiritual edifice. They were the family of five, attending Mass every Sunday without exception. To say nothing of the parental pride they felt as their children participated in the Mass: their young altar-server-twins assisting the priest, draped in the white outer garment of the church girded by a coloured cord at their waists, each colour depicting the liturgical season. They experienced equal pride when their daughter became a reader at church, as natural a task for her as breathing. This is the very building in which Paul acted as parish council member for years; Paul, as a young man, had also joined the Knights of Columbus based in this parish.

The Uninvited Guest

One Saturday morning after Paul's shower, Carol hears herself telling Rosa they will be attending Mass tomorrow. "It'll be nice to get out," she says, looking at her husband.

She has kept secret from Paul the central reason for the falling away of regular church attendance as it has as much to do with *her* heart as with *his* ailing body. Believing in a loving God is a leap of faith she cannot muster anymore, despite knowing, intellectually, that all faith is a leap. She has stopped praying too. That, she doesn't share with anyone except Barb.

As they're leaving the one-hour service the next day, a bottleneck occurs at the side door: a woman in a huge electric wheelchair makes her way slowly toward the exit and the outside ramp. They wait their turn.

Carol had noticed the woman in church before but from afar; today, she cannot help but notice the joystick that is attached to a shoulder strap and sits prominently like a microphone just below her chin. It's what she uses to control her chair: she scrunches up her chin, placing it on the joystick, then pushes to manoeuvre the chair.

Carol notices her beautifully manicured fingernails but it's off-putting because her arms and hands sit pale and motionless on the wheelchair handles. The woman smiles at Carol and Paul, before joysticking her way down the ramp.

It's the Fletchers' turn next. Rosa turns Paul and his wheelchair around at the top of the ramp, controlling the speed of the chair by bracing it against her body, as she and it descend backwards. They meet the joystick-woman at the bottom of the ramp, two big chairs trying to align for a visit— one motorized, one not.

Carol opens the conversation. "You're new here, aren't you?"

"I started coming a few months ago. I didn't much like the priest who comes to say Mass at Clarksview. That's where I live. I love Father Francis though." She repositions her chair to face them more squarely. She takes her chin off the joystick saying, "My name's April."

"I'm Carol, this is my husband Paul, and this is Rosa, our caregiver... we've been coming here for years."

Rosa addresses April. "You're sure good at driving your chair."

"I've had lots of practice," April says, her mouth and eyes crinkling into a smile.

No one utters a sound for a few seconds.

"I was in a manual chair when I was first diagnosed with MS, that's multiple sclerosis, by the way." She gets to her point. "Graduated to this chair over ten years ago now."

Carol looks down and sees Paul flinch. She decides not to share Paul's diagnosis with the fellow churchgoer. April does not ask either.

As they leave April waiting for the handicapped transit bus that will take her home, it's as if they are walking against gale-force winds. Carol tries hard to focus on their side transfer to the front seat of the car, rather than on Paul's face.

And so, Paul gets his second preview of what this chronic disease he's facing daily sometimes looks like, the first courtesy of his wife's insistence on attending the MS support group.

A deep silence settles in the car, like fine dust on a Sunday drive over a country road. The silence lasts the rest of Sunday. Even into Monday.

"Wish I hadn't mentioned April's driving," Rosa says to Carol every day for the next week. "Then Paul wouldn't know how long April's had MS."

Ultimately, they become fast friends with April. She's marvelous company: smart, witty, and funny. Eventually, April's manicured nails are not off-putting at all. Carol loves them. Later in the year when she meets April's daughter, she loves them even more.

"Last year, my mom sabotaged my birthday present to her," the young woman says. "I wanted to hire an LPN to come in once every two weeks and give Mom an extra bath."

She then tells Carol that her mom nixed the *Licensed Practical Nurse idea* and asked her daughter to hire an esthetician to do her nails instead.

"Ah, there's a woman after my own heart," confesses Carol with a grin.

Eventually, they get introduced to April's sidekick, and then there are two: April and Marcel.

Marcel is a feisty French-Canadian, younger than the lot of them, living with slight cognitive impairment as well as compromised mobility—the aftereffects of a stroke. He swears like a sailor, in French, of course, when his quick temper flares. He powers his wheelchair by virtue of superb upper body strength honed through years of hard work as a pipe fitter in the Fort McMurray tar sands.

April and the irascible Marcel are a team. They invite the Fletchers into their circle.

Carol and Paul enter. Hearts full of love, of fear, but mostly of gratitude that somehow, against all odds, life moves forward. Unpredictable as hell, but forward. Like the lone flower that clings to life, in the sparse dirt atop a mountain.

The Fletchers go to visit the extended care home where April and Marcel live. Go *back* really—as it's the very place Paul once volunteered, serving drinks to the residents along with his fellow Knights of Columbus. There is even a slight possibility that April had been served her rye and coke by one of these knights, perhaps even Paul.

But now they are April's guests on *bar night*, which, coincidently, is still held on Thursday evenings. The drinks are served to them by members of Paul's own fraternity, who welcome their fellow brother warmly, but warily too.

The visit becomes a pleasant Thursday evening routine that fills their time.

The continuum of life is manifest: Paul and his family unwittingly become part of the handicapped community. Not something they foresaw, nor wished for. But it's okay.

Alongside April and Marcel, no one seems to notice that Paul is young for a wheelchair and sits tall in it, or that Carol is short and youngish to be pushing it. No one even asks *why* Paul needs a wheelchair.

Everyone at Clarksview is different—all needing help, is how Carol makes sense of it. Maybe that's why it's so easy for them to fit in there. It's where they belong.

One Thursday evening on their way home from bar night, Carol entertains a stray thought: *Does April have a list of things that she can still do on her own? It would be much shorter than Paul's list, for sure.*

And who would write it for her?

Chapter 9: Pride Cometh Before the Fall
1996

Come September, a fire marshal visits Carol's school to demonstrate how to get students in wheelchairs safely out of the building in case of fire. Carol arranges a home visit on the spot. Something, she believes, the Fletcher household needs to know.

The upcoming visit gets rave reviews from Paul. It's a throwback to when Paul had made their young children fire smart. In bygone days during Fire Prevention Week, Paul would take their three children aside and calmly discuss the ways their family could prevent fire. He would take the exercise a step further, arranging a muster point—the wooden structure behind their garage that housed their garbage cans—where the family would gather in safety if the unthinkable happened.

Carol does her homework before the fire marshal's visit. She remembers having seen the fire extinguisher in the garage and she places it within easy reach in their downstairs storage room. She even spends some time purging the storage room of its boxes and old journals as, in her mind, clutter and fire are inextricably intertwined.

Carol makes sure that Darryl's and Rosa's shifts overlap so that they can both be part of the fire drill, paying them overtime. Darryl cranks Paul's bed to sitting position so he too is part of the conversation.

The marshal arrives on time. He is thorough. He tests both smoke detectors, checks a few electrical cords, and pokes around the furnace room. He avoids the storage room altogether.

The main demonstration begins. He reminds them that they could not use the elevator under any circumstances, if there were a fire. He's impressed that they have a mechanical bed which can be lowered inches from the floor, making the manoeuvre he's about to demonstrate much easier. The fire marshal asks Darryl to gently pull Paul by his ankles to the foot of the mattress. The marshal then twists the lowered mattress slightly off its frame.

"Next, you would pull the mattress right off the bed, onto the floor, and slide it to the nearest exit—your patio doors, in this case." He describes, rather than executes, the actual manoeuvre as no one in their right mind would drag a six-foot-two man through two rooms to a patio door unless necessary.

"These hardwood floors would make sliding the mattress much easier," the marshal says as he adjusts it snugly back on its frame. Darryl cranks the bed back up.

The marshal looks at the two women in the room and addresses Rosa first.

"Given your weight and height, you'd probably need help with this manoeuvre." He hesitates only a moment. "You too, ma'am," he adds, glancing at Carol.

He turns to Paul. "Your home is truly barrier-free. The lip between the inner and outer patio doors is pretty much non-existent. Impressive."

"Our reno guys were excellent," Paul tells him.

The Uninvited Guest

Just as the drill is winding down, the marshal asks if they have a fire extinguisher. Carol—pleased to finally get a chance to have her responsible-wife-debut—runs to the downstairs storage room to retrieve the extinguisher.

She hurries back to the bedroom, not wanting to keep the man waiting, and she hands him the extinguisher. He takes it and stops dead.

The fire marshal turns the red cylinder toward Darryl and says, "Read this."

Darryl reads aloud, "Propane torch."

Carol struggles to make sense of what's happening; the quizzical look on the faces of the caregivers and the fire marshal make it plain that they cannot believe that she has mistaken a *propane torch* for a fire extinguisher.

But Paul can. He knows exactly how his wife's mind works: she'd have avoided reading the canister the minute she saw it *assuming* it to be a fire extinguisher. Confident stupidity—he'd seen it before although he's far too tactful (and happily married) to call it that.

A perfect stranger, a man he'd met a mere thirty-five minutes ago, puts his fire-marshal-hand on Paul's black trousers before leaving and says, "Good luck, sir... with everything."

Paul chuckles. Seems like his fear of fire has left the building, at least for now. This encounter leaves him bemused.

When Carol tells this story to Barb, Barb insists that she would not have come to Carol's defence *if* there had been a trial. "You would have been guilty as charged."

When Carol and Paul's adult children hear this story, they shake their collective heads and do not want the story told at all; after all, it's their father who was in danger. But, as is the way with their zany family, the story gets told and retold—mythologized into yet another legend in their colourful family

71

history. Carol's mother Sarah laughs maniacally, each time she hears it.

Carol is certain the fire marshal is still telling the story too.

"The wife seemed sane enough at first, and that seemingly sweet husband at her mercy... the two caregivers looked responsible... what a peculiar home."

Pride cometh before the fall, thinks Carol each time the story is repeated.

Needless to say, the Fletchers find the *real* fire extinguisher immediately after the marshal's visit and hang it strategically by the back door.

The propane torch, they giveth away.

Chapter 10: Brave New World
1996

Watching April await the wheelchair accessible bus every Sunday at church is the impetus for the next metamorphosis in the Fletchers' lives. Equally important: transferring Paul from the car to the wheelchair will be near impossible in the winter snow.

The bus seems a practical solution. Paul agrees.

Carol swings into action and contacts the local accessible bus service.

The rules of the road on this transport system are explained during the initial phone interview with an agent. "The client needs an attendant during transport unless he can manoeuvre his own wheelchair... a family member, homecare worker, or even a friend needs to ride along." He adds that DATS stands for Disabled Adult Transit System.

The agent's use of the word *disabled* startles Carol. *Is it better or worse than being handicapped?* she's debating in her head, making it hard to concentrate on the questions she's being asked over the phone.

Suddenly Carol's bravado about being part of the handicapped community slips away.

Applying for DATS feels like going into the abyss.

As usual, Paul takes Carol's hand firmly saying, let's jump. Probably his love of vehicles helps pave the way.

Before long, the white minibus is pulling up to their house. DATS—the bright blue letters on both sides of the vehicle reveal to the neighbours what's going on in the Fetcher household.

Carol's graveyard humour is her way of coping as she tells anyone who will listen that she's always been in this whole handicapped gambit for the parking spot, and now they even have their own chauffer.

The side transfer from the wheelchair to the front seat of the Fletcher car becomes a welcome thing of the past. A DATS driver is now in charge. He goes to their elevator door, pushes Paul from house to bus, then up a ramp and into the vehicle. The driver secures the chair with straps attached to hooks built into the floor.

They find out soon enough the necessity of those straps: a few of the DATS drivers take corners as if they were wannabe race-car drivers, leaving clients fending for themselves in careening wheelchairs. Many clients, including Paul, are not able to clutch the handlebars of their chairs. Clenching one's teeth probably doesn't have the same effect.

They quickly drop the assumption that taking DATS is akin to taking a cab, delivering you directly to your destination: once you're on the bus, you're held captive indefinitely as someone else may need picking up or dropping off. The result is that Paul and his attendant end up spending a fair bit of time sitting and waiting on the bus. Arrival and departure times are complicated too: a built-in half-hour window—waiting to be picked up by DATS at home and again at one's destination—makes the trip time consuming.

The entire procedure requires patience—the patience of Job. The only one in the family with anything close to that

The Uninvited Guest

degree of patience is Paul. They eventually grow accustomed to the waiting, sort of.

What's harder for the Fletchers is the cleanliness (or lack thereof) of the wheelchair accessible vehicles. And the body odors permeating the air is a constant feature of each ride.

One day riding on DATS, it dawns on Carol how spoiled she has been: for the first decade and a half of their marriage, Paul lived by his cleanliness-next-to-godliness value when it came to the family car. DATS does not even pretend to aim for cleanliness: their clients have the choice to venture out in a smelly bus or resign themselves to being housebound. No contest, really.

And so, DATS—another set piece—creeps into their lives.

A small bonus: the fare on DATS is reasonable, appealing to Paul's frugality. The downside to using DATS had not occurred to them until the family doctor pointed it out. Spending that much time in one position in the wheelchair make the chances of Paul getting a bedsore pretty much inevitable. Yet another set piece to their lives.

One snowy Thursday evening, Paul and Rosa (Carol drives down by car) arrive at Clarksview for bar night on DATS.

This must be as close as the handicapped, elderly, and infirm get to feeling like regular folk, it occurs to Carol, *like the general public must be doing down the street, at the local bar.*

"A couple of years ago, I went to this place called William Watson Lodge," April says in between sips of red wine from a straw held to her lips by an attendant. "It's in the Kananaskis mountains."

Carol is not exactly sure how far away that is.

"You have to be handicapped to stay there," April adds.

Carol laughs. "Well, we've got that part right."

Marcel interrupts. "Is your beer cold?" he asks Paul. "Mine's warm."

April continues with her story about the holiday lodge, but she's interrupted by Paul's coughing episode. She waits patiently before explaining that she had hired a homecare worker to drive her up to the place to look after her for three days. Some of her family joined her. Bedrooms galore. An accessible bathroom. The works.

"It's really affordable too," April insists. "But it's a circus trying to get the place booked. Only one day for booking. You can get a busy signal for hours, literally, before getting through."

Carol sees that April had Paul at the word mountain. He stops imbibing, and coughing.

Carol's mind races: *maybe writing down the word disabled finally has some payoff!*

A hodgepodge of ideas swarms in her head.

Carol gets right on it and after navigating the difficulties of getting through on the phone line to book the place, the family has a date circled on the calendar for the following summer: four nights and five days at the William Watson Lodge, a gem of an idea, courtesy of April.

The lodge mails out a few brochures. They discover that it was the Alberta politician Peter Lougheed and his wife Jeanne—along with other key supporters, back in 1981—who were instrumental in developing a recreational area in the mountains that would be accessible to those with disabilities. Jeanne was obviously more than just a pretty face on the arm of her politician husband.

"The facility is subsidized by the Alberta Heritage Trust Fund," Carol continues reading from the brochure, "and is made up of twenty-two accessible cottages, boasting eighteen kilometres of wheelchair-accessible trails, six campsites, and picnic sites. Available to every handicapped Alberta citizen or senior over sixty-five, every second year. Open year round."

The Uninvited Guest

"Eighteen kilometres of trails," Paul says. "Wow." He asks how they'll get to Kananaskis.

Carol had not thought of that until this very moment. *DATS certainly won't take us there*, she thinks to herself. She has a few months to figure it out though, as the snow blows its way through late November and December.

***

Before they know it, Heather's January 15 birthday is upon them.

As Carol cuts birthday cake and Bruce hands out pieces to the family, a second reason to celebrate comes up.

"We're getting married," the grinning couple before them announce, almost in unison.

Both sets of parents gleam with joy. Heather had suggested inviting Bruce's parents to this birthday and now Carol knows why.

"I'm graduating soon and might even have a teaching job by fall so we figured a mid-summer wedding would work," Heather says. "With Bruce already teaching we figured we could swing it."

How the world has changed, Carol can't help but think. The memory of a young Paul squirming before his prospective mother-in-law, asking for Carol's hand in marriage, flashes through her mind.

First things first though. Carol brings up Paul's incessant coughing to the family doctor a few weeks later who recommends a swallowing test.

A family wedding on the horizon gives the doctor's suggestion an urgency.

Who knew they were supposed to be worried about coughing anyway?

Mobility, yes. Numbness, yes. Leg spasms, yes. But coughing? Carol never remembers reading about coughing in any of the pamphlets given to her by the family doctor.

Three weeks later, Carol gets a call from the Glenrose Clinic where the swallowing test is booked.

"Could Paul be here Monday morning, 10 a.m.? We've had a cancellation."

"We'll make it work." *We need to get this done and out of the way.*

Later that day, Carol cancels her Monday session with her students, all the while feeling irritated. Irritated at MS. Herself. Paul. Life. She doesn't know at whom. But she's darn irritated.

"I'll go with Dad on DATS," Heather says, adding to Carol's irritation.

"I thought you had an exam that day."

"It's the day after," Heather says. "I never told you, Mom, but I had so many questions when Dad was first diagnosed that I was too scared to ask." This is indeed news to Carol. Heather continues, "Maybe it's time to get some answers."

On Monday, Heather and Paul ride to the clinic in DATS. Carol and Rosa meet them there.

An X-ray technician greets them in the waiting area and leads the family to an examining room, its centrepiece a fluoroscope, an instrument used for taking X-rays of the body in motion. Rosa pushes Paul squarely in front of the machine, returning to the glass partition the family were instructed to sit behind.

The technician, Susan, introduces herself and unhurriedly takes Paul's history. Before this appointment, Carol had reminded herself not to talk for Paul, as she is more and more apt to do, what with his increasingly weak voice. She holds her tongue.

Next, Susan talks them through the test.

The Uninvited Guest

"As you eat and ingest fluids, I will film it. Think of the X-ray as a camera making a movie of your eating, drinking, and swallowing, especially your swallowing."

Paul nods.

"I've added a small amount of barium to the drink I'm about to give you—it's a dye that makes images show up on the X-ray. No worries though, it's tasteless and harmless. Let's begin with the hamburger."

Paul enthusiastically welcomes the burger, even at 10:30 in the morning. Carol mentions that Paul is fond of eating; his daughter and homecare worker vehemently nod in agreement. The technician says that it's a nice change from the wisecracks she usually hears about it being hamburger and not steak.

The process begins. Paul bites into the burger held to his mouth by Rosa who scoots away as he chews and eventually swallows. "Sorry I can't eat faster," Paul says.

"Take your time, no hurry," the technician reiterates. "Just eat as you usually do."

The fluoroscope films. Continuously. At one point, Susan directs Paul to turn his head to the right before he swallows. Now to the left. He obliges. "Better," she says. They have no idea what she means.

Then various liquids are systematically introduced into this mid-morning test. Juice. Some coughing begins. Water. Coughing. Milk. More coughing. A soda pop is next. Paul's coughing begins to sound like choking. The technician stops the fluids.

Next, she does something that none of this family have ever witnessed before. Susan takes a chalk-like powder—thickener, she calls it—adding it spoonful by spoonful to the next drink she prepares for Paul. She puts one spoonful in Paul's mouth, then moves behind the machine to film as he swallows.

In time, the technician switches back to solids—the hamburger having been cut into pieces now and fed to him with a plastic fork and spoon. She films some more. Paul's tired though, mostly from the coughing.

Mother and daughter sit very still. The ceiling fan sounds to Carol like a 747 coming in for a landing. If Paul feels awkward being fed, it does not show. All Carol sees is a man who loves to eat, whose only anxiety is to get on with the business of finishing his burger.

The test takes a turn: the technician prepares to usher them into a doctor's office adjacent to the testing room, advising them that Dr. Andrews will address the test results.

Despite his exhaustion, Paul manages one question. "Can I take the rest of the burger with me?"

The technician laughs out loud. "In all my years of administering this test, no one has ever asked to finish the burger. Ever."

"Would you like fries with your burger?" Carol jokes with her husband, trying to lighten her heavy heart.

The technician says she can't see any reason why Paul can't take the burger with them. In about twenty minutes, the doctor opens the door briskly. Paul has finished his burger.

Quick introductions are made, then Dr. Andrews turns on a TV-like monitor and brings up the images of Paul's swallowing for all to see.

They are mesmerized but they don't know exactly how to interpret what they are looking at. Dr. Andrews gets to the point. "Some of your food and most of your liquids are getting into your lungs," he says to Paul directly.

Next, he gives a layman's description of the process of healthy swallowing, looking from family member to family member, pointing to the screen.

"Muscles in the pharynx contract rhythmically, like waves. This motion pushes food into your stomach. Your throat muscles, Paul, are being compromised due to MS resulting in weak and disorganized contractions that don't always take the food and drink to your stomach." He continues, "Turning your head to the left alleviates this somewhat but I think it's only a matter of time—I cannot say how long—before this measure will be ineffective." The doctor delivers his final analysis. "Because some of your food and most of what you drink is getting into your lungs you are at risk for aspiration pneumonia, Paul."

The solutions given them by the doctor that day propel the Fletcher family into an even stranger *brave new world* than they could have imagined.

"Turn your head to the left when you swallow, as much as possible," the doctor says. He glances at Rosa. "It would be good if someone could feed him, so that he could concentrate on his swallowing." He takes Rosa's silence as consent, then continues. "All his fluids must be thickened because they're sneaking into his lungs."

Dr. Andrews turns to Paul and Carol. "You must protect those lungs," he says. "You don't want to get pneumonia... and I'm sure the last thing you want is a feeding tube."

They are struck mute. Even the doctor stops talking. It's uncomfortably quiet. And so, the swallowing test is complete.

Everything is getting in, into Paul's lungs, is the only thing that Carol can think as she watches Heather and Paul board the DATS vehicle.

On the car ride home, Carol is tempted to ask where a feeding tube goes and what it does exactly. Rosa would know; after all, she's a nurse.

But Carol is afraid to ask. She *does* ask Rosa how she feels about having to feed Paul though.

"I'd be okay... I did it in Chile with a few of my older patients... should I ask Paul first?"

Carol cannot think of the right answer to her question. So much for being organized and in control of everything.

Over the next weeks, the idea of a feeding tube is the elephant in every room of their house. Strange as it seems, Paul never mentions it. He is busy getting used to being fed.

They were supposed to have flowers, organza dresses, tuxes, toasts to the bride, napkin holders, place-settings—important things on their minds. Now, one ugly detail hangs over Heather's wedding: who will feed Paul at the wedding?

No father of any bride she's ever known, in all of Christendom, has had to be fed at his daughter's wedding.

Carol picks up thickener the next day after school at the Healthcare and Rehab Centre. It's the only concession she is willing to make regarding the swallowing test results.

Can you even thicken Champagne? she asks herself, as she places the tin of chalklike powder on the kitchen counter, tucking the silver container behind the toaster.

Chapter 11: May I Have This Dance? 1997

They can resist as much as they like but what's the alternative, really. The doctor's words at the swallowing test become the law of the land. Like much else in their lives, it's an ultimatum with only one real choice.

So, Paul is fed. He does not question it or lament it. Not out loud, at least. The one doing the feeding, Darryl or Rosa, puts a manageable bite-size piece on a fork and pops it into Paul's mouth. He controls the pace of his eating with a slight nod of his head, after careful and deliberate swallowing—sometimes turning his head left, other times not. Carol is shocked at how much energy it takes for the simple act of swallowing.

Another game changer: all of Paul's liquids are thickened and spoon-fed to him. Coffee. Juice. Milk. Even his weekend beer and wine. It renders everything into varying shades of goop; no polite way around it. Paul never comments on the flavor nor texture. Nada.

Carol has much to say on the newest adaptation in their lives, all in the privacy of her head though: *Being fed as an adult is not part of the equation of life. Well, maybe at ninety years old or something. Not in your forties. It's horrible. To watch. To think about. Paul loved eating.*

"To be fair, he still does love eating," says Carol to all three of their children, trying to bring equanimity to the strange new reality.

The new reality brings up questions among their children that have apparently been brewing for some time. All three come to consensus: it's no longer safe for their dad to be home alone for any length of time.

"What if he starts choking?" Glen says.

"And if he falls, he cannot get up," adds Heather. A fall is Nate's concern too but it's more about breaking bones rather than being stranded on the floor.

Carol listens and then she takes action. The loss of control she's been experiencing since the swallowing clinic is assuaged. *Finally, something I can do*, she thinks with relief.

The next day she and Paul discuss the possibility of once again extending Darryl's end time. "Two extra hours is a lot to ask when he's going to night school," Paul says.

But Darryl agrees to the extra hours.

The sighs of relief are audible over the phone, when Carol relays the news to her children.

Carol calls the placement agency to set Darryl's additional hours. "The extra hours qualify you for a program called self-managed care. It's still more cost-effective to have your husband managing with homecare rather than being institutionalized," the woman says as easily as if talking about the weather. "You will be assigned a case manager who will come to your home monthly to sign paycheques, fill out paperwork for tax deductions, workers' compensation, and the like."

In the days that follow, Carol feels like they are now running a small business and keeps expecting a government official to appear at their door to tell them that they need a secret handshake to join this club. Yet another club. *The government*

The Uninvited Guest

will have no place in our bedroom, Carol jokes in her head as if to hold the insanity of their lives at bay.

The joke alludes to a guarded occurrence: Paul and Carol have been having a secret Saturday date night for some time.

Soon after Paul's retirement, when normal living began to fall away, including sex, Carol and Paul savoured their Saturday nights alone in the house. She and her husband would share a meal made more special by their eating it at the small round table in front of their patio doors rather than in front of the TV.

Paul would sit in his wheelchair—a non-issue by this time—pulled right up to the table. Normal as heck. Carol paid attention to detail: from the extra special meal and wine, to using their good silver, to donning the table with a red and white checkered tablecloth. A flickering candle atop the table completed the atmosphere of an outdoor Paris café.

The next part of their date night was the *big* secret. It started out innocently enough (famous last words for every lewd tale ever told) with the Fletchers' penchant for family photos.

As Paul began spending more time in bed, Carol turned the three walls surrounding the bed into a gallery of sorts, featuring family photos from every era of their lives. These photos were a good distraction when he wasn't sleeping.

One Saturday evening before bed, as Carol changed up some of the photos on the gallery wall, she wore her light cotton nightgown.

While she worked, Paul expressed more pleasure in what her flimsy nightgown revealed than in the photos. With time, the event evolved (or should she say devolved) so that a picture was hung every Saturday evening, whether or not photos even needed replacing. Paul got the bright idea that less is more, so Carol often ended up wearing nothing but a bra and panties, never even getting to the nightgown stage.

"You realize that if someone rings the doorbell," she laughed one evening, "I can't answer it dressed—I mean undressed—like this."

After the newest photos were safely hung, Carol crawled into the hospital bed beside Paul, shivering.

"You have the body of a twenty-year-old," her husband would say without fail.

It's ludicrous the lengths to which a middle-aged woman will go to for a compliment.

Paul broached the topic of their lost intimacy—the thing Carol had been papering over since the addition of the hospital bed in their bedroom—head-on, as was his way with most things in life. Through his *actions* he told her that he was still her husband, was still attracted to her, was still a sexual being, handicapped or not.

They reinvent their lost intimacy, *remaking* love, as it were: holding hands, cuddling, and lying in each other's arms—even in a cranked-up hospital bed.

Of course, Paul's arms and legs and hands hamper his cuddling ability. No matter. Carol has arms and legs and hands enough.

One evening after book club, Carol makes a catastrophic error: she shares with Barb a few tidbits from the couple's date night. She pays the price dearly. Every week on the way to book club, Barb greets her, with a wink and a nod, saying, "So, how did Saturday night picture-hanging go, Carol?"

Serves me right, Carol thinks, blushing every time she's asked the question, as if on cue. But on this Saturday date night of their *brave new world*—the first time Carol must feed her husband—the hideous necessity is making her apoplectic.

Carol could not bear to set up the small, round table by the patio window. Rather, Paul sits in his lift chair for dinner, staring at the TV, while she sits perched atop a bar stool, legs crossed, chest tight. She's a hair's breadth away from bursting into tears.

She clumsily feeds Paul the lasagna she'd made earlier that day, missing his mouth once and hitting his teeth twice.

As usual, Paul leads her to a gentler place by doing what needs to be done. Simply eating. With each bite she feeds her husband, Carol feels less like a circus act and more like a couple again. Bite after bite, in the imposed stillness and quiet of their reconfigured lives, she finds, dare she say it—contentment? Or is it fulfillment? Or acceptance?

Don't quibble, for heaven's sake, she tells herself.

Gratitude floods over her followed in seconds by heart-wrenching sadness. This is an ugly, debilitating disease—that brings them to their knees pretty much every day. The cost is high. Too high. Especially for Paul.

Paul's voice takes her out of her reverie. "I'll join you in a drink if you don't mind thickening some red wine."

"Of course," Carol responds, chastising herself for forgetting her manners. Because Carol has not yet mastered how much thickener to add to a drink, the wine ends up a virtual red jelly. Obviously too much thickener. She spoon-feeds it to Paul anyway.

"Sour," is all he says as he screws up his face after swallowing. *If Ann were here, she would giggle,* Carol thinks.

Does the thick red concoction even remotely taste like wine? Carol ponders but dares not ask.

Of course, Carol is eventually prancing around the bedroom—scantily dressed, freezing. She fastens another family photo to their gallery wall. And Paul is enjoying the view. And, of course, they cuddle before sleep.

Date night. Another Saturday date night.

***

A very public, not private Saturday night is looming on the horizon as Heather and Bruce's wedding day draws near.

Ideas float around and coalesce, but one detail is non-negotiable: Heather wants her dad to *walk* her down the aisle. Obviously, she's been thinking about it.

"Would you be willing to push Dad's chair down the aisle, Nate?" she asks her brother on a family visit. "Be Dad's legs as I walk beside him?"

Carol must remember to wash the sheepskin arm rests on Paul's chair, a day or so before, so that they are as pristine as Heather's wedding dress.

Paul has a job too: just be there.

It sounds harsh, but his food intake will be scrutinized, starting the day before the wedding. Big coughing episodes wreak havoc on him, almost always requiring a day or two of recovery. The strategy of extensive resting before the big day is easier to implement: Paul is resting of his own volition lately.

Heather does not need her dad stolen from her because of things they can control, thinks Carol.

In one regard, though, they have no control: Paul must be fed in public. So far, only the closest of family have witnessed Paul being fed. Carol wonders whether Paul is dreading it as much as she is. He's mum on the subject.

The complicated transportation needs for the wedding day are left to Carol: she books DATS for the early afternoon church service with a ride back to the house, taking into account the ridiculous wait times. As well, she books the transportation service for the ride to the reception hall in the late afternoon, plus back home at midnight, the latest ride DATS offers. If they're lucky, Paul will last that long. She has no plan B if he must leave earlier, but she keeps that secret.

They decide to forgo the Friday evening rehearsal at the church.

The Uninvited Guest

"I'll get the logistics from Father Francis, Dad. Where and when to proceed down the aisle," Nate insists. "No worries."

Between the two of them, Rosa and Darryl figure out who will share what responsibilities for the day, an integral part of pulling the whole thing off. Carol is no longer befuddled when she reads or hears about a wealthy individual, who upon dying leaves a vast fortune to a homecare worker or a companion, much to the chagrin of a blood relative. Under harrowing circumstances like chronic illness, a new kind of family can be forged in which blood is not what binds them.

Heather and Bruce, too, are fully cognizant of Rosa and Darryl's importance for their big day. One request, agreed upon by everyone, is honoured by the couple: as long a time as possible to rest between the marriage and the banquet.

The day begins with the wedding gods smiling down on them: a big blue July sky, with a slight breeze to moderate the temperature. Carol knows they dodged a bullet as a hot day could have made it impossible for Paul to sit in his chair for any length of time, to say nothing of having the strength to eat or talk.

Exacerbation be damned, Carol proclaims to the gods, metaphorically shaking her fist at them.

The church service goes smoothly. The marriage is as lovely as they had all imagined it would be and the couple's excitement palpable. With Nate's assistance, Paul *walks* his daughter down the aisle, drawing soft applause and a few *aahs* from the crowd. Even though the wait time for DATS is shorter than usual, they manage to fit in a quick family photo after the marriage in front of the church they've attended for over two decades. All in perfect moderate weather.

But Carol makes a critical error: she dashes off to the banquet hall to check in with the caterers. That leaves Paul

89

and Darryl to their own devices, managing the preordained rest between events.

When Carol returns from the hall, Paul is in bed where he's supposed to be, but the mechanical bed is cranked up. In eating position.

Darryl is holding a poised forkful of food—and Paul is chewing.

"I don't believe it," says Carol, gritting her teeth like a rabid dog. "You're eating." She gathers steam. "You know you'll miss the reception if you aspirate. All the arrangements that Heather and Bruce made to maximize your rest time before the banquet, out the window. Your one job to rest, out the window." She looks gutted. "And you're eating!"

Hell, hath no fury like a woman scorned not by one, but by two men. Both have the decency to look sheepish; Carol storms out of the room.

The remainder of the wedding day puts Carol's worries to rest.

As the swirls of colour blur the dancers' movements—like in post-modern photos—the crescendos and decrescendos of the music bounce off the low ceiling and walls of the church hall, mingling with wedding guest voices. The smells of food and drink and warm bodies waft over the room as if in a warm embrace.

As the evening draws to a close, the band leader urges the crowd to grab a partner for the last dance. It ends up a family affair. Glen steps in to dance with his mom. Bruce dances with his daughter, a tired flower girl indeed. And Nate makes sure that Heather gets the last dance with her debonair dad, a carnation in his tux lapel, a bow tie affixed to his milk-white shirt, his shoes as shiny as bright stars—resting on his footrests. Nate sashays the wheelchair around the floor in time to the music with his sister perched atop her dad's lap, daisy bouquet in hand, white veil flowing, feet dancing in the air, both occupants spinning. And smiling.

That night Paul is sound asleep almost before his head hits the pillow.

Carol lays down her own head as a last mental image floats to the surface: Paul being fed, among their wedding guests. By Darryl.

And the sky did not come falling down. The sky did *not* come falling down.

Chapter 12: Beer Bottle Fight
1997

Six weeks after Heather's wedding, Carol and Paul fashion their own version of Thursday bar night in their backyard. "I can hardly wait to see Heather's wedding pictures," April tells Carol over the phone.

It's a hot August day. Carol is super organized. All-beef wieners sit safely in a cooler. Precut buns covered and protected from insects. Condiments lined up in their red, yellow, and green plastic containers, best-before dates religiously checked. Onions are fried, golden brown in butter, sauerkraut added as an option too; no respectable hot dog should be served without one or the other, or both.

Carol eliminates the plastic tablecloth that usually covers the picnic table, wanting the bare pine knots brazenly showing themselves off during lunch. It will be the perfect opportunity to point out that Paul built and stained the table. This is his show.

Mine too, Carol concedes.

"I'm happy to barbecue the hot dogs but you do know I've never used a barbecue before, right?" Darryl asks. "Never had the opportunity, actually."

"Never?" Carol asks.

The Uninvited Guest

"Nope. Not once. So I'm happy for any tips you can give me, Paul."

"April and Marcel should be here soon. Turn on the barbecue now," Paul says to Darryl. He's breathless by the time he explains the reason. "So it reaches the right cooking temperature in time."

"About what time are we eating?" asks Darryl, the men's conversation taking place in the safety of a shady spot on the patio, *exacerbation* no longer an abstract term in their lexicon.

When the DATS bus arrives, Carol wanders out to the front street to greet April and Marcel, watching as the driver unhooks the straps that secure both wheelchairs firmly in place. The driver manoeuvres Marcel's chair expertly down the ramp backwards, allowing room for April to joystick her own way down.

Carol wonders if April ever worries about unwittingly driving her chair off the ramp, which constitutes a cliff, in Carol's humble opinion.

Marcel takes off the minute he's free of the bus driver, forgetting all about his sidekick, it seems; Carol walks behind April to the backyard, the distinctive electronic *swizzing* noise of her electric wheelchair filling the summer air, sounding like a swarm of mosquitoes.

The rest of the visit is a swirl of activity. Three wheelchairs, five people, two of whom need to be fed. Carol plays bartender, as Darryl is busy manning the grill.

The drink of choice on this hot day is obvious: cold beer. Carol pours one for April into a pre-chilled glass, tipping the glass exactly as she's observed, not being a beer drinker herself.

Marcel turns up his nose at the idea of drinking beer from a glass. Luckily for them, he can hold the bottle. Carol thickens a Traditional Ale into just the right consistency, finding the sweet spot. She spoon-feeds the drink to Paul while intermittently holding up April's glass, a straw sticking out of the frothed beer. After a few sips, dark red lipstick stains the straw.

"Food's ready," announces Darryl.

He feeds Paul, cutting the dog into exquisitely small pieces, pre-empting the possibility of coughing. Carol feeds April, holding the hot dog to her mouth for her to bite into. *Why doesn't April aspirate?* she wonders. *She's got MS too.*

Thank goodness Marcel can hold and eat his own hot dog, although the patio underneath his wheelchair ends up smudged with green, red, and yellow stains by the time he's done. Carol notices Marcel's left hand move to grasp his beer bottle in between bites of his hot dog.

The cooking and feeding team forgo eating and drinking for the moment; it's just easier. Besides, they are left doing the talking as the other three eat away. And drink. And listen.

Carol points out the flower bed where their tulips come up each spring and explains that the bulbs are proving to be hardy because they are the very ones that Paul planted, years ago now. Carol wonders if Paul ever thinks about the time he fell beside the red tulips and the subsequent rescue by his daughter and neighbour.

Carol glances at her watch just as April asks about the wedding pictures.

"Let's get started," April insists. "Before we have to leave."

The pictures end up taking a long time—enough for Darryl to spoon-feed Paul the last drops of his beer—because April keeps asking Carol to identify people in the photos as well as commenting on what people were wearing. Carol flips through the photo album, skipping a few pages trying to speed up the process.

"I wish I could have found a caregiver to work for me the day of Heather's wedding. I wanted so much to be there," April bemoans. Carol stops skipping pages.

The Uninvited Guest

Marcel shows no interest whatsoever in the wedding photos. He wheels himself off to the garage, nursing the beer nestled safely between his legs; Carol can see him through the open door, inspecting the workbench and the assortment of garden paraphernalia hanging on the walls.

About fifteen minutes before Marcel and April must be at the front of the house waiting for DATS, April asks Carol to retrieve her wallet from the knapsack hanging from the handlebars of her chair. "Please take out the bus ticket and pin it to my blouse. The bus driver will see it there."

Darryl begins to collect the beer bottles as Marcel returns from the garage. He motions for the bottle between Marcel's legs.

Instead of giving the bottle up, Marcel's hands—his pipefitter-hands of yesteryear—double and redouble around the neck and body of the beer bottle, his hold on it now absolute.

The minutes tick by. April tactfully reminds Marcel that it's time to go. Still, he does not let go of the bottle.

April's tone of voice gets firmer. "Marcel, you know that DATS will leave us behind if we're not out front on time and you can't take the beer on the bus." The words fall on deaf ears.

Darryl kneels in front of Marcel and does what he must: peels—one finger, then two, then three—from the bottle.

Marcel is losing this battle, and he knows it. He grunts. Condensation from the beer bottle drips onto his tan summer trousers; sweat drips from Darryl's furrowed brow.

Marcel makes a last-ditch attempt, sliding three fingers lower on the bottle for more leverage, but in the end, the beer bottle comes loose.

April and Marcel arrive on the front sidewalk as DATS pulls up. Carol stands and waves at her departing guests once the

95

driver has loaded the two into the van. Then she rushes back to the backyard.

"My first ever beer bottle fight," Darryl confides, glancing from Paul to Carol.

"Marcel's stroke...," says Carol. "Well, he doesn't always know the boundaries."

Paul gets the last word on the August barbecue.

"Can't really blame a guy for wanting to finish his beer." He smiles. "Especially on such a hot day."

Carol begins clearing the picnic table. *If only Paul could hold a bottle of beer in his hand, never mind fight for it. If only.*

Chapter 13: They Laugh and Laugh
1997

They have one more summer promise to keep: their Kananaskis holiday.

It's Nate who solves the problem of how to get Paul to the holiday resort.

"Have you considered renting a wheelchair accessible van?" he says to his dad over speaker phone one evening. "You could sit in the wheelchair on the way down to the mountains just like you do in DATS." Paul's eyes widen at his son's suggestion and Carol's heart beats a little faster with excitement.

Nate keeps talking. "The only thing, Mom... will driving a bigger vehicle stress you out, especially a van?"

"Every car we've ever owned has been pretty big. I think I'll be fine."

"Oh, and by the way, I don't think Julie and I will be able to join you in Kananaskis."

"Oh no, Nate. Is everything okay?"

"No need to worry, Mom. Something's come up. Be sure to check into the van though."

For the entire evening, both parents brood and wonder why it is that Nate is not joining them on the family holiday. They stop fretting by morning because Paul is anxious to act on his son's van idea and says, "I'll get right on it."

Paul asks Darryl to phone around to price check van rentals and by the end of the next day, the van is booked.

"I rented it for an extra day so that we can practice with the ramp and the wheelchair straps before the trip," Paul explains when she arrives home.

The holiday plays right into the happily-ever-after-story Carol constantly tells herself. Here they are, like any other Canadian family—off to the mountains. Okay, so leaving a mechanical bed at home to sleep in barrier-free accommodations might not sound like much of an adventure, but she can only assume that the mountains will be visible from at least one room in the cabin. Compensation enough.

Finally, it's departure day. Darryl easily straps Paul and his chair into the van after their earlier practice run. Carol feels smug. Things are falling into place.

Turns out though, the van ride is a torture test. Not because Carol's driving a bigger vehicle, either.

Until this moment, Carol had not realized how much effort it takes for Paul to sit upright and how unsupported his head is. *Now I know why April has that headrest on her wheelchair.*

With every bump and curve in the road—every movement actually—Paul's head weaves and bobs, even worse than on DATS. Must be the speed on the highway. Soon his chin sags into his chest. To add insult to injury, Paul's leg spasms are worse than usual. Carol wonders if he's taken his medication to reduce spasms. "Did Paul get his baclofen this morning?" Both homecare workers nod in unison.

After a moment Rosa says, "But I think that he might need an increase in dosage; the pills don't seem to be controlling the spasms anymore."

The Uninvited Guest

They decide to pull over at the next rest area and transfer Paul to the front seat. Darryl pulls out the ramp from the van and backs Paul down it. He sidles the wheelchair next to the open passenger door.

The homecare workers had started using a specially-designed belt to execute side transfers ever since Paul had stopped being able to use the steel poles to bring himself to standing. They had, of course, brought the belt along for the side transfers at the lodge.

Darryl now places it firmly around Paul's waist, grasps it tightly on either side, then lifts Paul to standing, using the momentum to further swing him into the passenger seat. A nifty move when done correctly.

After the transfer, Rosa and Darryl sit next to each other in the back of the van. Paul dozes off almost instantly after the one hour of whiplash he's just endured; his legs spasms settle down, too.

The wheelchair sits, fastened to the floor, empty and bouncing all the way to William Watson Lodge. Macabre.

Carol knows how terrible Nate is going to feel when he hears of their van fiasco; he was so sure that his dad would love a ride in a rented vehicle. They learn a nasty lesson that day: even when away from home, they are dependent on many aids to make Paul's life manageable, including something to hold his head in place. A wheelchair headrest will be ordered the minute this holiday is over.

I hope the remainder of our holiday is not as fraught, Carol thinks, gripping the steering wheel harder.

Just as Paul rouses, they pull up to the William Watson office. Carol goes in but her nerves are still vibrating from the drive.

The staff at the lodge turn out to be marvelous. It ends up being exactly like checking into any other resort.

It's when Carol's driving to cabin number twelve that she feels an emotional pivot, like this whole thing may yet turn out to be a good idea.

Carol picks a parking spot directly in front of the cabin. It's on a large, paved driveway, the first indication of how wheelchair-friendly this place is. From the outside, the cabin looks a lot like a Swiss Alps ski resort, down to the wraparound cedar deck and railing.

They get Paul out of the van, utilizing the transfer belt successfully for a second time that day. He's recovered enough from his harrowing ride to request a spin around the wraparound deck. The mountains surround them. A barbecue sits out front on the deck. A huge gas barbecue, in fact. Looks brand spanking new.

"Wow," Paul says, ogling it. "Gotta use this thing while we're here." He turns to Darryl and adds, "I'm going to sit here and enjoy the view."

The mountains or the barbecue? thinks Carol as she unlocks the door to their accommodations. She gestures for Rosa to go in first.

Eventually, Paul is resting in the biggest bedroom, with the fully equipped barrier-free bathroom nearby. The rest of their family converge on the cabin in fits and starts. Angie and Sarah arrive before Bruce, Heather, and Ann, with Glen and Tracy following fast upon their heels. The gang descend into happy chaos, bringing in cooler after cooler of food (they certainly won't go hungry) and suitcases galore. Ann insists on peeking in on Papa but he's sound asleep. Snoring.

Each bedroom offers a slightly different view of the Kananaskis mountain range, notices Carol, as the last shreds of her skepticism about the facility melt away. There is now no room at the inn as each bedroom is filled; eleven people in all means someone will sleep on the living room sofa bed.

The Uninvited Guest

Rosa suggests to Darryl that she will take the shift when Paul wakes. Darryl thanks her saying, "I think I'll go check out the lake."

Carol remembers her mother's concern before the trip that bringing two caregivers was too expensive. Carol had pointed out that they would have to be paid at home anyway, so no. Carol made clear that the lodge was as reasonably priced as April had indicated when telling them about the place. "Besides," Carol had told her mom, "there is no way one worker could manage Paul's care over five days."

Soon, Paul is up from his rest and busy too: sitting in a lift chair almost identical to the one they have at home, staring at the mountains from the corner of the living room. Carol is overcome. *Thank you, Peter Lougheed, and thank your wife Jeanne for us too. My husband can rest his head as he sits in this wonderful place that our family will call home for the next five days.*

Sarah asks early next morning, "So, what's on the agenda?" When Carol was a teenager and tried to stay in bed longer, her mom would tell her, "You can sleep when you're dead." Sarah was all about shocking children into good behavior, self-esteem a non-existent notion in that era.

"How close can we get to the lake?" asks Paul.

"There's a lake here?" squeals Ann. "A real lake?"

Darryl interrupts the squealing. "It's completely accessible by wheelchair. The trail's a bit steep near the water but accessible. Totally."

So, the entourage head to the lake. They stroll confidently, knowing that some smart engineer made sure that the William Watson Lodge guests would not be stymied a mere metre from their desired destination—the lake—by a curb or gravel or any other obstacle.

On the walk down, Carol, Rosa, and Sarah lag, the larger group hurrying on. As chance would have it, the dawdling women meet a family of three on their way. What can't be missed is the odd-looking wheeled contraption the dad is pushing, a cross between a baby stroller and a wheelchair.

The families exchange pleasantries. The mother introduces them to the occupant of the contraption. "This is Joey."

All three of them momentarily hover over the contraption, greeting him with both a "hi" and a wave.

"How old is your son?" Carol asks the mom, straightening up.

"Four."

They continue on the path in silence for a while. Then, as they approach a hill, the dad jauntily pushes his son faster, turning to them saying, "We'll probably see you down at the lake... Joey loves it there."

Until this moment, it had never occurred to Carol what it must be like to have a handicapped *child*. An entire lifetime of handicap, a marathon compared to their own MS journey, a mere sprint.

How in the world do they bear it? Carol wonders. *He's just a bit younger than Ann.* After the family is well out of earshot, Sarah asks, "Could he talk, do you think?"

The trio walk the rest of the trail in silence.

When the women arrive at Lower Kananaskis Lake, they see the others marking their territory: setting up lawn chairs and placing a towel for Ann on the rocky beach typical of a mountain lake.

"Where's the Hawaiian white sand?" Sarah asks jokingly.

The lake is nestled right up to the base of the mountains. A perfect contemplation spot, especially with the backdrop of the little-girl sounds—of dipping in and out of the freezing mountain water, filling her green pail with rocks, pretend fish, and weeds—juxtaposed with the lulling lapping sounds of water washing ashore.

The Uninvited Guest

Carol points out the small island in the middle of the lake, sparsely populated by a few tall pines. Someone in the group decides it must be named.

"Ann's Island, of course," says Sarah.

Does every family enjoying this shoreline, name this island anew? wonders Carol.

The lake is a big hit.

The next day, the holiday activity is one that Paul hand-picked himself: a nature presentation at the nearby provincial campsite, as advertised on the information sheet they'd received at the lodge office when they checked in.

"It starts at eleven, so we'd better get going," he says, anticipation written all over his face. What a glorious antidote for the long days of indoor inactivity that Paul experiences at home.

Despite the number of side transfers it takes to get him in and out of the van and into his chair, Carol and Rosa and Darryl drive Paul across the busy highway to the nature presentation. Safer. The rest of the family walk over to meet them.

They settle on the main level of a beautiful semicircular amphitheater with concrete seating of about four or so rows cascading up. They are seated in the heart of the forest. Amid the mosquitoes. The smell of bug spray is heavy in the air.

The first part of the presentation is didactic. Identification of local plants, trees, and foliage. Like being in the classroom. Ann rests her small blond head on the arm of Paul's wheelchair, which happens to be at exactly the right height.

The park presentation gets better. For the next twenty minutes the Fletcher family is treated to a clever and obviously well-rehearsed interactive skit called *Weeds are Flowers, Too.* It's comedic. Informative. And engaging.

Brown knapweed, blueweed, marsh thistle, sow-thistle, chickweed, ox-eye daisy, and, of course, the pernicious dandelion. Who knew there were so many weeds under attack? They laugh and laugh under the midday open sky.

Soon after their return to the cabin, Sarah is still digesting the skit and asks Angie and Ann if they'd like to join her on a scavenger hunt.

When the impromptu naturalists get back, they sort through the treasures they've collected. "I'm sure the guy said these were ox-eye daisies," Angie says to Ann.

Sarah arranges the collection of mountain weeds in an empty pickle jar and plunks them down in the middle of the dinner table, saying, "There. It works."

Would the naturalists from the amphitheater consider this yet another attack on weeds, being plucked from their environment? Carol wonders.

The highlight of Ann's Kananaskis holiday is the easiest of all to pick out. It's the wraparound deck which she turns into a track, a racetrack.

Bruce leans against the rail timing her laps as she circles the cabin umpteen times. "Was I faster this time?" she yells.

Carol's forever memory that she'll take from this holiday is almost as easy to pick out as Ann's.

It starts out with a few of them flanked around Paul in his lift chair in the living room.

"The mountains are beautiful," Paul states. Then adds, "But they're a bit speckled."

"What?" asks Carol. "What are you talking about?"

He reiterates, saying, "The mountains are speckled."

Heather figures out Paul's riddle first. "Oh, you mean the *windows* are dirty." She chuckles.

Paul rearranges his face into a wry grin.

The Uninvited Guest

There's so much in Paul's life that they cannot fix, that they are excited—giddy even—when there's something they *can* fix.

In no time at all, the bucket brigade is out on the front deck, armed and ready to go. To wash the picture window and 'unspeckle' the mountains. Heather reaches the places that Carol, Sarah, and Angie can't. In about half an hour, the pristine mountains emerge, to say nothing of the squeaky-clean cabin number twelve windows.

Paul smiles. "Not speckled now..."

They laugh and laugh under the living room skylights.

For their last dinner at the lodge, Glen announces that he's going to marinate and cook steaks. *Steaks*, thinks Carol, *yikes. Something Paul has not eaten since before his swallowing test.*

Glen barbecues the steaks to everyone's preference, not an easy task given the number of dinner guests. Paul never leaves his side. The next best thing to cooking himself, it seems, is watching his son do so.

Carol and Ann cozy up in Paul's lift chair, far from the barbecue. Carol reads *The Cat in the Hat* to her granddaughter snuggled up to her, awaiting the call to dinner.

When dinner is ready, Heather cuts her dad's portion of steak into itsy-bitsy manageable pieces. He gets it down, eating slowly, turning his head to the left as he chews before each swallow.

Carol is on high alert the entire time, nervously anticipating Paul's first cough, and wonders if anyone else notices how hard Paul must concentrate to swallow his food without aspirating.

At the dining room table feast, they share the story about the window-washing for those who missed the event.

"You washed the windows today?" Tracy says, with a guffaw. "Really?"

"Oh yes we did," teases Angie.

They laugh and laugh under the cathedral ceiling.

The board and card games are quieter on their last evening at the Lodge, Paul the centre of gravity despite being relegated to spectator.

After a walkabout next day, Carol locks the door of the cabin on the dot of 11 a.m. and Darryl pushes Paul to the van. In the blink of an eye—four minutes actually—Paul is a passenger in their rented van. They've learned their lesson: the empty wheelchair is strapped in place, piled high with things so as not to bounce all the way home.

They do not leave their hearts in San Francisco, as the song goes. But be it duly noted that they do leave them at William Watson Lodge, in the majestic mountains that tower above Lower Kananaskis Lake.

Chapter 14: Nate the Builder
1997

The family are tired after the holiday as are Darryl and Rosa. Except for Paul: he seems energized by the William Watson visit. "Too bad we're only allowed to book every second year at the lodge," Paul says forlornly one evening.

Days later, Paul and Carol are still reminiscing about the family holiday when they hear from Nate.

"I'm thinking of coming up on Labour Day... I took a few extra days, so it'll be for a week," he announces over speaker phone.

Hmmm. How curious that he can take a whole week off now but could not join us in Kananaskis, thinks Carol.

Apparently, he has a surprise for Paul, something he's been wracking his brain about for months—trying to decide what he could build for his dad.

"I want it to be practical," Nate tells his mom privately over the phone, "not like the decorative stuff I'm usually working on in the shop. Dad watches a lot more TV these days—in the sitting room—so I thought I'd build a TV unit so he can watch from bed too."

"That's a great idea," Carol tells her son. "But keep in mind, the bedroom is small."

"Exactly," Nate says. "That's why I thought I'd go up. I designed a unit to hold both TV and VCR that will be suspended from the ceiling. Dad will be able to easily watch his shows from bed."

Now I can't even imagine life without the ease of a mechanical bed, Carol thinks. She can't help but hearken back guiltily to the pert occupational therapist that she had mocked.

Carol tells Heather all about Nate's visit and his plan.

"It will be good to put the TV in the bedroom because your dad's spasms are worse when he spends too much time in his lift chair. As soon as he's lying in bed, his legs settle down."

"Oh," Heather says. "I didn't know his leg spasms were increasing."

In that moment, Carol realizes that she keeps a lot of her concerns about Paul from her children. *Are her protective secrets good or bad?* she wonders.

Early in Nate's planning, he had asked Carol to measure three things: the width and height of the wall he intended to use, the size of the unused TV sitting in her study, and the size of the VCR. He'd also asked the location of the nearest plug in the bedroom. Carol had conspiratorially given Nate the information. She'd let Darryl and Rosa in on the ruse, frequently using them as cover when she was committing her crimes and could not put Paul on speaker phone.

A few days before Nate is set to arrive, Carol asks how he plans to get the TV unit home on the airplane.

"It's in pieces," he explains. "It'll be easier to transport that way and I thought Dad would enjoy watching the assembly."

Nate's right. Paul's interest is piqued the moment Nate arrives with the oversized suitcase he hauls into the sitting room. "What do you have there?"

Nate opens the suitcase and places varying sizes of finished wood on the floor; Paul's eyes crinkle as he smiles.

The Uninvited Guest

"What beautiful cherry," he says, as Nate does a mock-up of the pieces.

"It'll be glued together... no nails," says his son proudly. "I'll glue it tonight so it has time to dry. Can I use your clamps?"

"Of course. I think I would have liked being a wood worker," Paul says.

"You would have been a great wood worker, Dad."

Both father and son fall silent. Shouldering their own heavy thoughts.

"Do you have the name of an electrician?" Nate asks his father, breaking the melancholy. "This socket has to be moved before installation."

"We can call the guy we used at the dealership," Paul says.

Three days later, the electrical work is complete, the pieces glued together, and the installation begins.

"Remember how strict you guys used to be about TV watching when we were growing up?" Nate asks. "No TV before school... No TV during dinner... and here I am building a TV unit for your round the clock viewing pleasure. Go figure."

"And now, we almost always eat in front of the TV," says Carol. "No one could have predicted this." And she means more than their change in TV watching habits.

The last day of Nate's stay, the project complete and functional, he and his dad are watching TV together for the first time in the bedroom when Carol arrives home from work. She hears Steve the Crocodile Hunter say to Paul and Nate, "Isn't she a beauty?" in his heavy Australian accent as he wrestles a croc out of the water. Carol plops down on the bed beside Paul; Nate occupies the easy chair, just to the right of the cranked-up bed. They all watch the end of the program together.

Before leaving for home, Nate takes a picture. "Going to add this to my work portfolio."

The day after Nate's departure to Vancouver, Carol and Paul host a Saturday get-together to thank April for recommending William Watson Lodge. When April and Marcel arrive, a parade of three wheelchairs, and a total of four people make their way down the hall in single file.

Paul shows off the TV unit like a proud father standing (a figurative phrase, by now) on the sidelines of a baseball field, after his son has hit a homerun. All agree. Nate hit a homerun.

"It's like a piece of art," April says.

"I like the dovetail joints," Carol says.

Marcel spies the VCR. "You could record hockey games and watch them all night. That's what I'd do." He grins.

The talk then turns to their summer trip. The questions begin.

"How many times did you go to the lake?"

"Anyone take a dip in the lake?"

"Did you visit the amphitheater across the road?"

"Who barbecued?"

"What about those decks?"

They answer every question and add a few details: window washing, Ann's Island, *Weeds are Flowers, Too,* Paul's barbecue super-powers (albeit supervisory), timed laps around the wraparound deck. Some activities need more explanation than others.

Paul tells them that he's been reading about the Kananaskis Mountain Range since he got home. "Because of how the plates in the earth collided millions of years ago, they pushed the rocks up differently. Not as high and jagged."

April's most interested in Paul's discovery. "I always wondered why the Rockies look so different from the Kananaskis Mountains."

"Like inverted bowls," is Paul's assessment of the mountain formation.

The Uninvited Guest

The Fletchers don't say that the van ride down to the mountains was hellish; they don't talk about the four-year-old helmeted Joey in his curious vehicle on the trail; they don't say that they saw more makes and models and sizes of wheelchairs than they knew existed; they don't say that they have come to recognize that there is an entire world of handicapped who exist, that they knew not of, nor wanted to, if truth be told.

Carol doesn't tell them of the bio she read: William Watson, the namesake of the lodge, born in 1949. An injury at birth rendered him handicapped. Against all odds, he became a lawyer. But he never got to article, never mind practice law, as the world was not yet ready for a lawyer in a wheelchair.

As the Saturday visit winds down, April suggests a grand plan: "In two years, let's do a group holiday to the lodge. You'll love the place, Marcel."

Deep down, Carol knows this won't happen. She can't say why not, but she just knows.

***

A few weeks later Nate calls.

"Don't put me on speaker phone, Mom. I need to talk to you first." Nate sounds disoriented. "It's just not working. Julie and me. I moved out. I'm sleeping on my buddy's couch."

"Oh no," escapes from Carol's mouth. "Oh no."

"I'm looking for a small apartment." He seems to be trying to collect his wits. "You guys have enough on your plate... don't worry about me, Mom." Nate sighs. "I'm throwing myself into work. Tell Dad I'm sorry." She hears an intake of breath over the phone. "So sorry."

"I wondered why he didn't mention Julie when he was here, unless I asked about her," Paul says.

"I should've figured it out," Carol answers. She's annoyed at herself. Guilt follows close on the heels of her anger. "I seldom ask to speak to Julie when we call." She squeezes Paul's hand. "And she seldom asks to speak to us anymore."

The phone rings. "I'm on my way over," says Heather. And then there are three. To commiserate.

Heather admits that she knew about the tension in Nate's marriage, but he'd asked for confidentiality. "Now you know why they didn't join us in Kananaskis. Just too hard to put on a happy face for the family."

Glen and Tracy are the only other ones in on the situation.

Paul turns to Heather and asks, "What do you think Nate needs from us now?"

"A little space," she says. "You know how he overthinks everything—he feels like he's let you guys down, especially you, Mom." Her last words before she leaves for home are meant to be reassuring. "They'll figure it out. Don't worry."

Carol takes a page from her son's playbook and concentrates more on work. But she also keeps a close ear to the ground, to catch how Paul is handling his son's marriage breakup. She occasionally seeks out a different perspective from Sarah or Angie. Her mother and sister put their heads together to figure out a way to distract Carol and Paul.

One must know this about the two women. They are zealots, believing a good craft can cure just about anything, including broken hearts. To this day, the scrapbook that the two made for Paul and Carol's 15th wedding anniversary graces the couple's coffee table, rather than being relegated to die in their basement like some tacky homemade craft.

Sarah and Angie scour the craft stores around town, settling on a glow-in-the-dark solar system designed to stick on the wall or ceiling of a child's bedroom.

The Uninvited Guest

Paul gets to be part of the cosmos installation, watching as Darryl, standing on a short ladder, sticks each piece of the heavens exactly where he's told by these two crafty women. Paul gets to be amateur astronomer simply by looking up, no telescope necessary at all. After one particularly difficult day, Paul says, "I like how the Big Dipper ended up right over my head." He points with his eyes as he says this, lest Carol miss it.

Thank God for small mercies, she thinks as she glances over at her astronomer husband who seems to have turned his attention to Saturn and Mars.

Chapter 15: A Standoff at the Calgary Zoo
1998

Early February, Dr. Sneider, tells Carol that although he cannot safely increase the dosage of baclofen for Paul's leg spasms, he thinks he may have an alternative: a researcher he knows is doing a study in hydrotherapy and how it affects leg spasms, especially in people with MS. The aim of the study—increasing one's quality of life, drug free.

Carol puts the doctor on speakerphone. "It's not realistic to think that you could ever get off baclofen, Paul," the doctor cautions, "but the hydrotherapy might bring you some relief from the spasms." Before he signs off the doctor says, "Think about it, and contact my nurse if you're interested."

Paul is intrigued by the word *hydro*. Carol has forgotten how much time Paul had spent in and on the water in his youth. Entire summers at his childhood family cabin, jumping off the pier into Hanmore Lake. Paul and his brother built a canoe in their teens, a bright red one in which Paul eventually taught each of their three children to row.

And just like that, Dr. Sneider has added a new member to his colleague's study group. The adage rings true: *when the student is ready, the teacher appears.*

The Uninvited Guest

Paul might imagine too, that with water, water everywhere, a canoe might just pop up.

But no canoe pops up; it's more like the Loch Ness Monster. Darryl relates the story to Carol when she arrives home from work. "DATS got us there early which was good. I wheeled Paul to the pool deck. Most participants were walking." He pauses momentarily before continuing, "I couldn't get Paul onto the seat that lowers people into the water. There was nothing for him to hang on to. The instructor noticed immediately and told Paul that if he's unable to be in the pool unassisted, this study isn't for him."

Another box to tick in the litany of things Paul is forced to give up.

Water.

Even hydrotherapy.

Dr. Sneider calls shortly thereafter to apologize. The researcher had not realized that Paul has an advanced case of MS, he tells Carol.

Paul has an advanced case of MS.

Carol finds these words startling even though they shouldn't be.

She covers Paul's ears. Doesn't tell him the researcher's assessment of his condition. Nor does she quote the researcher's words to the rest of her family.

The rest of the year drags on. What really gets the Fletchers out of their doldrums is Glen and Tracy's invitation to visit Calgary. The couple are in the throes of housebuilding.

"We'd sure like to hear what you and Dad think about our new house," Glen says over the phone. "The builder just completed one that is very similar to what ours will look like... he said he could show it to you and Dad whenever we like. I know it means another van rental, but I really think it would be great to have you and Dad come down."

Carol had once heard a road trip described as *windshield therapy* and the family could sure use a little therapy right now, especially since the hydrotherapy went awry.

Nevertheless, it involves a lot of planning. Will an accessible rental van be available? Do they stay two or three days? If three, that's too much care to expect from one person. In that case, can Rosa join them? And how will a hotel work for all of them? And Paul needs an accessible room.

The whole thing is dizzying.

Eventually though they are in a Calgary hotel restaurant sipping morning coffee, Paul's thickened and being spoon-fed to him, of course. The *joie de vivre* written on Paul's face makes the gargantuan effort worthwhile. Including bringing two caregivers and the restless sleep Carol had on the queen hotel bed beside Paul. She cannot believe that she misses her futon.

The good news: Paul does not experience even a hint of a coughing fit throughout breakfast.

When they arrive on site to see a facsimile of the house that Glen and Tracy will build, the house builder is punching in the code on the garage door. He drives off once they have gathered inside the garage, telling them he'll be back in an hour.

Carol spies three steps in the garage leading to the door to the house. She panics. *Is the door even wide enough for the wheelchair to get through?*

It takes a while before they figure out how to get Paul in.

First, they put the wheelchair brakes on so that the wheels don't spin. Rosa stands just inside the house at the top of the steps ready to receive the wheelchair. Darryl hangs on to one side of the chair while Glen does the same on the other side. They coordinate the lift moving from step to step and eventually place the front wheels of the chair on the landing at the top of the steps. They pause and rest; the wheelchair, with Paul in it, is heavy. After a few moments, Darryl and Glen lift the back wheels onto the landing. Rosa unlocks the brakes and then rolls the chair toward her. Paul is finally in the house.

Had there been railings on the stairs or had the door been slightly narrower—well, Paul's tour would have ended in the garage.

But they're safely inside. Mission accomplished. Just as well too, as Carol is near her limit of how many more obstacles she can face.

She tries to calm down and enjoy the home's features. It helps that Tracy is excitedly narrating the tour, informing the group about the debate she and Glen are having about the Brazilian hardwood floors beneath their feet.

"We're seriously considering these floors for our house—a tad red for our taste, yet the more we see them, the more we like them."

The high ceilings and two-story windows, the island in the kitchen—all are noteworthy. It brings to mind the house shopping she and Paul did as a young couple and what fun it had been. Of course, the 1970s house was a bungalow, the very one they still live in today.

Carol eyes the flight of stairs to the upper level of the house with trepidation. Tracy invites Carol and Rosa upstairs to view the bedrooms. Paul shows no interest in joining them. He seems to know it would be near impossible.

In time, Paul's body begins to sag.

As she descends the stairs, Carol notices Glen bending low, listening to his dad. She wends her way over to intervene, but only if necessary.

It is necessary.

Carol knows how difficult it is to understand Paul once his fatigue sets in, something Glen rarely deals with firsthand.

Paul keeps glancing toward the garage door they had entered. He can't point, but it's that vicinity of the house that has his attention. He's trying to say something.

Darryl asks, "Do you want to go back to the van?"

Rosa asks Paul if he's feeling ill. All of them are trying to decode Paul's words.

Then Carol spies it. The culprit. A hand-printed sign graces the wall, just inside the doorway. It reads: "Please take shoes off before entering."

That's it. Paul nods in agreement as Carol points out the sign to her troop.

The long drive down yesterday, the confusion of booking three hotel rooms side by side, Carol's fear of Paul's coughing fits, not sleeping well, stairs to navigate, the dreaded long journey home, the tension of seeing her son and daughter-in-law's reaction to a much sicker man than they've last seen—all of it comes crashing down on the world-weary Carol.

"You want us to take off your *shoes*?" She digs in. "For heaven's sake, Paul, your shoes aren't even touching the floor." She catches her breath. "They're on your footrests... the sign doesn't mean you!" Carol sighs, exasperated.

Back outside at the cars, waiting for the builder to return, Carol's family stands, awkwardly trying to recapture the pleasant mood of the visit.

Glen tries to put a happy face on the ordeal.

"You always were a stickler for following rules," he says with a genuine smile.

Tracy adds her own version. "You live by the gentleman's code," she says brightly.

Darryl sides with Paul too. "You just want to do what's right."

Rosa stands by Paul's chair silently.

As excuses fly around in every direction, Carol stands her ground: "Besides, your shoes aren't even dirty."

The Uninvited Guest

Next morning, Glen pushes his dad for the second day in a row. Father and son traverse from one animal enclosure to the next at the Calgary Zoo, the place Paul had requested they visit as they had many times before as a young family (and many other zoos, for that matter) every chance they got. It's a beautiful April day, the warm air hinting at the promise of summer.

A peacock brashly crosses right in front of Paul's wheelchair, dragging its six-foot velvety blue feathers behind it. It stops, turns, and seems to look directly at Paul. The two get into a staring match.

Paul blinks first, by giggling. The peacock seems offended, puffing itself and its feathers to its most imperial self, before strutting off in righteous indignation.

"I think you lost that one, Dad," Glen says, laughing.

Nothing else that afternoon compares to the peacock encounter.

After saying goodbye to Glen and Tracy, Paul conks out the moment they hit Highway 2 North towards home.

"The traffic is heavy," Carol says. It's all the energy she has for conversation. She turns on the radio.

The Sunday talk show host poses her question for the next two-hour discussion: how would you rate last year's snow removal in Calgary? Carol is irritated and changes the channel abruptly from station to station, searching out some soothing music.

What a mistake. She hears Elvis Presley crooning *"for I can't help falling in love with you."*

It's their song. It's all Carol can do to stay in her lane on the busy highway as she feels a flush of emotions: wanting to be held in Paul's arms as in days of yesteryear, yearning to be somewhere, anywhere but driving this van. What about twirling around a dance floor, Paul strong enough to lift her slightly off her feet as he had on their 15th wedding anniversary?

Paul sleeps right through their song.

Once in Edmonton, they drop Rosa off at her house; Darryl's shift ends after he feeds Paul dinner and prepares him for bed.

The next day, Heather drops in to hear about their Calgary visit. Carol fills her in with details including the take-your-shoes-off fiasco at the show home. Heather is amused, but not surprised. She knows her dad.

Heather is tickled pink by the peacock-standoff story. "Dad, maybe that peacock recognized you. We visited that zoo every year when I was little!"

Paul smiles between breakfast bites, tired, but happy.

Paul and the peacock, thinks Carol, *both captives, in their own right.*

Later that same day, they hear from Glen and Tracy.

"We're so thrilled you came down to see the house," Glen says on speaker phone, never mentioning his mom's meltdown at all.

Months later, well into October, the Fletchers get a lovely photo in the mail: Tracy and Glen, arms linked, standing together proudly outlined by the doorframe of a large garage piled high with boxes. The house is near completion.

The sharing of the picture is a kind of hospitality. Tucked inside the envelope is an invite:

Christmas Day Dinner
Location: Tracy and Glen's new house
Time: 2 p.m.

"Can't wait," is the postscript scrawled on the bottom of the invitation.

Carol does not put the Christmas dinner date on the calendar, afraid of jinxing it.

Chapter 16: Health is a Crown That Only the Sick Can See
1998

It doesn't work: Glen and Tracy's Christmas dinner is jinxed anyway.

MS is doing the talking *again*.

Darryl informs Carol almost daily that Paul sleeps through breakfast. On weekends, she watches Rosa try to rouse him as he nods off between bites of lunch.

Even with all the precautions they are taking, a coughing fit accompanies pretty much anything Paul swallows, including the thickened water that he is spoon-fed to get his pills down. One day as Paul seems to be coughing up a lung, he mentions that his chest hurts.

The busyness of Carol's school year and maybe some magical thinking, allow Carol to ignore the empirical evidence piling up before her eyes.

It's the last symptom that dashes cold water in Carol's face, bringing her to her senses: fever. A fever so high, Paul is barely able to lift his head or speak.

"Has he been like this all day?" Carol asks Darryl when she arrives home from school, a mere week away from the Christmas break. Darryl nods. "I'm calling an ambulance."

Paul's thick, dark brown eyebrows rise as she dials but he says nothing.

Fifteen minutes later, two burly men are walking down the hallway to their bedroom, leaving a gurney at the front door. They are brusque. No formalities whatsoever and then, in reaction to the presence of the mechanical bed, Carol supposes, they ask, "What does he have?"

"A fever," Carol answers. "Oh... and multiple sclerosis."

The paramedics check Paul's vitals, documenting them on a clipboard. Carol asks if they would like their homecare worker to help get Paul onto the gurney, as he's difficult to move. The suggestion seems to get their backs up. "We've got this," the burlier of the two says.

They park the gurney parallel to the bed. They roll Paul over on his side, placing a sheet beneath him. They turn him to his other side and the sheet becomes a kind of sling. As one of the attendants cranks the bed up, Paul opens his eyes, seemingly unaware of what's happening. Carol reminds her husband that they're going to the hospital.

Both attendants take up positions on the right side of the bed grabbing the sheet firmly, the gurney between them.

"One... two... three..." they count, as each man lifts on cue. Between mechanical bed and gurney, Paul lets out a blood-curdling wail that makes the ambulance attendants stop midair, looking like they don't know which surface to aim for. It sounds like they've broken Paul.

They choose the gurney, all the while asking if Paul's okay. He nods weakly.

"Does your husband have a chest injury?" they ask Carol. "Does he usually talk louder?" "When did the fever begin?" Frankly, they look and sound scared.

The two men wheel Paul down the narrow hall, one behind the gurney, the other leading the way. They take him out the

The Uninvited Guest

front door and down the snowy steps after having determined that the elevator will not accommodate the gurney. The two attendants load Paul into the ambulance, slowly and carefully so as to avoid hurting Paul.

Carol searches her purse for pen and paper, jots down two phone numbers and hands them to Darryl who stands beside her on the road, the doors of the ambulance wide open.

"Call Heather at her school. They will get her out of class if you say it's an emergency," she advises. "Then call Rosa so she doesn't come to work this evening."

"For sure," Darryl says, taking the numbers. He's visibly unnerved.

One attendant and Carol step inside the vehicle, seating themselves beside Paul.

"My husband's neurologist is at the University Hospital. Is it possible to go there?"

"No problem, we'll get him there, ASAP." Seems like Paul's deep chest howl did the paramedic in.

As the driver pulls away from the curb, he turns on the siren, startling Carol.

She reaches for Paul's hand as they pull away. It's burning up. *Why, oh why, did she wait so long?* She bites her lip, trying to calculate exactly when the fever started.

Paul sleeps all the way to hospital. It scares Carol that he's not checking out this vehicle and its paraphernalia.

The handoff from paramedics to hospital staff is quick. Carol senses their discomfort.

"Hope things go okay for your husband," they mutter as they place Paul's chart on his chest.

They wave meekly before slipping away.

Relentless questions follow. From all sides. It sounds to Carol as if everyone is talking underwater. Timelines blur.

123

People pass every which way, nurses, even policemen, among the chockablock gurneys.

Carol is brought out of her thoughts when Heather rushes toward them. She leans over her dad's stretcher.

"Hey, Dad," she squeaks in a voice filled with unshed tears. "What's up?"

Carol feels reassured by this familiar greeting that her daughter uses every time she sees her dad.

Heather plants a kiss on Paul's forehead and takes the metal chart off his chest, placing it at her father's side.

The daughter-father greeting is interrupted by a nurse who leads them to the registration desk. The first thing the triage nurse asks for is Paul's healthcare number. Carol is flustered, not even having thought to bring Paul's wallet in which the card is kept, but Heather has the wherewithal to name her dad's neurologist. The nurse types in Dr. Wilby, giving her instant access to all the information she needs.

Next, she asks them to describe Paul's symptoms. Carol tries to go backward from most recent to a few weeks previous as the nurse's fingers fly over her keyboard. "Fever, difficulty talking, and fatigue."

"And he's had no appetite lately," Heather adds.

Carol squirms as they complete the litany.

"Looks like the paramedics took Paul's temperature... did you take it earlier in the day?" the triage nurse asks.

"No," Carol says, dropping her eyes.

Before Carol knows it, she and Heather are whisked away through double doors to a section of curtained-off cubicles, each barely large enough for a bed and a few chairs.

"Can't say how long it'll be before the doctor sees you," says the gurney-pushing nurse.

It seems that they have bypassed the packed waiting room entirely. *Is that a good thing or a bad thing?*

The Uninvited Guest

"Should we wait until after we see a doctor to call Nate and Glen?" asks Carol noticing that Paul has dozed off again.

"Might just scare them if we call now," says Heather.

"But what if they feel left out?"

"Do what your gut tells you, Mom."

Carol turns to the person she has relied on for sanity all her married life, gently shaking his shoulder.

"Paul, do you think we should let the boys know where you are?"

He opens his eyes before answering Carol's question. "I think they'd like to know I'm here."

At that moment, a nurse enters to hook Paul up to a heart monitor and start an IV drip, explaining both actions to Paul who barely opens his eyes this time round. Heather asks the nurse where the nearest pay phone is before scooting away.

The doctor enters the room moments after Heather's return. "I'm Dr. Johnston and this is my resident, Dr. Fenton." He stirs Paul from his slumber to ask the same question Heather had asked her dad earlier. "What's up?"

Paul glances at Carol after every question the doctor poses, so she begins answering for him. As she's doing so, she remembers that Paul has recently mentioned experiencing some pain in his chest. The doctor's eyebrows arch.

Why, oh why, did we wait so long to bring Paul in? The word *negligence* crosses Carol's mind.

"How much walking does he do?"

"Well... none," Carol says sheepishly.

"But he does stand momentarily when he does a side transfer into his wheelchair or his bed or his lift chair—many times a day actually," Heather adds. "He needs help with it though."

Carol finds her voice, trying to rehabilitate the doctor's impression of the Fletchers. "His homecare workers religiously

125

do leg exercises twice daily. And he goes out to visit friends or out to dinner, quite often." She hesitates. "He's on baclofen."

"Not walking, though," the doctor reiterates, almost under his breath.

Next, he begins the physical exam. Presses everywhere. Legs. Feet. Neck. Abdomen. Listens to his heart. Lungs. Checks his ears. His throat. Asks Paul to open his eyes, shining light into them. He returns his attention to Paul's legs.

"Non-ambulatory makes him prone to vein and pulmonary embolism," he says to his resident.

"The first step is to conduct a Doppler ultrasound," the doctor says, then turns to look at Carol. "Not walking makes your husband susceptible to pulmonary embolism. We'll check for signs of anomalies in the veins in his legs... the ultrasound transducer is a handheld device that can be done right here in emergency to check the blood flow."

"What's a pulmonary embolism?" asks Heather.

"Medical term for blood clots," the doctor replies. "A clot could start in a vein in his leg and travel to his lungs. We'll also check his lungs with the portable X-ray right here in emergency too." The doctor pauses. "And, of course, we'll order blood work. He'll be taken up to a room as soon as possible."

The word lungs make a lightbulb go off in Carol's head. "Oh, I almost forgot," she says, placing her hand over her mouth. "We took my husband to the swallowing clinic last February... and the doctor there said he was at high risk for aspiration pneumonia."

The doctor frowns slightly.

"That's why we feed my dad small pieces of food," Heather jumps in, "and thicken all his liquids."

"Important to know," the doctor says. "I'll arrange for a lung specialist to see him as soon as he's up in the ward."

The Uninvited Guest

Heather directs a loaded question to the emergency room doctor, seconds before he departs. "I have two brothers who live out of town... should we tell them to come?"

Heather's innuendo is obvious: how serious is this?

The answer is a momentary reprieve, it seems: "You could," the doctor states. "But you could also wait a day or two... to see how things go."

Chapter 17: Room 301
1998

Carol sits beside Paul in room 301. Heather is probably still in bed as she insisted on staying with her dad until he was safely settled, around 3 a.m. apparently.

Carol vaguely remembers being handed a phone late in the evening with her brother-in-law John at the other end, insisting he was on his way over to take her home for some rest. She cannot remember if she slept last night. She looks down: she's in different clothes, so she supposes so.

Paul stirs. Carol shoots up in her chair and leans over the bar that separates them. It seems higher than the one at home and makes it difficult for her to reach over to kiss her husband. She grabs his hand instead.

"Hi honey," she whispers, "I'm here... I'm here."

"Did you tell Darryl not to come to work today?"

"I did," Carol answers. Paul dozes off as if satisfied with the answer to his question.

The room is alive with sounds. Occasionally, a beep ushers in a nurse—her scurrying shoes heralding her appearance—to silence a machine. A dripping IV hydrates Paul. Also dripping into Paul's veins is an anticoagulant called heparin, to ward off blood clots they've been told. A large plastic bag hangs at her feet on a low bed bar, collecting Paul's urine. She must always remember to sit on this side so that no one else sees it.

A call button is clipped to the pillow, left of Paul's head. Carol makes a mental note to tell the next nurse that appears that Paul cannot reach up to press a button.

Paul is wearing a faded blue hospital gown and Carol can only imagine the difficulty the nurse would have had getting it on him. Carol hopes Heather didn't witness the ordeal. She's been keeping the difficulty of dressing Paul hidden from the children, her need to protect them as alive as when they were six-year-olds crossing a busy street.

She also wonders if Paul is past being embarrassed by the invasions of privacy foisted upon him, time after time?

Heather arrives and lands a kiss on her dad's cheek, just that much taller than her mom to make it manageable over the shiny chrome railing. He opens his eyes and smiles broadly at his daughter.

"Your room has a nice big window, Dad."

He turns his head to the window and Carol can't help but notice how much effort it takes for him to say, "Which direction are we facing?"

"That's east," Heather says, pointing. "I stopped at Tim's this morning. Parked near the Jubilee, just west of here. And Whyte Ave is southeast, about two blocks away." Nothing wrong with her dad's head, especially his sense of direction and she knows he'd be interested in these details.

The exertion of the conversation puts him back to sleep.

"Glen should be here by mid-morning," Heather reports to her mom. "Depending on traffic. Tracy can't leave until she ties up some loose ends at work. She'll come when she's able. Nate says he'll wait to see how things go here but asked to be kept in the loop."

Heather informs her mother of another morning call. "When I called in your absence this morning, your principal asked if Dad could have visitors."

"Hopefully, we'll be home before there's time for that to happen," says Carol.

Time warps in the hospital: drags, helter-skelter, then drags again.

The doctor in charge eventually appears. He's an internist, Dr. Brownly.

He voices his concern. "The Doppler ordered by the emergency room doctor last night seems to be showing anomalies in the veins in your husband's left leg, but it's an inconclusive test." He looks down and reads Paul's chart. "Dr. Johnston has written here that your husband is non-ambulatory, is that right?"

Carol nods.

Dr. Brownly continues and his voice seems to rouse Paul.

"Even though you had a portable X-ray of your chest last night, Mr. Fletcher, we need an X-ray with you sitting up." Carol glances at Heather wondering if her daughter is thinking what she is: Paul can't sit up.

"We'll continue the anticoagulant that Dr. Johnston ordered until we know more." Dr. Brownly puts his hand on Paul's shoulder and says, "We're hoping a blood clot has not already passed to your lungs."

The words *blood clot* supplants Carol's worry about Paul's inability to sit up for the X-ray.

After finishing the physical exam, the doctor bustles out of the room, leaving Carol and Heather wondering what to do next.

When Heather moistens her father's lips with a swab or adjusts his pillow or puts her hand on his brow, Carol waits her turn. Then cranks the bed up or down, changes Paul's

The Uninvited Guest

hand position, smooths the bedclothes. Heather peers at her mother's actions through troubled blue eyes.

Paul looks the same. Sleepier, perhaps. And sleeping more deeply, perhaps. Carol's rationale for the deep sleep is that he's exhausted from all the hospital commotion.

The next hour is interminably long. Thoughts swirl in Carol's head; she feels dizzy.

Heather strokes her dad's hand and wipes away tears from her eyes.

"We never thought to ask the doctor how to treat a blood clot in the lung," Carol says.

"We should start writing things down," Heather says. "To remember what to ask. And we need to tell somebody that Dad cannot sit up on his own."

A few hours later, Glen steps into the hospital room, changing the family dynamic. He looks every bit as haggard as his mother and sister. Pursed lips. Furrowed brow. Curly hair still dusted with snowflakes—his grandpa Steve's unruly hair, not his dad's neat wavy-do.

He bends and gives his dad a big but gentle hug, looking like he will not let go. Carol cannot help but think of Jacob—wrestling with the angel Gabriel to wring a blessing from him.

Breaking the silence, Glen says, "Tracy sends her love."

Paul's eyes are open so Glen continues. "You have to get out of here, Dad. It's almost Christmas and you're supposed to be at our new house for dinner."

It takes Paul several minutes to muster the strength to ask two questions. "Busy roads? Company car or your own?"

Safe topics.

After Glen has explained the details to his dad, Heather breaks the spell.

"Glen," she begins, "the doctor was here this morning. He said they found irregularities in the veins in Dad's leg. Might mean a blood clot has already moved to his lungs. And more clots could form."

Glen's blue eyes dart to his father. Paul's eyelids flutter open briefly and then close, as if to protect him from the doctor's words.

"But he's talking," Glen says. "He seems okay."

Glen looks directly at his sister, seemingly unable to process what she's telling him.

Carol breaks in. "Nate is waiting to hear some news before he books his flight. I think we should call him."

Heather offers to call. Glen sits down and says, "I'll stay here. With Dad...."

Upon returning, Heather reports, "Nate will be here ten tomorrow morning," She sits in the chair closest to her dad. "He's coming on WestJet."

Time seems to revolve around the opening of Paul's eyes. Carol decides to let her son and daughter do the fussing each time he opens them.

She's preoccupied trying to sort out who needs to be told what. Especially Rosa and Darryl. Carol's irrationally afraid they'll start looking for other jobs. But it seems inappropriate to voice these concerns now.

A nurse enters the room, rousing Paul. "Someone will be in shortly to take you down for X-rays," she says.

Reliving the howl that erupted from Paul when the paramedics moved him, Carol jumps in, her voice rising in volume as she describes her husband's inability to move on his own. The nurse cuts Carol off.

"They use a Hoyer Lift to transfer him to the X-ray table," she says before leaving.

Paul dozes off immediately.

"What in the world is a Hoyer Lift?" Heather asks.

"Beats me," says Glen.

The Uninvited Guest

"As long as it doesn't hurt him," says Carol.

***

An hour later, two porters arrive to wheel Paul to the X-ray room; Carol asks if they can accompany Paul.

"Of course," the men say amicably.

"But only one customer to a bed," one of them teases.

It feels good to stand and specially to walk, thinks Carol. She'd recently read that some of the best contemplation happens when humans walk. But Paul can't walk. Hasn't been able to for a long time. Carol cannot imagine how it must feel. Being pushed, everywhere. By many folks too. Thankfully, Paul's okay for the moment, sleeping right through the jaunt to the X-ray room, as his son helps by navigating the shiny IV pole, through threshold after threshold.

Just as they arrive at their destination, a white-coat technician comes out of one of the rooms.

"Paul Fletcher?" she asks. She scans the three bystanders and anticipates their question.

"You're welcome to join him."

The X-ray technician wheels forward a bizarre-looking stainless steel monstrosity. A patient lift, they are told. The bottom is a U-shaped base on wheels, called C-legs, which get pushed beneath a gurney, a bed, a chair—whatever a patient is being moved to or from.

The family stares. The spine of the thing acts as the main support, and attached to it is a short arm, sitting parallel to the C-legs. Affixed to the end of this arm is a mast, of sorts, with four thick black hooks dangling from it. This umbrella shaped piece looks space-age-sturdy—not something that might collapse in a strong wind.

The technician is matter-of-fact, seemingly not sensing their shared horror at the look of the lift, at all. She explains to Paul that she must move him from his hospital bed to the X-ray table. She further explains that the red mesh material she's placing behind his back, buttocks, and legs creates a cradle of sorts.

"It's called a sling." The technician prattles on. "Don't worry though, this sling can hold as much as three hundred pounds, and I know for sure you're not near that."

Paul nods and says, "Okay." It's his go-to word these past forty-eight hours.

The technician looks over at the family. "I could use some help to support his back," she says. "To keep him sitting upright for the X-ray."

Heather and Glen step forward as if in a trance, donning the lead apron protectors they're handed. They now look to Carol like soldiers from the Middle Ages, ready for a call to action; the only thing missing are broadswords.

Once the woman has the sling under the length of Paul's torso, she takes its two long tie-like pieces, pulls them taut and criss-crosses them at Paul's crotch. "I'm criss-crossing the ties so that you don't slip through and end up on the floor."

The technician pushes the stainless-steel lift toward Paul in his bed, stopping the umbrella-like piece over his chest, efficiently attaching the sling loops to the mast hooks. She pumps the hydraulic handle and poof—Paul rises from the bed.

The moment of lift.

"Oh," escapes from Carol's mouth.

Probably one of the most useful aspects of the sling becomes visible as Paul hangs in the air: an acrylic half-moon piece inside the mesh supporting Paul's head tilts him almost to sitting position.

The Uninvited Guest

Some fancy engineer invented this state-of-the-art thing, is all Carol can think. It reminds Carol of the stork-delivering-a-baby image she has seen so many times on congratulatory cards at the birth of a baby. But rather than being swaddled in a blanket like a baby, Paul is swaddled in a red and black mesh sling, swaying slightly.

"Now that you're safely in the sling," the technician says, "I'm going to move you over to the X-ray table, Paul."

Carol tries to read Paul's face. He's awake. His curled fingers hang onto the wide border of the sling as if it's something he's done all his life. His sterling silver wedding ring catches Carol's eye.

Paul is lowered to the table. The technician says, "Relax your legs on the table, Paul." Turning to Glen and Heather, she says, "This is when I'll need you to hold your dad in a sitting position." In one fluid motion, the sling is unhooked, and the Hoyer-Lift backed out of the way by the technician. "The sling would interfere with the X-ray," the woman explains further, as she tucks it below Paul's hips, its long straps dangling on the floor.

As Glen and Heather struggle to hold their father still, the technician rushes over to her X-ray machine, taking pictures—more than one.

"All done," she says brightly, as if she has just taken a family photo to be sent out as a Christmas card. "But just hold on to your father a minute longer and I'll check the images. I don't want to have to put him through this again."

"Almost done, Dad," Heather says.

"We got this, Dad," Glen confirms.

MS has forged a role reversal: the son and daughter reassuring the parent he'll be okay.

The technician's voice interrupts Carol's thoughts. "The X-rays are fine... let's get you back on the bed."

Heather and Glen slink back to stand near Carol. The stunned family hold hands watching the lift routine in reverse, their protective eyes following the technician's every move.

One thing for sure, this woman has done this many times before. She's good at it. Before long, two porters have the Fletcher family back in Paul's room.

He's safe. Away from hydraulic monsters.

Carol can't wait to sit down. But Glen and Heather suddenly have somewhere else to be, urgently, it seems. Carol is sure she hears crying; she sees Glen's arm slip around his sister's shoulder as they leave Paul's hospital room.

I could never have imagined such a thing, Carol thinks. It looked so routine, which was perhaps the most horrifying part of it.

Objectively, Carol would personally like to meet the inventor of the lift, congratulate him on his ingenious ergonomic invention: Paul was not hurt in the X-ray transfer at all.

Subjectively, she wants nothing to do with his invention. And she means it. End of story.

Paul sleeps soundly, exhausted, no doubt, after his flight into outer space. She's dying to know what he thought of it.

Carol can't shake the feeling that this Hoyer Lift experience is a turning point of some kind, like the ones she's heard people describe as life changing. The life they *had* morphing into something *else*. Carol hopes she's overreacting. Her sighs are heard only by the pale green walls of Paul's hospital room.

In the months to come, Carol learns the full story of this invention they've encountered in hospital: Ted Hoyer himself was a quadriplegic. The very man who invented this beast, hence the name. Hoyer Lift.

But she's far and safe from that information on this Hoyer Lift hospital day.

Chapter 18: There Are No Atheists in Foxholes
1998

The Christmas season is surreal, festive surrealism at its worst. Carol simply cannot figure out how her family got here. Nate arrives from Vancouver, but he can't seem to get his footing. When he arrives at the hospital, they try to fill him in on what's transpired thus far, but he gets defensive. "Why am I always the last to know anything in this family?" *His recent divorce is making him more emotional than usual,* thinks Carol.

The family tension sinks into insignificance though on December 23. It begins with a dust-up between Dr. Brownly, the ward internist, and the lung specialist, Dr. Chung.

It's as if the doctors forget that the family are in the room, privy to their differing opinions.

Carol squirms in her chair.

Dr. Chung insists that the chest X-ray they've done shows a whiteout effect on the right lung. "Indicative of pneumonia. Aspiration pneumonia. That explains the fever... he should have been on antibiotics from day one. Just hope the blood clot theory in the legs didn't sidetrack us."

Dr. Brownly sounds defensive. "Pulmonary embolism is a real possibility. This patient is non-ambulatory... and the

Doppler exam found anomalies in the veins of the patient's legs the night he was admitted, confirming our assessment."

"But that doesn't explain this latest chest X-ray," Dr. Chung insists, his exasperation showing. "Or the fluid buildup in his lungs. Or his fever."

Dr. Brownly doubles down. "I think he should still stay on the heparin, at least, for now."

He looks pensive before adding, "Maybe he had clots that are now complicated by pneumonia."

In the end, the doctors compromise: an antibiotic will be introduced immediately to treat what appears to be pneumonia, but Paul will remain on heparin to address the blood clot concerns. Both drugs will be used, for now.

Suddenly Dr. Chung seems aware of the family. "We'll begin an antibiotic immediately."

Carol feels relieved about the antibiotic although unnerved by the doctors' disagreement.

Mere mortals after all, not gods.

The family holes up in Paul's room the rest of the day. When someone asks Carol a question, it takes her a moment or two to realize that they are talking to her. The incessant paging of announcements in the room and hallways doesn't help.

They are working out a roster to make sure Paul has a family member by his side as much as possible. Glen's main concern is to get Tracy here from Calgary; Heather and Bruce are discussing when to bring Ann up to see her Papa. By now, a nurse has administered a second dose of antibiotic through the IV line in Paul's hand. He's sound asleep.

Carol and Nate are drafted for the first shift of the official bedside vigil. Early on the morning of the 24th, they sit at arm's length from Paul. He does not open his eyes once. Carol tries to regain some perspective by telling herself that *things could always be worse*. She remembers looking down her nose

The Uninvited Guest

at the drivel she had read in the self-help books a friend had tried to interest her in, but here she is—using the cliché at Paul's bedside.

And lo and behold, things get worse. Dr. Chung rushes back into the room to say that they've re-examined the X-rays and have decided the fluid build-up in Paul's lungs is more substantial than they first thought. It must be drained. Immediately.

Nate asks what is involved. "We introduce a very fine needle midway up Paul's rib cage, on the side of his chest," the doctor explains. "We freeze the area so he shouldn't feel any discomfort. If anything, the release of fluid should ease his laboured breathing." As if speaking to himself, the doctor adds, "We'll send the fluid to the lab for culture, to confirm that the bacteria is responding to the cephalosporin we've just put him on."

Dr. Chung looks at Carol for the first time with a hint of sorrow in his eyes. "This pneumonia is turning out to be peskier than we first thought. And Paul's lungs are compromised by the MS... but we don't know how compromised." He leaves the worst for the last. "We'll find out how strong his lungs are soon enough. It wouldn't hurt to tell your family to prepare for the worst."

The doctor slips away, lest they ask for more explanation, it seems.

***

Prepare for the worst? Surely Carol's heard wrong. He can't mean what she thinks he means. There's no way. You die *with* MS not because of it. The neurologist told them so when Paul was diagnosed over six years ago now. You live with it for years and years.

139

Besides, *pneumonia?* That's for old people. And Paul's not old. And anyway, pneumonia is treatable.

"Mom, we've got to get Heather and Glen here," Nate is saying. But his voice sounds far away. And makes no sense. This is what it must feel like to be tortured. You disassociate.

"I'm going to find a phone and call them."

Carol leans over her husband's bed the minute her son leaves the room. She lowers the shiny bar that separates them and crawls into the bed beside him. This is her chance.

"Don't die honey," she whispers in his ear. "Please Paul. We need you... we all need you." Her voice crumbles. "You can hang on... I know you can... you must. Please, hang on."

Carol has no memory of how it all happens. Nor how much time has passed. But eventually people keep appearing in Room 301 as she sits holding Paul's hand.

John and Barb appear first. Barb looks stricken; John is in fighting mode. "How did he get *this* sick *this* fast? Are the doctors sure?"

Carol proffers no answers to these rhetorical questions.

John continues, "And I thought he was supposed to have such strong lungs?"

When Sarah arrives with Angie, Carol finds her tongue and tells them that she's sure Dr. Chung is mistaken. He doesn't know Paul. How positive he is. "Paul's going to wake up and start asking which way is east or west or north or south on the street below," Carol insists. Her mother and sister look at each other—as worried about *Carol* as they are about Paul, having no idea what she's talking about.

Glen shows up with Tracy who's just arrived from Calgary. Finally. Tracy's face registers shock as she gazes at her father-in-law for the first time in months.

Heather and Bruce and Ann appear next. They lower the bar on the bed; all three take turns leaning over to give Paul

The Uninvited Guest

a kiss on his forehead. Papa's usually chatty granddaughter is silent, which scares Carol. Carol's fear is heightened further when Paul's former partner George arrives, bends over, and looks like he's saying goodbye to the man he spent years selling cars with.

Suddenly, the family is ushered into the hallway and told that the procedure to drain the fluid will take at least an hour. They follow the leader into the lounge. One gowned patient sits reading. They crowd to one side of the room, dominating it. The family members are all talking over each other, as if unleashed by some fury inappropriate to express in front of Paul. The gowned patient gets up and leaves.

It's as if being thrust into the hospital lounge changes Carol's centre of gravity. She's thinking about the outside world which is busy celebrating Christmas Eve.

"We have to call April," Carol says. "She can't find out from someone at church. That would be horrible. And Rosa and Darryl need to know too."

The family are making their way back into Paul's room after his right lung has been drained, when Rosa and Darryl arrive as if summoned magically by Carol's thoughts of concern.

Some visitors stand, others end up sitting beside Paul. Some hold his hand. Sometimes his right. Sometimes his left, which showcases his wedding ring.

"He slept right through the draining," the nurse informs them as she cranks up Paul's bed slightly, checks his IV, and rearranges the bedding. Paul sleeps through Rosa and Darryl's visit as well.

Eventually, the visitors leave, some tear-stained; Glen, Nate, Heather, and Carol remain.

The day of December 24 passes and turns into night, *the night the doctor hinted could be one of Paul's last.*

141

Because she does not know what else to do, Carol reverts to her old life: she prays. She bows her head, as if she's back in her parish church and suddenly comes to a realization: there are no atheists in foxholes. She couldn't have imagined this cliché would ever having anything to do with her. But today it does and now she knows it's true.

Please–please give us another chance. I didn't know how sick he was. But I'll take better care. Honest. I'll get it right. Call an ambulance sooner. Much, much, sooner, I promise. Please, God. I've learned my lesson. Please turn back the clock. Give me one more chance. Don't let Paul die. I'll get it right.

At around 3 a.m. on Christmas morning, Paul's fever breaks. He begins making groaning sounds in his sleep, moving his head, opening and closing his mouth, although not uttering a word. Carol awakens her family members from their light dozing.

By mid-morning Paul is opening his eyes too, and when he drifts back asleep, it's not as deep. By afternoon he's looking around, albeit with gaunt cloudy eyes.

Dr. Chung comes by and looks as relieved as they are. "Nice to see you awake, Paul."

Paul looks at him, no words coming forth never mind any sign of recognition of who is talking to him.

Carol and Heather follow the doctor to the door, like dogs begging for some scraps.

"We're cautiously optimistic that the antibiotics are working. His fever's subsiding, so he seems to be out of the woods."

And just like that life turns again, leaving them on their feet rather than Humpty-Dumpty-upside-down.

Glen swabs Paul's cracked lips. When Paul smiles sweetly at his son as he's done all his life, Carol is beside herself. *He's all there,* is all Carol's heart sings out to her. *He recognizes his son.*

Paul's first words are fitting. "I'm hungry."

Everyone in the room breaks out into laughter. That's it. Paul is okay. He's hungry. He's back.

Though much is taken, much abides. The words from *Ulysses* that she'd read as a young woman (and didn't even know she'd remembered) take up the space in her head as she watches her husband come back to them.

Chapter 19: Enter, *The Beast*
1998

Paul is window gazing again. And talking (albeit with difficulty), interested in the lives of every visitor who appears at his bedside. The Paul they recognize is emerging.

A cheery nurse says to him early one morning, "We're working to get you out of this place." Paul smiles at her. "Soon."

The hospital swings into full gear on the road to Paul's recovery. It's impressive: a physiotherapist introduces leg and respiratory exercises to Paul's routine, a social worker has been assigned to them, a dietician discusses Paul's food choices for easier swallowing, and a gastroenterologist, for who knows what, joins the team. Carol is mostly dealing with the hospital bureaucracy now, with her family support, of course. New territory for her. Luckily, Carol is entitled to a paid leave at work.

One day in the hospital gift shop she purchases a yellow notebook in which to write the myriad of questions that cloud her head, to say nothing of the myriad of information thrown at her at every turn. Soon the notebook is overflowing with doctors' names, names of meds, follow-up appointments. She adds the name of the social worker they're assigned but is still confounded as to what role a social worker could play in their situation.

Talk about being wrong. The first thing Nadia does is help them sort out what to do about Rosa and Darryl while Paul is hospitalized.

Carol explains, "Rosa and Darryl are the best caregivers. They covered three shifts between the two of them: weekdays, weekends, and evenings."

The social worker suggests that Darryl and Rosa take their shifts at the hospital to get used to Paul's new routine. His new shower and toilet routine, his exercises, his meals.

When Carol broaches the idea with Paul, he says, "What a good idea." Relief floods Carol's body. He insists on paying them their regular salary for the time that they will spend at his hospital bedside.

The topic she does not broach with anyone is something one of the team doctors had asked while Paul had been in the shower. "Have you considered a nursing home for your husband?" He sounded emotionless. "His care will be extensive."

It was a jarring question, like the wind unexpectedly slamming a door shut.

The social worker's suggestion seems to Carol the alternative solution to the nursing home idea: Rosa and Darryl will get to practice, as it were, the nuances of Paul's post-hospital extended care. Then, Paul can go home, and Carol can go back to work.

Carol is excited about something else too: the voice of reason in their marriage is making decisions again. But, the comfortable well-looked-after wife role... well, that's gone, it's plain to see. *Just as well,* she thinks, *my wifely-role-hat doesn't fit quite the same anymore.*

So, Darryl begins feeding Paul the hospital breakfast and lunch. Rosa often brings homemade dinners. She feeds him small amounts, forkfuls at a time, which often takes more than an hour. Despite this, life seems to be getting back to normal in these busy and noisy surroundings.

"Baby steps, Mom, baby steps," Glen keeps reminding his mother as she tells him she can't wait for them to be in their own home.

The lung doctor stays involved, explaining that the pneumonia looks to be clearing. Carol still skips out of the room for any Hoyer Lift transfer by *the beast*—as Carol now calls it. At present, it's a mainstay in Paul's life: used to put him on a bedpan or to take him for a shower. Still takes two people though, as someone must push the lift, as well as the IV pole. The lift has not been used to place Paul in a wheelchair much yet, simply because he can only sit—even with support—for mere minutes at a time. Carol locks Paul's growing dependence on the lift safely into a throw-away file in her head.

Dr. Brownly is still concerned about blood clots. "We'll abandon the heparin only when we're sure the oral Coumadin is working," Carol hears him say to Paul. "Which you'll continue once you are at home, of course." *Another thing to write down*, thinks Carol.

Carol's personal favourite in the hospital all-star lineup is the physiotherapist: he's young, has a great sense of humor, and an ease with Paul that's endearing. When they meet him, he says, "Call me TJ, everyone does." Carol keeps meaning to ask what TJ is short for. TJ tells them that he's read Paul's chart and knows what he was able to do before the pneumonia super bug hit. "You need your superpowers back," he tells Paul as he bends his legs, emphasizing that movement is medicine.

Later Carol reads what TJ wrote under assessment on the exercise sheet he's compiling for his patient: *future wheelchair*

The Uninvited Guest

transfers unlikely. It's the word *unlikely* that Carol wishes she had not seen.

As way turns into way and 1998 becomes 1999, Carol stands in the hall just outside the hospital room waiting for Paul to be transferred to a wheelchair via the Hoyer Lift—no side transfer possible, just as TJ had predicted. As she waits, Carol now wonders if Dr. Chung was covering his bases when he insinuated that Paul might not make it much beyond December 24.

The nurse brings Carol back from that horrible day to something much more pleasing: it's Paul's first real venture out of his room since he got here other than the X-ray department or shower room, that is.

"He's all ready to go," says the nurse, giving over the wheelchair to Carol.

The couple finally escape Room 301.

Off to the healing gardens, no less, on the main level of the hospital.

Paul says wistfully, "Sorry I can't push the IV pole."

"I've got it," Carol says, trying to hide her ineptitude at making the procedure look easy.

Paul asks to sit by the waterfall he spies as soon as they enter the gardens. The sound of running water, a salve to the wounds of this couple.

An Edmonton arborist has done his magic. Little staked cards identify each plant in the healing gardens. The arid section has cacti, some looking like candles. The tropical area sports a few exotic orchids sprinkled among ferns. Even the outdoors become part of the gardens: huge floor-to-ceiling windows frame tall evergreens sporting wisps of snow. A snowman sits a few feet from the hospital window. Carol wonders if the visitor who built it, is still visiting.

Of course, the couple cannot live in the healing gardens. Soon they are making their way back upstairs.

***

Next day, TJ sits before them looking uncomfortable. Paul takes his suggestion better than Carol.

"I don't want to spend the rest of my life in a bed," he declares emphatically. The longest sentence he's mustered in a long time.

TJ picks up where Paul left off but aims his sales pitch at Carol. "The Hoyer Lift is used in long term care facilities all around this city, giving people with mobility challenges like Paul's a chance to be up and around."

Depends on what you call up and around. Carol clenches her fists as hard as she can, working hard to control the snarky words ready to roll off her tongue.

TJ continues, "I'm not sure of the numbers in terms of home use, but from what I've seen, your caregivers are more than capable of using it." TJ runs his hand back and forth across his neck. "And for now, at least, you cannot manage any wheelchair transfers, Paul."

Carol is enraged at the never-ending loss of agency in their lives; Paul, on the other hand, is preoccupied, seemingly trying to process the mobility solution introduced by TJ.

And then, the sales pitch goes the way of all good retail pitches. "And it's of almost no cost whatsoever to you folks because Paul qualifies for a lift through a government program." Paul and Carol do not speak after TJ's departure. They need to go back to the healing gardens. Right now.

Of course, Carol fills out the forms the social worker gives her the next day, as she has come to terms with Paul's assessment of the situation: what's the alternative, really?

The Uninvited Guest

Soon she is arranging a date and time for the Hoyer Lift to be delivered to their house. "Put it behind the shower curtain," she tells Darryl, who awaits its delivery at the house.

And just like that, *the beast* sneaks into their lives. But this stainless-steel contraption is not like some adorable floppy-eared puppy sneaking into a family's heart. Carol finds it soul-crushing.

Funny that she doesn't want to know what TJ stands for anymore. One day her daughter sets her straight. "Don't shoot the messenger, Mom. It's not TJ's fault." She then comments on what Carol has already figured out. "Isn't that how April is moved around in her place?"

Rosa and Darryl have not actually performed the Hoyer Lift transfer due to hospital insurance regulations, but they've watched like hawks, especially Darryl.

The weeklong efforts of the hospital staff—aimed at getting Paul home—have been impressive. Incidentally, these efforts will also get Carol back to work—and Rosa and Darryl back at their house caring for Paul—and Heather and Bruce and Ann coming for Sunday dinner—and Glen and Tracy driving up from Calgary—and Nate calling from Vancouver—and Barb and Carol going back to book club—and Sarah and Angie coming for lunch—and April and Marcel coming for tea.

That's ridiculous, Marcel doesn't even drink tea. Her daydream stops dead in its tracks.

Carol almost misses the last land mine they step on before leaving the hospital because she spends that last Thursday morning at home. She's finishing up laundry and tidying up the house, even going so far as to file the bills to the right of Paul's lift chair before departing for the hospital.

Upon her arrival at the hospital, Carol finds Rosa feeding Paul hard-boiled eggs for lunch. Moments after she arrives, he claims, "they taste like rubber."

Dr. Sutherland enters the room, and they become acquainted with the first woman doctor on Paul's team. She goes headlong into her talking points with aplomb. The only way they even know her name is from the lanyard dangling from her neck.

"My report indicates this patient had his first swallowing test in February 1997 and was told at that time that he was a high-risk candidate for aspiration."

Carol responds to the accusatory-sounding statement. "Yes, that's why we've been thickening my husband's fluids ever since, as well as cutting up his food into tiny pieces."

It's the next talking point that unnerves Carol completely, especially the callous tone with which it's delivered to Paul. "Thickening your fluids and cutting up your food are not enough... now that you've had pneumonia. A feeding tube is the safest way to avoid aspiration."

Paul just keeps eating what Rosa places in his mouth, as if he's not even heard the ultimatum. The lunacy of the doctor telling him that he can no longer eat as he finishes his lunch is not lost on Carol.

She must hit back. "Then why was my husband brought food trays after his aspiration?"

"Unfortunately, your husband had already been assigned a modified diet *before* he was diagnosed with aspiration pneumonia." Dr. Sunderland pauses only briefly. "In the chaos that ensued...." The doctor holds her ground. "Well, from here on in, it's a risk—a high risk—given the state of the patient's lungs."

The doctor takes about five minutes more explaining how the feeding tube works and where it goes and who would put it in. Carol stops asking questions and stops listening too, hoping that the gastroenterologist cannot tell the latter.

The Uninvited Guest

After the doctor leaves the room, Carol breaks the silence. "Well, she certainly won't win any bedside manner awards."

And that's it. Paul does not acknowledge the gastroenterologist's visit at all. That evening he asks Carol if she would mind bringing up the chicken rice bowl she usually orders from Earls. They share the dish, as it's far too much food for Paul.

It seems that Paul has made an executive decision, as in his business days of old. He intends to keep eating, at least for the time being. She suddenly remembers that this is the second doctor who has introduced the idea of a feeding tube to the family.

Carol feels it her motherly duty, though, to fill her children in on Dr. Sutherland's recommendation. But she does not make it sound unequivocal, as had the doctor. It's more like something they may need to deal with, down the road... if necessary.... It's the lie she's telling herself, trying hard to believe.

Discharge papers are ordered and signed by the lung doctor.

Because Paul is now considered quadriplegic, he qualifies for an ambulance ride home. A nurse uses the Hoyer Lift to transfer Paul to the gurney brought up by the two EMTs.

And now, I have two quadriplegics in my life, Carol thinks as she witnesses the transfer from hospital bed to gurney.

The nurse's last act is one of kindness. She covers Paul with a heated blanket. "You haven't been outside for a long while and it's cold," she says.

On the eighth day of January, slightly before noon, they depart from the heated ambulance garage on the hospital's main floor. And no one even claps.

The ambulance attendants reverse engineer the Fletchers' pre-Christmas ambulance ride to the hospital; this time the

151

transfer from gurney to bed is chest-pain free now that Paul's pneumonia is cleared up.

Heather shows up around dinner and just happens to witness Paul's first transfer from his bed to his lift chair. The two women watch as Darryl slips the sling beneath Paul's body, positioning it. If Darryl feels pressured by their watching this maiden journey with the Hoyer Lift, it doesn't show.

Darryl's only hesitation occurs when it comes to figuring out how to crisscross the straps on the sling between Paul's legs before attaching the loops to the actual lift and hoisting him in the air, lest he fall through. He solves it. In about ten minutes, Paul is sitting in his chair and *the beast* is parked behind the shower curtain ready to huff and puff into action at a moment's notice.

Heather especially seems to be keeping a keen eye on her dad on his first evening home.

Did Heather make the same bargain as Carol had—to keep an eye on Paul all the rest of her livelong life through—if he survived?

Probably.

Chapter 20: Swimming
1999

Their old life has been lopped off, a necessary amputation to save their lives.

Not even a remote chance of doing a transfer to a bed or chair without the Hoyer Lift. Even with help. Unfortunately, TJ was right.

The urinal is Paul's means of peeing. The toilet is useless as he cannot sit on it or hang on to the grab bars for support. For a bowel movement he must be hoisted, for God's sake, over the commode chair (aka the shower chair), by the Hoyer Lift. And if Paul ever gets to go out again, he will have to wear a condom catheter and urinal bag under his pants.

With the red beast their only means of transfer, their Saturday date nights are over; no more picture hanging. Carol cannot manage the Hoyer Lift transfer on her own, so bedtime is a three-person affair from here on in.

The third person seems to have been waiting in the wings: Rosa has a friend looking for some extra hours. His name is Armand, and he soon joins the Fletcher roster for the Saturday and Sunday evening shifts. He's a quick study with the Hoyer Lift, because of his work at an extended care centre in south Edmonton.

The painful hospital experience seems to have created a vessel for black grief, guilt, exhaustion, but mostly fear. Does the vessel have room for rebirth? Carol has no idea.

This new life involves a night nurse too; Carol was not even aware of this provision in her healthcare plan until one of her co-workers alerted her to it. Given the seriousness of Paul's illness, the agency sends an RN, not an LPN, a bureaucratic decree which must be heeded. The RN basically comes and sits beside Paul or in an adjacent room, all night long. A different nurse every night.

"What a waste of money," Paul says to Darryl within earshot of Carol as she walks across the sitting room. "Imagine a nurse sitting there watching me sleep. I can't believe these insurance companies." Paul isn't done. "For twelve weeks, watching me sleep." That's how long this health benefit lasts. Carol tries to justify the presence of an RN by reminding Paul of how many times they were warned about the inherent danger of bedsores.

"A night nurse is perfect because she can adjust the pillow behind your back, and turn you from your left side to your right a few times each night." She tries to cement her argument. "I can't do that in the middle of the night, especially once I'm back at work."

Paul's not giving up easily. "Very expensive pillow change," he says to Carol, as sarcastically as she's ever heard him speak.

It probably doesn't help that Carol moves to the downstairs bedroom, feeling uncomfortable sleeping with an RN sitting in their bedroom or next to it.

Is *this* what Paul is really fussing about? It feels reminiscent of when their marital bed was replaced by a mechanical one. That, and the fact that their home is now truly Grand Central Station, as previously described by their daughter when she moved out.

The Uninvited Guest

Carol wonders if Paul's waste-of-money muttering about the night nurse is his way of venting about the direction his life is taking. Who could blame him?

Carol is angry at herself for having bought into Dr. Wilby's prediction of 'manageable lifestyle changes.' Her guess is that Paul did not buy in, but he—even he—could not have imagined this, she speculates. All semblance of a normal life feels gone. They are alone in their home for a total of six hours a day: two early morning hours, one hour just before dinner, and three late evening hours.

Carol keeps reminding Paul (and herself) that the night nurse is temporary: they'll graduate eventually, and she'll be back in her futon, sleeping next to Paul. It's a goal. Besides, Carol's new downstairs bedroom is just off the laundry and furnace area. It's cold.

On their second day home from the hospital Carol answers the phone to find herself speaking to the gas company representative.

"It has come to my attention that your payment is overdue." Carol can't think straight. She listens on. "However, it's in arrears only by a month, it appears, so how can we arrange for you folks to correct that?" Paul is sitting feet from her in his lift chair in the sitting room and guesses the gist of the conversation.

When Carol hangs up the phone, Paul asks about the bills that were left sitting on the table just right of his lift chair when he went into hospital.

"I filed them."

"You what?" Paul asks, shaking his head slightly. *The only part of his anatomy he can still shake*, thinks Carol morbidly.

"Well, before you went to hospital, remember how you were trying to get me doing more of the budget stuff... I put the bills in the file folder." Carol suddenly realizes her error. "Are you saying that those bills were unpaid?"

When Carol expresses consternation that the natural gas could have been turned off in the coldest month of the year in one of the coldest provinces in Canada, Paul sets her straight.

"Well, no, actually, there's a law against turning off the gas during the coldest months of the year."

Glen and Heather aren't one bit surprised about their mother's gas bill gaffe but do try to talk to her about her level of stress.

One morning in the shower Carol finds herself crying. She's glad she's downstairs so no one can hear her as the crying turns to weeping. As tears and water run over her body, she's angry, frustrated, sad, but mostly scared. She once was a woman living an orderly life. Her role and place in the universe secure. Not once did she have to worry about servicing a car or waiting ridiculous amounts of time to leave the house because her husband was being dressed—only to sit on a DATS vehicle and wait some more. Nor did she have to balance a cheque book or pay a bill or call doctors or order medicine or watch sad things going on all around her.

She leaves the shower only when the hot water has run out. Guess this is where her level of stress is at, she'd like to tell her children.

Stressed or not, Carol has a long list to attend to before her last five days of leave from work come to an end. A follow-up appointment with their family doctor, being key. Truthfully, the Fletchers never received a conclusive diagnosis before they left the hospital. They're filling in the blanks: the fever disappeared when Paul was put on antibiotics, so he must have had aspiration pneumonia. He's on Coumadin for the prevention of clots in his legs. Guess he had that too. Maybe Dr. Sneider will have more answers for them.

The Uninvited Guest

The doctor suggests a house call, after hearing the family's concerns about exactly how to get Paul to his office.

This loving deed by the family doctor just may be Act 1 of their rebirth story on the road to Damascus, thinks Carol hopefully.

Two days before Carol's return to work, the Fletchers get a drop-in visit from her mom. Carol feels instantly rejuvenated, a tiny bit of her old life creeping back as Sarah had a habit of showing up unannounced for tea.

But it leads to some drama. Since Paul's hospital stay, he's been even more difficult to dress than before: his body now dead weight—not an exaggeration, at all.

The caregivers dispense with his street clothes in favour of a bedsheet. They simply cover him once he's seated in his lift chair. He has his undershirt, underwear, and socks on, of course.

Well, Sarah takes one look at him and expresses her dismay. "Whatever are you wearing, Paul?" Paul's mother-in-law frowns crookedly at him. "What kind of a fashion statement is that?" Carol's mother has lived an entire lifetime out loud and today is no exception.

"We're just getting our bearings," Carol says, justifying his attire by explaining how shell-shocked they've been since back from the hospital.

Sarah shows no mercy. "So, Paul is going to wear a sheet for the rest of his life?" Paul chuckles throughout his wife's defence. The next day Paul is fully clothed, his shroud gone. And every day thereafter. Back in the land of the living.

Paul and Carol need their very own healing gardens. That's what Carol tells Glen one day over the phone. And her concerned son promises that soon—one of these weekends—he and Tracy will come to Edmonton to install an aquarium in their sitting room. An idea, he says, that has been brewing ever since he'd spied one in the hospital lounge on his dad's ward.

Carol can't wait to tell Heather about an aquarium, to heal them all.

When Glen and Tracy arrive a few weeks later, Glen explains that the aquarium must be installed in two stages. "Water in the tank today. Next weekend, I'll bring the fish." Glen sprinkles white rocks on the bottom of the tank. They have a grand time distributing the trinkets he bought. Ann gets to decide where the treasure chest—lid slightly ajar, with its gold coins spilling out—will sit. And the fake rock and plants are placed too. Heather steadies Ann as she stands on a chair, little-girl-fingerprints marking up the glass. Grape stands below wanting to be part of the action, barking sharply. Carol has long since acquiesced on her *no dog in the house rule*.

Paul enjoys every moment of the setup. "Check the pH level," he says to Glen. It reminds Carol of Paul supervising their three children's school science projects. "It has to be just right."

The aquarium, still fingerprinted from Ann's visit, sits for one week, awaiting new life. *Kind of like us,* thinks Carol.

***

Before they know it, Glen and Tracy are back in Edmonton.

"The pet store cautioned me not to overdo it," Glen explains. "Start with a few fish and gradually add more over time." He holds the plastic bag filled with mostly orange fish up to the light, the better to see them. "Otherwise, they'll all die from shock."

Yikes. Let's not use that analogy for our lives.

Ann tries to count the fish as they swim every which way in their new home. As Carol leaves for the kitchen to cook lasagna (a welcome activity from her old life), she hears her granddaughter giving the fish names.

The Uninvited Guest

They eat in front of the aquarium to avoid a Hoyer Lift transfer in front of Ann. The dinner atmosphere is a bit like watching a silent movie, the only sound being the running water coming from the plastic tubing, busily bubbling in the top corner of the tank.

"Zen-like for sure," suggests Carol.

After dinner, the family play a board game. Paul watches. As the evening wears on, Armand inserts himself into the sitting room scene and says that Paul needs to be readied for bed.

"I'd like to read the booklet that came with the new aquarium," Paul tells his newest and competent homecare worker. "Just for a few minutes."

Armand performs the pre-reading ritual: places Paul's reading glasses on his nose, folds the booklet open—cracking its spine—and placing it on Paul's beanbag table. He rearranges the lift chair slightly to the correct reading position before placing a pillow beneath Paul's lower legs, to take pressure off his buttocks. He places a smaller pillow behind Paul's left shoulder to keep him from leaning over. With the ritual complete, Paul begins reading.

Suddenly Ann lets out a squeal, saying excitedly, "Papa's moving his legs, Papa's moving his legs!" Her eyes beam.

After a few moments of pregnant silence, they get it. Ann thinks he's *choosing* to move his legs and moving legs means he's getting better. Maybe she thinks he'll be able to walk, maybe even run.

She doesn't know that these violent painful jerking movements are manifestations of a message from brain to legs gone awry. She knows nothing of baclofen. Or the central nervous system. Or a scarred myelin sheath.

"Did the hospital make Papa all better?" their sweet grandchild asks her dad and step-mom.

The reality is shattering. Armand's repositioning of Paul's legs probably brought on his leg and foot spasms.

It dawns on Carol that this little girl never knew Paul walking. A line can be drawn in Paul's life—those who knew him walking and those who did not.

On certain days, Carol herself has difficulty visualizing Paul walking even though she watched him do it for over twenty years.

But on this day, a little girl erased the line between her papa's two lives, making all their hearts beat a little faster.

As they leave for home, Ann throws a goodbye kiss to Natalia and Jordan, the fish that she named earlier in the day. And then they are gone. Only the gurgling water in the aquarium makes a sound.

Carol retrieves the Hoyer Lift from behind the shower curtain for Paul's trek to the bedroom. Once Paul is in the sling, swinging free, he asks Armand to sidle him up close and personal to the fingerprinted aquarium glass to look at the newest creatures in their lives. He stays there for a few minutes, the light from the aquarium casting him in a spotlight, long legs dangling free, toes pointing awkwardly downwards, not ballerina-graceful at all. Carol is forced to grow new beliefs, the old ones falling away. *Is this Paul's new standing?* Carol asks herself, with a deep ache.

Paul is pleased with the aquarium. And Carol is pleased with her son and daughter-in-law for making it all happen. And pleased with her daughter and son-in-law and granddaughter for adding to the fun. But mostly, Carol is pleased with Paul.

His transition to this lopped-off life seems as natural and spontaneous as what the fish are doing in their new home. Swimming. It's what fish do. It's what Paul is doing.

On Monday, Carol returns to work, not quite healed, but better.

Chapter 21: The Knight in Shining Armour
1999

Three weeks after Paul's wardrobe malfunction—that is, the bed-sheet fiasco—Carol waltzes into Paul's bathroom with folded towels, seemingly startling Rosa. She has one of Paul's shirts draped over the vanity next to the sink, scissors in hand.

Rosa's mortified look matches Carol's inability to process what she's seeing. Rosa sounds panicky.

"I picked his really old shirt, only this really old one... to cut... down the back...to get it on more easily. I'm sorry. I should have asked you first... I'm so sorry."

It takes a couple of seconds longer than it should before Carol is able to say to Rosa in her most soothing voice: "It's okay. If you need to cut Paul's shirts to get them on, just do it."

And for the first time ever, the two women embrace, treachery their bond.

Carol goes out and buys a few new shirts because as strange as it sounds, she finds them easier to cut up. Nevertheless, it feels sacrilegious, like ripping apart a church vestment. They do the dirty deed out of Paul's sight and he never mentions or acknowledges what he must have, by now, figured out.

The good thing that arises from this event—like a phoenix rising from the ashes—is that Carol is ever more resolved to confront the dressing difficulties the homecare workers are struggling with. It's something she can actually do.

As chance would have it, Carol notices some of the jocks around the junior high she's working in wearing athletic pants. What really catches her eye is that they seem to have snaps down the entire outside leg, right up to the waistband. She approaches the Phys Ed teacher and very soon orders two pairs for Paul from the sportswear catalogue the teacher keeps on his desk.

They are a dream to put on. Carol casts aside the notion that athletic pants usually hug athletic bodies, not frail, lifeless legs. *So what?* she thinks.

"They're so shiny," Carol overhears Paul saying to Rosa as she dresses him after his shower.

He's right, they are shiny. They're a light material too, thinks Carol, *so they can only function as Paul's indoor wardrobe.* Carol still needs to work on his outdoor wardrobe. A little evil voice in her head asks if it's even worth it: will her husband ever really go outdoors again?

Carol ignores the voice. A few days later, she scours the phone book, finding a company named Stitchery House which touts itself as specializing in clothing for the handicapped. Before long its owner, Betty Paulsen, is at their house, a tape measure hanging around her neck. Carol likes that she speaks directly to Paul as if he's a person.

She has fabric samples aplenty and there's Carol—who has never graced the doorstep of a fabric store in all her life—fingering and admiring cottons and linen/rayon mixes and merino wools. She picks heavy brushed cotton for the trousers—deep navy—the new black, she's told by Betty Paulsen.

Paul comments on the colour. "It won't show dirt."

The Uninvited Guest

Carol purses her lips. *When in the world will he ever be in touch with dirt?*

The seamstress suggests the trousers be lined for warmth and comfort. Carol asks Rosa to pick out the lining. She chooses a beautiful red and blue checkered flannel, which will be seen only by the official dressers. Equally unseen will be the condom catheter with its collection bag and the white compression stockings, mainstay items in Paul's post-hospital wardrobe, the latter being a precaution against his ever-present nemesis—blood clots. The best thing about the trousers is that no one would guess that the entire length of each leg has snaps down the outside and inside crotch area too, made invisible by overlapping two-inch seams.

The finale of this new wardrobe phase of their lives culminates with Paul's early birthday present from his daughter-in-law. Tracy has a degree in design and was born to sew, with or without the degree. She purchases a deep-plum Eddie Bauer suede jacket and opens the seams the entire length of its sides as well as the inside length of each arm. It's as arduous and painstaking a task as it sounds. Tracy sews heavy Velcro along the exposed seams, the integrity of the jacket remaining intact. The finished product is impressive. Carol sends Tracy a picture of Paul in the handsome jacket, penning their heartfelt thanks on the back.

The garment works like a charm. The donning of a jacket necessitates a subtle forward movement of Paul's body in his wheelchair, which he can no longer do. The beauty of this wardrobe piece, though, is that one single homecare worker can lean Paul forward slightly, while tucking the back of the jacket in place. The sides of the jacket are then easily velcroed up. Next, each of Paul's arms is placed on his chair's armrest and wrapped with the open sleeve. The sleeves are velcroed into place.

To Carol, Paul ends up looking like a knight in shining armour, sitting atop his mechanical wheeled horse. All that needs to sound is a bugle, summoning him to war.

Oh yeah, he's already at war. With his body.

Just as one problem gets solved, another appears on the horizon.

Early one afternoon, Carol takes a call at work from one of the night nurses. "Paul is up most of the night and I think it's because he is sleeping too much during the day." Carol wants to snap back, "What else does he have to do?" but listens instead. "I think you have to make sure his homecare workers are not letting him sleep all afternoon."

Carol controls herself. "Thanks for letting me know... I'll look into it."

But she doesn't. Even an insinuation criticizing Darryl or Rosa is beyond the pale. Carol and Paul cannot live without them, and yes, even Armand. End of story. Full stop. They can and will eventually live without the night nurse. *Soon*, is what Carol's imagining.

After she calms down, she thinks more clearly. She institutes home movies into Paul's routine, three afternoons a week on Nate's home-built VCR unit in the bedroom. That'll do it. She forbids movie popcorn though; just too easy to aspirate.

One Tuesday afternoon weeks later, Carol arrives home earlier than usual due to a cancelled meeting after school. Images of a home movie are flashing in the darkened bedroom. She plunks herself down in the small cream-coloured armchair to the right of Paul's bed, whispering a soft hello so as not to interrupt the home movie.

Right before her eyes, Paul is chopping wood at a campsite. He stands tall, long arms and legs accentuating the statuesque frame that Carol had completely forgotten he had. He raises the axe well above his head, brings it down to cleanly split the wood with deliberate aim and precision, the yellow raw pieces gleaming on the tree stump he's using as the cutting base. His fluidity with the axe shows that he's done this before. He's good at it.

She has the urge to escape: every split a blow to Carol's heart.

She has another urgent need: to replay this frame repeatedly, over and over again. The axe over the head, Paul raising his arms this high or even that high. The animated man she's watching on screen is incongruous with the man lying next to her in his hospital bed watching himself chop wood.

Carol chooses escape: to make herself a cup of tea in the kitchen.

By the time she re-enters the bedroom, Darryl is giving Paul a foot massage, the end of shift ritual that has developed over the years.

Finally, it's couple time. They are alone. She snuggles in close to Paul. She must know.

"Doesn't watching our home movies make you sad?"

Paul seems surprised by the question. "Why would they make me sad?" The question reverberates in the air like a plucked violin string. "I like seeing what I used to do."

Carol stuffs her sadness in the overflowing lock box in her heart.

That evening Paul asks her to call Nate. "Put me on speakerphone. I want to tell him I'm watching the home movies in order." Nate answers after one ring.

Even the vast number of home movies to watch does not hasten the arrival of spring. Paul has not been outdoors since his ambulance ride home, almost two months ago now. Carol senses some cabin fever—different from a physical fever, thank God—and she's right. Paul tells her one day that he'd like her to book DATS.

"I'd like to go down to the old dealership to see George and the new cars."

Carol wishes it were the faint hope clause that Paul had written into the dealership sales contract coming true, and that Paul were well enough to sell cars a few days a week. But no, that's in the annals of impossibility.

They don't get to the dealership until early summer. And it's a disaster anyway. The DATS ride is an unimaginable ordeal because of Paul's weakness. And besides, once they get there, George is out for the day and there is only one person who recognizes Paul. And even she does not comment on his new wardrobe.

Chapter 22: The Hoyer Lift Rebellion
1999

Fall and winter are interminably long: it's as if the Fletchers are caught in a dream sequence. Paul is the first to awaken from the dream.

One morning, he makes a simple but unusual request.

"I'd like to sit in the living room this morning instead of the sitting room." And the routine—of going from bed to the West Wing—that they'd adhered to both before and after his hospital stay is broken. Paul instructs Darryl further: "Could you please park my wheelchair facing the front sidewalk?" And there he sits for the remainder of the morning. Even requesting to be fed his lunch there in front of the bay window.

This window becomes Paul's eyes on the outside world. No TV. No radio. No newspaper. Paul has long ago given up on the audiobooks that Glen recommended as they leave him exhausted rather than entertained. It's the concentration that makes it so, Carol supposes.

He spends much of his time in the living room staring at their front yard pole-light, the one that they had installed just after buying their house, with its brass plate bearing the Fletcher house number. Passersby and dog walkers—the latter holding leashes and the ubiquitous plastic bags in

167

hand—frequent the city sidewalk. Cars run east and west on their busy avenue in plain sight.

And just like that, Paul discovers a new coping strategy.

It takes some time before Carol realizes the magic of it.

One Saturday, he chooses to sit at the dining room window overlooking the backyard so he can watch their neighbour Dale shoveling the back sidewalks (which he does regularly these days). Dale waves almost every time he looks up and sees Paul in the window. Carol shakes her head, smiling as she pours her morning coffee.

Paul also spends time peering through his bathroom window after his Saturday morning shower. Their reno team had the foresight (or dumb luck, she's not sure which) to install an oversize window in this room—bringing Paul yet another angle of their backyard, including the narrow flowerbed where he once planted tulip bulbs. He gazes through the glass awaiting both spring and the tulips.

The window on the world works.

Paul still occasionally chooses to sit in the West Wing staring at the fish in his aquarium. From that vantage point, he can also see his deck, often catching Carol exiting the garage door.

What isn't working are the four steel poles scattered throughout their home. It's well past time to remove them, getting rid of any evidence of Paul's walking, or, should she say, standing days.

Carol cannot believe how aggrieved she is to get rid of them. What she wouldn't give to have Paul grab a hideous steel grey pole one more time. Reach up and pull himself to standing. One more time. She'd snap a photo, even. She does not mention the dismantling of the poles to Paul, and he never asks where they've gone.

Christmas comes and goes again, this time without either a hospital stay or a visit to Glen and Tracy in Calgary. *The beast* has put a stop to all such endeavors. Carol finds out soon though that Paul is not letting *the beast* kibosh his need to forge ahead with his life. Something is going on. Not a one of the family is privy to precisely what—yet.

A Wednesday, three weeks before Easter break to be exact, Carol snuggles into Paul's shoulder for their late afternoon hospital-bed chat, and the workings in Paul's head are revealed. "I've been thinking," he begins, "Now with spring coming, and warmer weather, maybe we could try to get me into our car. With the Hoyer Lift. A little trip to Smoky Lake would be nice and we wouldn't need to rent a van."

It takes more than a few moments for Carol to get her bearings.

"I don't think that thing is meant for outdoors." Her thoughts whirl around in her head. "The Hoyer Lift is meant to move you around in the house."

Paul comes forward with an obviously well-thought-out defence. "You're probably right. But we'd be trailblazers if we used it outdoors."

Carol is dumbfounded. On two accounts: the idea of using the Hoyer Lift outdoors and Paul's calling them trailblazers.

Now she can't rest. Maybe never will again. *Let me get this right*, she thinks to herself. *Paul had to be cajoled by his daughter to use the wheelchair; he resisted giving a house key to a homecare worker; he began using the Hoyer Lift only when there was no other choice. And now, he wants to go dangle in the sling, outdoors. To get into their car.*

Later, when Paul is in his lift chair waiting for dinner, he asks Carol to fetch the instruction sheet that came with the lift. "I don't think I saved it," Carol says, annoyed he's even asking.

Paul glances at the rolling filing cabinet tucked beside his globe. "I had Darryl make a Hoyer Lift file."

Of course he did, thinks Carol, as she flips through the file folders, finding the instruction sheet in seconds. She reads aloud. "Transfer to bed. Transfer to chair. Transfer to toilet."

She scans further down the page. And notices the image of the Hoyer Lift on uneven terrain with a bold X through it, like the no smoking signs at hospital entrances.

She reads aloud in her omniscient voice. "*Warning–Lifts are primarily a transfer device, not a transporting device. Do no use on shag or thick-pile carpeting or outdoors on unpaved surfaces. Forcing lifts over obstructions can cause tipping.*"

Case closed, thinks Carol. Paul's as strict a rule-follower as she's ever met, and not to her chagrin today.

She hears Paul cherry-pick from her words.

"The instruction sheet says *primarily*. So occasionally it could be used for an outside transfer."

"Really?" says Carol. Not believing her ears.

Paul points out another loophole in the pamphlet. "And, it says unpaved surfaces, so maybe paved ones are okay."

The very next weekend, a spring day both by date and temperature, Darryl has replaced Rosa on her Sunday shift. Paul thought that the car manoeuvre might be easier for Darryl to manage. He pushes the Hoyer Lift with Paul cradled in its sling into the elevator. It looks weird to Carol as Darryl pushes the dangling Paul outside and down the sidewalk to the garage where their car—an unsuspecting participant in a rebellion—sits.

Carol opens the front passenger door as well as the back one. Darryl moves the lift toward the car. By this time, Carol has hopped into the back seat ready to help direct Paul over the front one.

But the swivel bar with attached boom and mast does not fit under the roof of the car. Darryl backs up the Hoyer Lift and lowers the mast and boom, leaving Paul's shoes trailing on the cold concrete garage floor. They try again. It's closer, a mere half-inch from the top of the car. But it's not going to happen. The car is too low; the Hoyer Lift is too high. No matter what they do.

Darryl pulls the lift away from the car. "Sorry, Paul," he murmurs as he pushes him back to the elevator door. "I'm so sorry."

They are stymied.

Chapter 23: The Chevy Guy Goes Rogue
2000

Anyone who truly knows Paul understands exactly what this Hoyer Lift defeat would do: spur him on. That's not surprising; what is surprising, though, is Paul's next move.

It's another car-dealership trip but not to visit his partner, George, or even his old dealership.

"I want to check out the Ford dealership on 97th Street," Paul insists, soon after their aborted attempt to get into their car. "To check out the competition."

Carol doesn't have to tell her children how strange this all is. It doesn't add up.

Rosa rides in DATS with Paul; Carol follows in the car. They pull up to the dealership at the same time. Carol watches the driver grab the handles of Paul's wheelchair to back him down the ramp. Paul's head falls forward. The driver pays no heed. Instead, he hurriedly bumps Paul all the way down to the sidewalk, head bobbing.

Rosa tries to intervene, but the driver waves her out of the way. Once he gets to the sidewalk, he hands Paul off to her. His duty done.

Does he ever see the handicapped as people? Carol wonders.

The Uninvited Guest

The dealership that they enter is newly built. Huge windows. And full of vehicles, of course, but Fords.

A keen young man greets them. "Welcome to our showroom," he says, probably hoping they're not tire kickers.

Paul confuses Carol by asking the salesman where their trucks are.

I thought we were here to see this year's new cars, thinks Carol.

The lad leads them to the trucks and swings into action. The art of selling. The first truck he shows them is a blue Ford F-150. Paul listens as the salesman lists its features. He interrupts to say that it's not the one he wants to see. *Something is going on*, thinks Carol.

The salesman immediately moves them a bit closer to the bay area of the showroom.

In the next truck, he demonstrates how the front passenger door of the vehicle opens in a traditional way whereas the back passenger door opens to face it (Carol learns only later that these two doors facing each other without a central structure are called suicide doors). The young man touts how handy a space this is for loading groceries or any other old thing into the back seat. "Like your wheelchair, sir, for instance," he says, motioning for Rosa to wheel Paul in closer to the vast space created by the novel doors. "You could hop in the front seat, sir, and throw your chair in the back."

He's got to be kidding. *Hop in the front seat. And throw your chair in the back.* How can Carol possibly explain to this salesman that which he cannot imagine? What she herself can hardly imagine.

Poor lad. Little does he know that he's talking to a quadriplegic. A man who won first place in a car rodeo when he was seventeen years old but can no longer grip a steering wheel, let alone hop in the front seat. A man who got to this dealership today on DATS, driven by a heartless driver. A man who drove many kinds of vehicles in so many different cities and towns, byways and highways, every chance he got. He even got to drive on the *wrong* side of the road in Australia, probably before this lad was even born. And this man, now sitting before this young lad, spent countless years in a car dealership, selling every model of Chevrolet imaginable. The lad also doesn't realize that Paul is guarding his driver's license in his wallet as the last verification of his driving existence.

What's wrong with a healthy dose of oblivion? Carol thinks.

"It's sure interesting the way the two doors open," says Paul.

"Sure is," agrees the salesman. As they leave the showroom, the lad waves goodbye, likely believing he's dismissed them from his life forever.

Once outside, DATS pulls up with a driver other than the one who got them here. Carol and Rosa breathe a collective sigh of relief.

A few days after the visit to the Ford dealership, just as Carol is about to leave for work, Paul asks rather softly, "Do you think you'd like to drive a truck?"

The question sets Carol off: *What are you talking about? I have a million things to think about. You. Our kids. My speech students.*

She puts down her black briefcase right in front of Paul's feet, trapping him. "Yes, of course... what else could I possibly have to do but learn to drive a truck?"

She grabs her briefcase, unintentionally swinging it up against Paul's legs as she leaves—without another word.

All day long, Paul's proposal nags at her; what nags at her most, though, is her insensitive reply to his question.

Paul has never, to Carol's knowledge, contemplated owning a truck. And now he's buying one. Well, asking if she'd mind driving a truck instead of a car—sounds like buying one to her.

A Ford. An F-150, to be exact. With a wonky back door that opens the wrong way, if memory serves Carol correctly. He doesn't ask his grown children's opinion. Just shares with them over the speakerphone what he's thinking. They're surprised, but not that surprised.

"Just because Dad isn't driving, doesn't mean he isn't thinking about vehicles," Glen says to his mom over the phone privately.

They call Nate with the news. "Good for you, Dad," is the essence of what Nate says over the speakerphone that evening.

It's Heather and Bruce and Ann who get to be part of the Easter Monday Miracle, in person.

Because that is how quickly they talk to the salesman-lad again. Carol finds the business card and calls young Neal. A bit of confusion occurs (the family is later informed) when Neal tries to explain to his boss that the buyer needs the truck at his home to figure out whether he can get into the vehicle. But, after a bit of wheedling—his being a salesman, and all—the red truck replaces their car in the garage, awaiting a rather unorthodox test drive.

Of course, the truck is more than high enough to facilitate the swivel mast and boom at the top of the Hoyer Lift; equally important, the lack of the structural post between the truck's front and back seat creates a chasm wide enough to allow the lift to get its C-base legs beneath the truck and more than close enough for a transfer.

As soon as Paul is comfortably seated in the truck, spontaneous clapping breaks out, reminding Carol of the Cape Canaveral Space Launch Tour the family had witnessed years ago. Only two people don't clap: Paul, who can't, and Neal, whose dropped jaw seems to be impairing his thinking.

Ann hops in the back seat between her dad and Carol. All are seat-belted up. Heather backs out of their garage, driving the red F-150 for the first time. They leave the salesman and Darryl chatting on the cold concrete floor of their garage.

The Fletchers buy this show room model so as not to waste time putting in an order.

And so, the Fletcher family get their wings. Red wings. Ford F-150 wings.

After Paul is transferred to his mechanical bed much later that evening, he asks Carol to call each of their sons, so he can share his bedtime story with them, the one with the happy ending.

"I first saw the commercial on TV. What caught my eye was the way the doors opened. After realizing that the car was too low, I thought the truck might just work for the lift." Paul sounds as pleased as punch. He continues, "I can't wait for George to come over... he won't believe I have a Ford parked in the garage."

Carol cannot help but be struck by the scope of Paul's imagination: he has found yet another cure. A truck.

Much more effective than the countless well-intentioned but annoying *cures* proposed to the family over the years. The exotic diet or juice concoctions or copious amounts of vitamins or manic exercise schemes or food supplements—or the positive thinking mantra, highly touted by so many. It was the latter that bothered Paul most—making like it was his fault his MS wasn't going away, that he should be able to think away his chronic illness.

Was Carol any better, really, than their well-intentioned family and friends with their harebrained schemes for dealing with MS? She shudders, remembering how sarcastic she'd been days before when Paul asked if she'd consider driving a truck. The question reminds Carol of another question he'd asked her when she was a mere eighteen and newly dating Paul.

"What kind of car does your mother drive?"

"Blue," Carol had answered wide-eyed and oblivious. "Dark blue."

Carol now believes that Paul was acting out the centuries old mating instinct to test their compatibility. Guess he decided to take a chance on her anyway. They married months later, days after her nineteenth birthday.

She smiles as she recounts this blue-car dating story to Paul before bed that evening. Carol adds, rather softly, "I'm sorry I was so sarcastic when you asked about driving a truck."

"That's okay," Paul answers. "It worked out."

Now she can sleep. In peace.

***

"Once the school year winds down, we can go for a ride in the truck weekdays as well as weekends," Paul suggests to Carol. He goes so far as to ask Rosa and Darryl to make a list of the places he's conjuring up. All the places he must go.

Carol is relieved to read how long the list is: it'll take years and years to complete.

Soon they are ticking items off the list—titled the Truck List—posted just above Paul's globe. *Gives globetrotting a whole new meaning.*

Now, the days fly by as they put the first miles on their truck.

It's much easier now for Carol to ignore the family doctor's most recent diagnosis: Paul has sleep apnea. It is only much later that Carol learns that MS could be affecting the respiratory centre in Paul's brain stem and is likely the origin of his sleep apnea.

One warm afternoon, the first Friday of her summer break, Carol goes grocery shopping. As she scoots round the store, Paul is sitting in the passenger seat of their F-150: vehicle-watching, akin to people-watching. All made possible by their wings. Darryl keeps him company.

Paul had asked Carol to aim the truck at the busy intersection when she'd parked. Facing the traffic, which waxes and wanes at each light change. Precious minutes in which to take in vehicle after vehicle.

When the groceries have been loaded into the back seat area, Paul points out the obvious. "Guess we should invest in a canopy. A shame to have a truck box and not use it."

"Yeah, maybe we should start a landscaping company this summer," Carol adds in jest. "Start delivering dirt or sod from the back of our truck."

She gets no response from her happy husband as they head for home from the grocery store.

Carol muses all the way home: seven years ago, their lives had pretty much been on track when an uninvited guest appeared, shaking everything up, casting everyone in new and instant roles.

Paul became the reluctant protagonist—test after test heaped upon his head, testing his mettle, and she took on the role of antagonist, being a natural at creating tension, and all. At times the children or their extended families have tried to shelter Paul, relegating him to the 'victim in need of protection' role, but he will have none of it.

Paul forges ahead controlling what he can, seemingly knowing when to give in. Not give up, but give in.

Carol has just this moment figured out what she likes about their lopped-off life: it's the dance they do. Choreographed. Moving closer to Paul. Pulling back. Three or four people some days. Sometimes more. Sometimes fewer.

This MS dance has reshaped their lives: it's graceful, sometimes unnatural—grotesque, even—but it's whole. And authentic. A dance of love.

Chapter 24: The Long Way Home
2000

Once the Fletchers have their fire-engine-red F-150, the yellow brick road leads them to their second William Watson Lodge holiday.

Two events shape this second Kananaskis holiday. The first: Nate joining in on the summer family fun and bringing along a girlfriend for them to meet. They are smitten with Kim as soon as they meet her—as smitten, it seems, as Nate.

The second momentous event of the holiday is spontaneous and occurs on the day they are leaving. As Carol, Rosa, and Paul sit at the intersection of the Trans-Canada Highway, Paul says in a quiet voice, "Sure would be nice to go by the Columbia Icefield on our way home, on Highway 93." So as Darryl turns toward Calgary, haven driven in his own vehicle, Carol turns at the sign pointing to Banff.

After the fact, Paul clarifies. "It's a bit further this way... might take a bit longer."

Carol realizes in that instant what she's done. But it's too late. Difficult to turn the truck around on this busy highway. Never mind deal with the disappointment on Paul's face if they abort this side trip.

They arrive at Lake Louise just under two hours after leaving the lodge. Paul says, "We haven't been here for so long." They view the historic hotel and the vacationers canoeing the tranquil turquoise waters of Lake Louise, the stuff of so many postcards sent around the world.

Carol stops short of driving to Moraine Lake, even though Paul points out that turnoff as well.

"We can't make another stop, Paul," she responds. "We'll never get home at this rate."

Paul keeps bringing up the view. The colours. Wonders aloud if they'll see any wildlife. He's talking more than usual.

Rosa reads a sign out loud: Hector Lake.

Paul jumps in as if he's an actor picking up his cue from Rosa's line. "I've read that this drive is one of the most spectacular views in the world."

"Has to be true then," Carol gibes, "if it's written down somewhere." She's trying to mitigate some of the growing apprehension she feels.

"Can't wait to get to Bow Summit, the highest point of the drive," Paul tells his fellow travellers.

Oh no, not another stop, thinks Carol. She hatches a plan. "Okay, we'll stop at the Summit, but we'll do your leg exercises there. You've been in the same position for too long." The stop takes twenty minutes. It's awkward trying to extend Paul's long legs in the truck cab, even with the seat pushed back as far as it will go. Carol parks discreetly so their newly-invented extreme mountain sport has no audience.

Rosa takes Paul's arms from the armrests and places them on his knees, hopping into the back seat as they pull away from the curb. "Your elbows need a change," she tells Paul.

The truck becomes eerily silent for the remainder of the ride to the Icefield, their designated lunch and washroom stop.

Paul, of course, has his catheter-bag attached to his leg and it won't be full, so no problem there.

Carol parks in full view of the Icefield, including the ice explorer visible in the distance, the one they had ridden in as a family multiple times, over multiple years.

Carol purchases lunch from the restaurant, bringing it back to Paul and Rosa. Carol and Rosa become a tag team. Rosa cuts up a hot dog (hard to do with plastic utensils), standing just outside the open passenger door feeding him. Carol thickens Paul's Sprite and spoon feeds it to him from the driver's seat in between bites of food.

They can't hurry the chewing and swallowing so the stop lasts nearly an hour. Paul does not take his eyes off the massive Columbia Icefield as he eats. Eventually, Carol wraps up the uneaten fries noisily in their waxed paper saying, "Sorry, we have to get going, Paul."

As they get a last glimpse of the Athabasca Glacier, Paul says dejectedly, "Looks like the ice is shrinking."

The receding glacier is an alarming sight, for sure, but even more alarming is that they left Kananaskis almost five hours ago. *The ninety kilometre an hour speed limit in the National Park doesn't help*, frets Carol. She is frantically trying to remember if Jasper has a hospital; she's pretty sure Hinton and Edson have only health care clinics, neither being a resort town per se.

But do they even treat blood clots in a clinic? wonders Carol.

Upon waking, Paul seems surprised that they bypassed the town of Jasper. He looks out the window just as they pass the ancient and somewhat decrepit Jasper Cemetery, a long train rushing by, parallel to the highway.

The next landmark makes Carol feel like they're almost home: Pocahontas Campground. Realistically, they have hours to go, but it's the familiarity of the resort that makes her feel their journey's end at hand: the modest outdoor pool was a favourite family vacation spot where all three of their children learned to swim.

Carol has a moment of panic when Rosa reads the Miette Hot Springs sign aloud, fearing that Paul might request a trip up that narrow and precipitous mountain road. But he doesn't say a word.

At last, they leave the National Park and cruise at 110 Kilometres per hour. The only thing holding Paul upright in the front seat, it seems to Carol, is the chest-high support strap that the Healthcare and Rehab people installed shortly after the purchase of the truck. The seatbelt certainly wouldn't be enough. Paul had railed against the support strap on the grounds that it would adversely affect the truck's resale value; Carol does not rue the day that she rallied in favour of the strap.

When they reach Hinton, Carol stops at the first phone booth they see. She and Rosa pool their loose change for a long-distance call. Rosa begins doing leg exercises on Paul as Carol slides from behind the wheel.

She calls Heather's number. No answer. She gets her mother on the first ring. Sarah begins crying the moment she hears her daughter's voice.

"Where are you?" Sarah asks, in a teary voice. "Are you okay?"

Carol explains that Paul wanted to go home by way of highway 93.

"An eight-hour detour? What were you thinking?" Sarah answers, her concern turning to anger. "I was sitting here wondering if I knew what you or Paul or Rosa were wearing when you left Kananaskis." Carol hears a deep breath. "The only reason I haven't called the police is because Heather convinced me to hold off a bit."

The Uninvited Guest

Carol rushes back to the truck. Paul is dozing. She does not wake him, nor does she relay her mom's hysteria to Rosa.

Luckily, they do not have to stop in Edson for medical attention. Almost three hours later they pull into their garage, just shy of eight o'clock.

Carol is brain dead; Rosa mute; and Paul, well, Paul is thankful.

"Last year when I was reading about the Highway 93 route, I was thinking that I'd never be on that road again." With effort, Paul lifts his head. "Thanks for taking the long way home, Carol."

Here she was, fussing throughout every minute of the trip, while this good and wise man did not squander even one second of the experience. Carol is humbled.

Chapter 25: Growing Up
2000

Paul's truck-cure is working; road trip after road trip with places to go and people to see. They are finally planning to fulfill the promise of a trip to see Glen and Tracy's now almost two-year-old home when Darryl says that they need to talk. Together—Carol and Paul. Tomorrow morning.

Since Carol does some of her best worrying at three in the morning, she gets little sleep before Darryl's early arrival.

It's twenty to seven in the morning. Paul is watching the local news. Carol is on high alert.

Darryl begins tentatively. "Well, I've just passed Math 33. I now have my high school diploma." He continues softly. "Just seems like the right time... I've applied to NAIT." Darryl stops talking and looks at Paul. Not Carol. "I want to be an electrician."

What he doesn't mention, and Carol finds out in the weeks to come from Rosa, is that he's already been accepted to the program.

Carol is beside herself. She doesn't know what to say but Paul saves the day.

"Good for you." It looks like Paul would up and shake Darryl's hand, if he could.

"Congratulations!"

Darryl focuses on Paul's reaction. "You've taught me so much, Paul." He looks over at the globe. "I think meeting you was one of the best things that ever happened to me... but now seems like the right time for me to go to school."

How does Paul love him? Let us count the ways:
Thanks for easing me into a life I was terrified of.
I'm glad you think we taught you a thing or two.
Another thing, you sure helped out with our renovations.
We're sure going to miss you around here.

Paul interrupts Carol's thoughts, sounding like a proud dad, hearing that his son's life is moving forward. "An electrician. Wow."

How in the world is he able to strike those *grace notes* amid this news?

Sensing Carol's dismay, Darryl tries some damage control. "I won't begin classes till fall, so I can stay another month, maybe a little longer. I'll help train someone, if you like."

In those moments, Carol realizes that in the end Paul's care is a job, and people leave jobs behind all the time, so why not Darryl? It's as if she's walking across a frozen lake and can hear ice cracking beneath her feet.

Barb calls that evening to check in because she knew about Darryl's prearranged meeting with Paul and Carol.

"It's even worse than I thought," Carol explains, out of Paul's earshot. "Darryl's leaving and can't work for us anymore... going to NAIT, full time this fall... don't think I'll be going to book club tomorrow night."

Barb gets militant. "Forget it... if ever you needed a 'Jane Austen' distraction, it's now.

I'll pick you up as usual, 7 p.m. sharp."

The next three calls are exactly what she thought they'd be like: horrible. It feels like she's telling all three of her children that someone's just died. "We're looking for someone new again. Sorry Glen. The trip to see your house is on hold. Again."

Next day, the calls don't get easier: Carol finds herself giving the gory list of the tasks involved in Paul's care to the placement agency they turn to for a new hire.

"My husband is transferred by Hoyer Lift," she tells the person over the phone. "Everywhere, about three or four times a shift, at least. He's fed solids and his drinks are thickened. He's hard to dress. He uses a urinal or a catheter and collection bag." She avoids the description of Paul's dangling over the commode chair waiting for his bum to be cleaned. "Takes tons of pills. Needs daily leg and arm exercises. Foot massages." *Even at this, it's an abbreviated list*, she thinks. "Oh, did I mention he's quadriplegic?"

The agency sets up a two-part process: an interview with Paul and Carol, and a hands-on training session with Darryl.

The procession begins. And it's not pretty.

The first person Carol and Paul interview is an outgoing, young woman. Carol completely overlooks her nails (claws would be a more apt description); it's Paul who points them out to Carol after the interviewee leaves.

"How would you like those things coming at *your* face every day?"

The young woman calls later that same day, anxious to hear whether she's gotten the job. Carol had thought to comment on the inappropriateness of her nails for this line of work but thinks better of it.

Carol lets her have her pointy pink nails but not the job.

Initially, candidate number two seems promising. The man explains that he's been doing homecare for years, in fits and starts, because he suffers a serious case of wanderlust. He works five, six months, and then is off traveling, Costa Rica having been his last destination. The man's adventure stories would

The Uninvited Guest

appeal to Paul's love of travel, for sure. Carol is so desperate to find someone that she convinces herself that they can figure out the vacation piece later—if the guy is good at his job.

Today the training session is introducing Paul's morning routine: a sponge bath and shave in bed. Just before starting Paul's dressing routine, the phone rings. While answering the phone in the adjoining sitting room, Darryl hears what sounds to be a commotion of sorts. He rushes back into the bedroom: the trainee has opened a bureau drawer and is frantically pulling things out, dropping socks and shorts on the floor as he searches for who knows what.

The part that completely defies logic, never mind disqualifying this man from the job is that the trainee uncovered Paul who now lies in bed half-naked, unable to cover himself with the sheet. He's staring straight up, perhaps looking from whence his help might come.

"What are you doing?" Carol hears Darryl shout as she's filling the dishwasher.

Carol rushes into the room. When she sees the situation, she hastily ushers the man out of the house.

Within a few days, the placement agency sends out another man. He outdoes hyper-Costa-Rica-man within half an hour's worth of training, if that's even possible.

He arrives at the door with his wife, asking if it's okay if she waits for him. Something about having only one vehicle. Carol obliges and invites the wife to wait in their living room.

The first demonstration of that day is as complicated as it gets: positioning Paul, in his sling and Hoyer Lift, over the commode chair for a bowel movement. Paul's need for privacy (and Carol's sensibilities) result in Carol leaving to cocoon herself in their downstairs rec room to read.

She's lost in her book club's latest pick when she hears Darryl racing down the basement stairs. The urgency in his steps startles her. As do his words.

"I told the trainee that we had to wait near the bathroom so that we could easily hear Paul when he's done. Instead of sitting down with me, he dashed off to get his wife." Darryl looks like he doesn't want to finish the story. "Before I realized what was happening, the man was back and slid open the bathroom pocket door to show his wife how Paul dangles above the commode chair."

"He—what? Is he gone?" Carol asks, trembling.

"No, I told him to wait."

Carol charges to the front door while Darryl veers off down the hall to Paul's bedroom.

"How could you? He's a human being not a circus animal," Carol says, looking the trainee right in the eye. He doesn't answer, just leaves to join his wife in the car. Carol latches the screen door behind him, trying to swallow her anger and suppress her tears.

Paul is quieter than usual for the rest of the day, only mentioning once how startled he was to see two strangers standing in his bathroom doorway. Carol is sad for Paul, and for all of them really, because they are at the mercy of many people to keep their lives in a delicate balance.

Later, brooding about the breach of privacy Paul had to endure reminds Carol of a documentary she'd once heard, touting the idea that Norway fares so much better in eldercare than other nations.

One detail from the piece made so much sense to Carol: trainees would be transferred in a lift during a training session. One such trainee who was interviewed afterward said she would never forget how vulnerable she felt being lowered into a tub via the lift, even in a bathing suit. Obviously, the Norwegians get it right.

The next morning Carol tells the agency not to send any more men applicants. She explains why briefly, but the agency coordinator seems more focused on finalizing what is becoming a drawn-out procedure—according to her.

Two women come next in the hiring process, in quick succession. The first is a chain smoker that leaves Darryl and Paul so often during the training session that the Fletcher backyard is in danger of becoming an ash heap.

The second woman hoists Paul in the air with the lift, only to have Darryl catch the fact that she has not crisscrossed the straps of the sling between Paul's legs as she had been instructed to do. Paul is momentarily in danger of falling through to the floor. The trainee is so traumatized by her error that she leaves, not able to complete her training session.

Afterwards, Carol wonders seriously if the fact that the woman left in reaction to her egregious error confirms that she may have been the right person for the job. At least she had a heart.

Finally, finally, the right woman appears.

Her name: Jessie. She is a qualified nurse (like Rosa), but her homeland is Jamaica. She's been in Canada longer than Rosa.

Jessie shares an apartment with her sister Bobbie, a quick bus-ride from the Fletcher home.

Carol asks Paul what he thinks about Jessie after the training session. "She seems to like the work," he replies.

When Carol tells Jessie that she is hired for the job, Jessie asks if she should wear a uniform to work. "No need," says Carol, remembering that Paul had asked Rosa not to wear a uniform since he was not sick.

And so, Jessie comes into their lives as Darryl leaves. Paul takes his absence better than Carol, taking life's buffets and rewards with pretty much equal thanks, which is his way. Besides, Paul is genuinely happy for Darryl. "I'm sure glad he's studying to be an electrician," he periodically remarks to Carol, for weeks on end.

One afternoon, the NAIT office calls for a reference for Darryl's apprenticeship program; Carol feels an urge for sabotage. She offers an olive branch instead: "He's a hard worker, mature for his age, and was never late for work, not even once. He'll make a great apprentice."

It's taken just shy of three weeks to hire Jessie who will work the weekday shifts—full time.

Rosa continues her evening and weekend shifts—full time.

Armand worms his way into their hearts more and more, Saturday and Sunday evenings—part time.

Carol goes back to speech therapy—full time.

Paul continues his MS Odyssey—full time.

And they begin anew. Yet again.

Chapter 26: Lift Off
2000

In this third or fourth iteration of their new lives—Carol's lost count—their house gets as quiet as it was when they were tiptoeing around a very sick post-hospital Paul. Jessie is not as chatty as was Darryl. She answers when spoken to. And she goes about her business quietly too. She seems genuinely comfortable feeding Paul. It's the look on her face as she moves the fork or spoon to and fro. One of the women who had fed Paul—as part of a training session—looked to Carol as if she wanted to stab him with the fork, the entire meal. In the eye.

Two weekends after Jessie is hired, Barb's elderly mother, Elvira, dies. Paul insists on attending the funeral, considering how much time they spent with her in the years before Paul's diagnosis.

"But it's a Greek Orthodox Mass," Carol informs him. "It will be long. Very long. Are you sure you feel strong enough?"

"She's John's mother-in-law. We can't miss her funeral," says Paul.

Carol acquiesces considering that Paul does not insist on much. Carol is unequivocal on a back-up plan though: it's her prerogative to deem when they need to leave.

Her next concern, perhaps her biggest, is using the lift outdoors without Darryl.

But Jessie insists, saying that she'll be fine, even when Carol explains that the trip will include three transfers, two outdoors.

"Are you sure?" Carol asks again.

"I think I'm ready to try the lift outdoors."

Because Sarah catches a ride with them, they're bordering on late for the 11 a.m. funeral, causing them to change their parking routine: they choose the designated handicapped parking spot right in front of the church instead of their usual discreet off-to-a-corner location. The transfer is smooth and they get into the church just in time.

The funeral is a proper send-off for a woman of her generation. One of the hardy disciplined folk who built this country—is how the priest aptly describes Elvira.

Many people seem thrilled to see Paul. Carol navigates the awkward moment or two when someone extends a hand to greet him (with no reciprocal gesture possible) by thrusting her own out instead.

Other acquaintances are visibly shocked at Paul's health decline; some avoid altogether the much-changed man they once knew.

By the end of the service, though, Paul is not holding up as well as he had hoped. Attending the burial is out of the question. And a return to the church lunch after the burial, a pipe dream. Carol firmly invokes her back-up plan, much to Paul's chagrin.

The funeral crowd spills out the front doors, some mulling around and standing in the September sunshine. Right in front of the handicapped parking spot.

Jessie easily pushes Paul on the paved surface, parking his wheelchair parallel to the truck. The crowd on the sidewalk thickens. It reminds Carol of the wedding dance crowds of

The Uninvited Guest

her youth when people slipped out for a smoke or a nip from a bottle.

Only this crowd is about to witness how two smallish women get a quadriplegic six-foot-two man out of his wheelchair and into the front seat of his truck.

Carol and Jessie introduce *the beast* to the crowd standing outside the church, by opening the tailgate and lifting the Hoyer Lift out of the truck box. At Carol's instruction, they turn the lift over in midair before setting the thing upright on its four wheels on the pavement. It's a heavy contraption, but Carol can see that Jessie is much stronger than she. This outdoor manoeuvre is new to Jessie, but she's managing just fine.

Paul sits patiently in his wheelchair, with Sarah standing near him, swatting mosquitoes away.

Under the pressure of an audience, Jessie gets confused with the sling, so it is Carol who arranges it behind Paul's back, tucking it under his buttocks and pulling it through to the front of the seat with its long ties. The one thing Carol remembers vividly from watching this procedure many times now is to crisscross the ties between Paul's legs. Paul is ready to be safely hoisted into the air.

Jessie pushes the steel lift directly in front of Paul's chair, opening its C-base legs wide to stabilize the thing on the pavement. Thank goodness the handicapped spot is pretty much pebble free.

Carol attaches the four loops to the four hooks hanging from the mast at the top of the lift.

By this time, Carol doesn't have to worry about Paul's potential embarrassment as she once did. He has come to terms with rejecting a life in bed in exchange for being transferred with *the beast*, any old place, any old time.

The crowd mutters, discussing what will happen next, is Carol's guess. Because truly, until you've seen the lift-off with this thing, it's a bit of a mystery.

Jessie pumps the hydraulic handle on the lift, the same concept as the old water pumps common on any Alberta farm forty years ago. Jessie pumps again. Did Carol mention that most of the crowd watching them is men? Many of them are farmers too, so any mechanical feat has a whiff of excitement to it.

Pump, pump again and this time Paul should clear his wheelchair seat, cradled and swaying above it ever so slightly.

Something is wrong though. Horribly wrong!

Paul is rising—as he should—but so is his wheelchair. The chair should not leave the pavement.

The crowd is none the wiser: heaven knows what they thought was going to happen to the wheelchair, once suspended in the air. It's the stork-delivering-the-baby image gone frightfully askew.

Carol quickly realizes the error of her ways: she forgot to undo the seat belt before putting the sling underneath him. Paul is being lifted in the air attached to his wheelchair by a seat belt. Many watching the procedure would be surprised to learn that wheelchairs even have seat belts.

It's more complicated than it might seem at first glance, because in order to *extricate* Paul from the chair, they must first lower he and his chair back to earth, undo the four loops from the four mast-hooks, then back the lift away from Paul. Then and only then do they have access to unzip his jacket and undo the seatbelt.

Once Paul is hoisted and swinging in the air as he's *supposed to be*—wheelchair firmly on the pavement where it belongs— Jessie wheels the chair out of the way. Carol pushes the Hoyer Lift to the truck door, swinging Paul in the sling over the front

The Uninvited Guest

seat: Jessie assists from the back passenger seat. Finally, Paul is in his proper place.

A faint murmur passes through the crowd.

Lift-off and landing complete.

The two women hoist the Hoyer Lift at the back of the truck, turn it on its side above the tailgate, and slide it into its rightful place, the empty truck box.

Carol folds the wheelchair with a thwack, angry that her chance to show off before a crowd was foiled.

As Carol drives away from the church, she glances at Paul and says, "I can't believe I forgot to undo your seatbelt before lifting you from the chair." She thinks back to how expertly Darryl had been able to transfer Paul to and from the truck.

"Too bad we aren't able to go to the gravesite," says Paul, bringing the focus back to the pioneer woman who will soon be laid to rest.

"I know John and Barb will understand," Carol reassures Paul. "But we made it to the church. We did it." *All because of the beast.*

Chapter 27: Two Men of Good Will
2000

The truck has given the Fletchers a semblance of normalcy and stability, enabling a summer full of activity.

As the leaves turn colour, Carol can fully immerse herself into the new school year; Paul seems to be recharging his batteries, content with the home routine, with his ever-present link to the outside world sitting in the garage.

This stability prevails throughout the next five months.

The Fletchers' routines are now established. Thursday evening bar nights with April and Marcel; Sunday dinners with Heather, Bruce, and Ann; frequent visits from their sons and other extended family. Paul's business partner George graces their door regularly—usually when Carol is at work.

These routines make Carol feel bulletproof.

True, they have not yet managed the visit to Glen and Tracy's newish home, that promise still unfulfilled.

But as the year on the calendar turns to 2001, another promise, which Carol makes to herself, looms larger on the horizon: she is determined to make Paul's upcoming birthday *big*. She doesn't want to admit (even to herself) that she's spooked by the urgency she feels.

She wracks her brain until serendipitously spying a billboard on her way home: *Explore the city by helicopter!* The idea is born.

Of all the losses Paul expresses, explicitly or implicitly, it's his loss of flying in an airplane that seems to sting most, next to driving, of course. Carol is determined to change all that. She wants to get him up in the air.

When she tromps through the snow in February to book the flight and explain their special needs, the earliest date she can book is March 4, two days after Paul's birthday.

Once Paul hears of the booking, he begins doing something that he's never done before—to Carol's knowledge, at least—in all their married life. He has a caregiver tick off each day on the calendar. Just about as surprising is that Paul does not even inquire about the cost of this birthday present.

They'd better enjoy it while it lasts, is all Carol can think, for she knows full well—to borrow a line from William Wordsworth—*the Rainbow comes and goes.*

Days before March 4, Carol puts all three homecare workers in flight mode too: they take extra care with what Paul eats to decrease his chances of aspiration and he must rest every moment he can. That's where the city tour brochure comes in handy. Paul spends his time reading the thing, sometimes simply staring at the sketch on the front of the brochure: a handsome helicopter, artfully hovering in a blue sky as depicted by some clever tour ad agency.

Carol reminisces about the old days when flying off somewhere was a big part of their lives. First thing Paul did when the family got on a plane was to pluck the info card from the pocket in front of him and confirm the type of aircraft they were on, the altitude they would reach, and so on. By take-off, he would have devoured all the stats on that card. She never once remembered him reading the menu before this info card, his love of flying transcending even his love of food.

Tour day finds Paul and his family at the municipal airport early, about an hour early, not sure exactly what to expect.

After the ticket agent in the office is reminded that the customer who's flying with them that day is handicapped (Carol had softened the word from quadriplegic to ensure he'd qualify for the trip), the pilot appears at the counter introducing himself. "Ben," he says, as he shakes Carol's hand.

"I bought my husband this trip for his birthday... he's sitting in our truck... with our daughter and a care worker," she chatters nervously. She then briefly explains that the lift transfer to the helicopter might take about ten minutes.

"I'll let you folks get your husband into the helicopter... you're my first flight today... I'm ready when you are."

The Hoyer Lift transfer begins. They're self-conscious. Will the pilot think they're crazy to have booked this trip when he sees what they must do to get Paul into the aircraft?

The pilot stands on the tarmac until they have Paul dangling in the sling. In the next moment, the pilot motions them toward the passenger side of the aircraft saying, "You'll have the best view from here." He wins Carol's heart for not acting as if this were a crazy idea.

The helicopter door seems to be just slightly higher than the truck, so Rosa, Heather, and Carol anticipate a straightforward transfer. They debate a moment or two about whether to remove the sling from beneath Paul, once they've got him seated. They veto the idea.

One less step, all three conclude.

Alas, they *are* stymied—as unequivocally as they were trying to get Paul into their car—except this time it's not the top of a car keeping Paul out, but rather the width of the helicopter door. No matter how wide they hold it open, it impedes their ability to get the lift close enough to get Paul into the front seat. They reset. Another angle. Another failure.

The Uninvited Guest

Hope is beginning to fade. Carol's shoulders tense.

The pilot intervenes, as up to this point he had remained spectator. "Doesn't look like it's working." He inspects the hinges on the door. "Hold on a minute," he says, leaving them stranded on the tarmac.

The weeping has not begun. But the women in the group are close.

Paul, on the other hand, still hanging in the sling, is peering inside the aircraft at the instrument panel, as if checking the dials before a flight, getting ready to fly this thing up and away.

Pilot Ben returns with someone who looks to be a mechanic, given his blue coveralls and the screwdriver in his hand. The mechanic ignores the family, focusing on the door. After a few minutes, the pilot says, "He can remove the door, but it will take a few minutes... you folks willing to wait?"

Are you kidding? Carol thinks, holding her breath. *You can take the door off? And you would? For Paul? For us?*

Carol's fragile faith—stitched together since Paul's hospital 'recovery'—takes a giant leap forward when she realizes that these two men, men of goodwill, with nothing at all to gain but to make the day of this quadriplegic man, are taking the door off this helicopter to get him into it. And they don't know this man from Adam. How patient he is. How well he is handling his illness. How much he loves aircraft and flying. But here they are, determined to get this man into this helicopter when it would have been perfectly reasonable to call the whole thing off.

Within twenty minutes Paul is co-pilot. Carol half expects Ben to hand off the flight to Paul, let him fly this aircraft. Well, maybe not, since Paul couldn't even shake his hand upon meeting him. But Carol knows that if the pilot could, he would. He's proven himself. He's gold.

Paul is alert, his head not sagging, probably adrenaline coursing through his veins, is Carol's bet.

The pilot heads east, flying over the industrial area of the city. Not a pretty sight, but a reality for this oil capital: smoke pouring out of tall stacks, adulterating the city cloud cover.

The helicopter heads right leaving the smoky industrial area in its rear, snaking along the North Saskatchewan River to the downtown core. Carol's stomach does a somersault, not because of the movement of the aircraft but because it occurs to her that the helicopter door will have to be taken off again before Paul can get out of this thing. Although if Paul has his way, he just might request to live the rest of his life in that co-pilot seat. Up in the air.

Carol's eye catches the glinting glass of the Muttart Conservatory pyramids and the Edmonton Ski Club appears immediately to the south.

Twenty minutes into the flight, Paul's head begins to sag. Heather asks Rosa who is sitting directly behind Paul if she could prop up her dad's head from her vantage point. Rosa's solution is creative: she utilizes the sling around Paul like the chest strap in the truck, pulling it taut to stabilize his shoulders, causing his head to rise slightly. *Good decision to leave the sling in place*, thinks Carol, as she watches Rosa hold it taut for the remainder of the tour.

The pilot speaks into his microphone pointing out the sights. The Low Level Bridge. Then the landmark High Level Bridge, built almost ninety years ago. Cars hasten over both bridges, drivers oblivious to the joy of one city man high overhead.

Kinsmen Field, where Paul used to take his children to play pitch and putt, comes into view. They head south to the university area, and Carol is reacquainted with her feelings of grief over a Christmas holiday spent on the third floor of the University of Alberta Hospital, the memories washing over her.

The Uninvited Guest

Flying west brings the group over the world-renowned West Edmonton Mall. They hover above the vast landmark for a few minutes.

The pilot catches up with the river again to fly over the original site of this city, Fort Edmonton. A place Carol recalls visiting with their young children, especially the ride on the historic train meandering through the Fort. Another memory—the sound of the high-pitched whistle, signaling each successive stop—enters her consciousness.

The pilot heads toward the last leg of the tour: the Edmonton Queen Riverboat, sitting low in the water.

It appears that Paul is doing yeoman's work trying to keep his head upright, as it now sags, almost at a right angle, to his chest. The pilot turns the craft left, for one last look at the river, as if saluting the Edmonton Queen before heading back to the municipal airport.

Paul takes his eyes off the windshield for the first time in their flight, attempting to lift his head to look in the pilot's direction, struggling to say something. His intuitive daughter quickly figures it out—not her dad's mumbled words, but rather, his intent. "My dad wants to say thanks for the tour," she says to the pilot, placing her hand on her dad's left shoulder as if to say, *I've got this covered, Dad.*

Pilot Ben turns to Paul and says, "Glad you enjoyed it."

The careful hovering and touch-down manoeuvre of the helicopter reminds Carol of Paul's parallel manoeuvre in a Hoyer Lift, done at least eight to ten times daily, into seat after seat after seat. The closest he ever gets to flying these days, until today.

The blades beat loudly overhead, slowing down. A slight vibration rocks the vehicle gently.

The mechanic stands by the side of the hangar in waiting.

Ben shares a minute with Paul before leaving his post, pointing out the various functions of the buttons and dials, two men sitting there as casually as two men might in a new car discussing the latest dashboard. Should Carol tell the pilot that, once upon a time, Paul sold cars for a living? No need, she decides. They've created their own moment.

Twenty minutes after the helicopter door is removed, Paul is back in the front seat of the truck. His head sinking deep into his chest.

As they leave, the mechanic looks up from his task of putting the door in its rightful place. He waves. Paul can't wave but he smiles; Heather waves at them too as she drives away in her SUV.

It's only then that Carol remembers that one of the main reasons that Heather had come along on this trip was to get a picture of Paul in the helicopter, a birthday picture. "Darn," Carol moans.

To Carol's surprise, a few weeks later Heather shows up with a framed photograph. She had snapped the picture when her mother had ducked in to use the washroom just before their flight, before Paul's head was sagging into his chest.

It's trick photography at its best: Paul sits smartly in the co-pilot seat looking into the camera, without a door to mar the shot.

Carol looks at Paul and smiles. She kept her promise. Paul's 51st birthday was *big*.

Chapter 28: Wedding Day Blues
2001

Promises of another sort—vows, that is—are on the horizon. Nate is marrying Kim. Soon. July 22 to be exact.

The happy couple have decided to marry in Edmonton even though Kim is Vancouver born and raised. Probably for Paul's sake is Carol's guess.

On the Victoria Day long weekend, Nate and Kim fly to Edmonton to finalize wedding arrangements. Carol asks Kim, "How do your parents feel about having your wedding in Edmonton?"

"It's their chance to visit Edmonton for the first time... they're excited," Kim answers, confirming what Carol had already suspected. Nate is marrying into a good family.

But first things first. Picking out and buying Ann's junior bridesmaid dress brings Carol to that happy place she'd always associated with weddings. Ann's dress is peach with a full and poofy chiffon skirt, a perfect dress for a ten-year-old. Ann suddenly turns shy when trying it on, realizing that she's the centre of attention.

By Saturday morning though, the pre-wedding visit is off the rails. Nate corners his mother to ask, "What's up with

Dad?" Her son is beside himself with worry, surprised by how much sicker his dad seems than when he saw him last.

"Maybe you guys are doing too much with Dad," he says, searching for answers. "Maybe all the truck rides are wearing him out, it's just too much."

What she wants to say is "maybe MS is taking over" but decides to hold her tongue, at least until *after* the wedding.

Before Carol knows it, all three of her adult children and their partners are huddling. Talking late into the night. Things get serious. "Are we being fair to Dad?" is essentially the gist of the concerns they share with their mother after their late-night meetings.

Carol believes that the final straw to what subsequently happens at their house is Heather.

She shares with her brothers, as well as with Tracy and Kim, a book she's reading called *May I Walk You Home?* Carol does not recognize either of the two coauthors: Joyce Hutchison or Joyce Rupp.

"It's filled with story after story," Heather explains, "of someone like a brother or mother or hospice worker—journeying with the dying but sensing that the person needs permission to let go... to leave them." By this point, Heather's voice is barely audible.

Carols knows this is hard evidence to repudiate, but somehow, she cannot square the story with Paul. Apparently, her kids can, though.

Before Carol has any chance to do damage control, they are planning an emergency family meeting.

Her kids probably don't know this, but Carol had attended many an emergency family meeting when she was growing up: her mother (a widow raising two young daughters) up and called emergency meetings as a matter of course. She remembers the exact tone of her mother's voice as she outed the culprit of some misdemeanor by articulating her full Christian name, countless times, throughout the ordeal. It occurs to Carol, at this very moment, that her mother could have been frightened, sad, or lonely, or even overwhelmed. But how could two little girls have known that?

The Fletcher emergency family meeting is scheduled for Sunday evening—two days before Nate and Kim's return to Vancouver. The children know that Sunday evenings are family dinner night in the rec room. They often roast smokies in their wood-burning fireplace, an indoor picnic, of sorts. Carol reminds them that dinner will be early—at five—since Armand needs to have their dad in bed by eight-thirty. She is grateful that her children are comfortable with Armand being present during the family meeting. He's been in their lives almost two years now.

Glen builds the fire; Heather roasts a smokie for her dad first off so as he has enough time to eat it slowly. She does not offer to feed him as she usually does on their regular Sunday evening dinners; a bit strange. Carol wonders if Paul notices.

Carol is out of sorts. The only sound for a long time is her knife, cutting the cucumbers, tomatoes, broccoli, and carrots, as she prepares a platter of vegetables and dip.

Paul is in his element. Surrounded by family and food and fire, three of his favourite things, as Julie Andrews might sing from the hilltops. These occasions around the fire remind Carol how wise a decision it was—Paul's, of course—to have the elevator go to the basement level.

Carol waits. The children wait. Paul is the only one not waiting. He does not know that this is a *May I Walk You Home?* intervention.

As the minutes drag on, Carol sees that she may have to set things in motion. After all, Armand does eventually have to get Paul upstairs.

"Nate has something to tell you," Carol turns and says to Paul. She repeats herself, a tad louder, not sure Paul caught her drift. "Nate wants to tell you something."

Paul shifts his head slightly to look at Nate. His son's mouth opens. No sound. Nate tries again and the words come... but floundering, like the whitefish that he'd so often caught on the countless fishing expeditions of his youth. The words are slippery.

"You know how important you are in our lives, Dad..."

Whew. The thing's in motion, thinks Carol.

The hushed room listens: "And how much we all—well—Kim and I want you to be at our wedding."

Nate continues using his pianissimo voice, the crackling of the fire almost drowning him out.

"But, if all of this is too... too much for you, Dad... and, and you can't..." He's almost there. "If you can't be at our wedding, if you have to go... well... we'd understand."

Carol is glad Nate didn't suggest that Paul could go meet his Creator—a description of death she's often heard.

Paul stops chewing. Swallows. Thinking. Always one to think before he speaks.

But his thinking time is shorter than any of them could have anticipated. Because Paul pretty much gives—as soon as he has no food in his mouth—his answer.

"I like it here." A momentary silence. "I sure like it here."

Such ordinary words. Not one more than four letters long.

And Paul, who is not given to repetition at all, said it twice.

No philosophical ostentation.

Five monosyllabic words.

Did he even address Nate's inuendo? wonders Carol.

So, Paul would like to wake tomorrow to the morning light, as it streams through their bedroom window and shines on the wallpaper that he put up so many years ago.

The Uninvited Guest

He would like to eat smokies next weekend that someone else roasts for him in their beloved fireplace that he designed and helped build, with his Italian bricklayer friend.

He would even like to paint this rec room because he was the last one to do so, and it could sure use a coat of paint.

He would like to fly down, or better yet, drive to Calgary or Vancouver a few times a year to visit with his two sons in those two cites that he loves so much.

He would like to meet Kim's parents at the upcoming wedding.

The emergency meeting comes to a screeching halt.

Paul will gather his strength, like the gleaner in the wheat field at harvest time, to attend every event, big and little, for as long as he can.

And when he can no longer do so, every one of those who love him, knows that he still wants to.

Because as he just said, *he sure likes it here.*

Nate did what he thought was the right thing to do—release his father, if need be. Walk his father home.

Paul answers in the only way he knows, directly speaking his heart's truth.

The rest of the evening is not quiet. It is still.

It's the weight of Paul's words descending upon their hearts.

Has Paul just walked them home? Carol cannot help but ask herself.

***

Nate's intervention words are unexpectedly prescient: Paul does not make it to the afternoon wedding two months later. Not because he's gone to meet his Creator, but because he has a coughing spell at breakfast the morning of the wedding. He's too weak to be dressed, and far too weak to be sitting in a wheelchair for hours. Even too weak to stay awake for the remainder of the day.

The family work hard so as not to turn the wedding into a wake.

They keep up appearances. If someone were watching the art gallery wedding that afternoon and did not know that the father of the groom was at home steeped in the aftereffects of an aspiration attack, they might not notice anything unusual. The casual observer would only notice the flowers and ankle-length organza dresses and the one white tux appropriate for an afternoon wedding.

An astute observer, however, might intuit the truth when the gallery staff appear, hastily rearranging the chairs in the front row, removing the space allotted for Paul's wheelchair. A big hole to fill in the intimate room. The "till death do us part" phrase might jump out to some astute observers and illicit a few gasps or furrowed brows.

Carol sits through the celebration with two hearts.

Sad for her husband and son: Paul misses the big event and Nate does not have his father by his side for his special day.

And relieved: they have avoided the necessity of an arduous donning of Paul's wedding clothes over a catheter bag and hose attached to his thigh that must be firmly set in place, lest it be dislodged. They've avoided at least four Hoyer Lift transfers to and from their home, five kilometres away. Carol is relieved of the fear of listening for the invariable coughing spell that would mar the wedding luncheon. She won't have to vicariously feel Paul's embarrassment when someone from Kim's family reaches to shake his hand to no avail. And this is the short version of her relief list.

Paul's new in-laws are keeping up appearances too. No sad pitying sighs or words of sorrow from them, thank goodness.

The Uninvited Guest

The wedding is still filled with smiles, hugs, handshakes as well as one particularly lovely moment: when their granddaughter Ann, exquisite in her peach ankle-length dress, presents the ring-pillow to her Uncle Nate who unties the gold band from its flowing white ribbon before placing it on Kim's finger.

Almost all the twenty-five people present at the marriage meander over to the Fletcher home after the luncheon. But they don't get to visit Paul. He's asleep. Thank goodness Kim's parents got to meet Paul a few days ago.

It takes until the next morning for Paul's body to replenish enough energy to say goodbye to the wedding couple, now dressed in their street clothes, off to a honeymoon getaway.

Well, at least they have new pictures to hang on their gallery wall. Which Paul will get to view. *Hopefully.*

Chapter 29: Yet Another Curve Ball
2001

Even before Carol gets to hang Nate and Kim's wedding photo on their gallery wall, she gets a call from Dr. Sneider.

"Give me a minute to put you on speaker phone, so Paul can hear too."

The doctor explains, "Your hemoglobin is low, Paul... but the good news is that it's borderline low—90 grams per liter."

"What's it supposed to be?" Carol queries, trying to remember if she's ever heard or read about hemoglobin before. Paul seems distracted. Or disinterested. Or something.

"About 110," Dr. Sneider informs them. "You're anemic, Paul."

"But why would he be anemic?" Carol asks.

"Could be a lot of things. Low protein, vitamin deficiency, inflammation." The doctor pauses. "Let's start with iron supplements." She hears the uncertainty in Dr. Sneider's voice. "We'll keep an eye on it with blood tests."

And so, another regimen is added to their lives: regular home blood tests. At least it's not something extra Carol has to do, per se. And she can pick up the iron supplements when she picks up Paul's baclofen and Coumadin and stool softeners.

The Uninvited Guest

Paul submits to the testing of his blood as if everyone he knows gets their blood checked at home on a regular basis.

Her kids are not happy with the doctor's curious non-answer about the reason for their dad's low hemoglobin. Carol downplays her own concerns so as not to incite a rebellion.

MS is finding yet another way of sashaying into their lives.

A week later, Dr. Sneider calls again to say that Paul's hemoglobin is about 80. He's speaking only to Carol this time. "He needs a blood transfusion. Immediately." Carol clutches the phone harder.

It's Jessie's turn in the truck with them, headed for the outpatient clinic where Dr. Sneider has booked a blood transfusion for his patient. Heather meets them there.

No one needs to explain the process to Paul once they're at the clinic, though, because he's very familiar with its reverse procedure: donating blood. He'd done so for almost twenty years before his diagnosis. Has a certificate to prove it, marking some milestone or other, probably shoved in a drawer somewhere. *I should resurrect it to add to our bedroom gallery*, she thinks, in the spirit of the comedian who pokes fun at what hurts in order to survive.

Either the clinic setting, or the procedure, seems to act as a trigger for Paul.

"I had just started donating plasma," he says to the nurse at his side, "when I had to give it up."

"So I'm guessing needles don't bother you, sir?" another nurse says, as she probes for veins. He smiles ruefully at her observation.

Funny, thinks Carol, *another loss in his life that had never been mentioned—until today.*

Over the next four hours, Paul receives two units of blood. Carol brings Paul lunch from the downstairs cafeteria; Heather feeds him sitting opposite the arm with the IV dripping blood into her dad's vein, concentrating on getting her dad's food into his mouth and hoping it's not getting into his lungs. Jessie thickens his Coke so he can take his pills. Since they have nothing but time on their hands, they take their time: Paul eats his tuna melt slowly, not coughing once. The small room is dwarfed by a metal storage unit, medical equipment piled almost to the ceiling on its five shelves. When Paul is done lunch, he asks Heather if she'd mind straightening the boxes of rubber gloves. Heather is confused, not making the connection to what Paul had been staring at during his long lunch.

"While I was eating, I noticed the boxes on the shelf." He catches his breath before his next statement. "The nurses here look pretty busy—so maybe you could straighten them up?"

Carol shakes her head and laughs out loud; Jessie utters a soft chuckle; Heather bends to her father's request, straightening the glove boxes, the gauze—all the paraphernalia on the metal shelves. Heather seems thrilled to be able to bring some much-needed order to her dad's life.

Hours after the transfusion, they are home and Paul turns into the energizer bunny. "I haven't felt this good since... since... I can't remember when."

"You certainly do look stronger. Your voice sounds stronger too," says Carol.

Paul wants Carol to phone everyone they know to share the news of his miracle *cure*. He listens to every call, his body not sagging and his eyes revealing his glee.

But within forty-eight hours Carol finds herself calling everyone back. "It didn't last. Paul is as weak as ever." The silence at the other end of the phone is deafening.

Carol sees the disappointment written all over Paul's face. It reminds her of a soldier's face soon after having witnessed a roadside bombing.

The Uninvited Guest

The Fletchers soon discover that the battery in the energizer bunny is recharged after each blood transfusion—but only for a limited time.

"The good thing is," Dr. Sneider explains, "we can keep doing transfusions for now."

***

The addition of blood transfusions to their lives makes Carol take stock.

For a few years, high on her anxiety list of living with MS—after reduced mobility, of course—was Paul's hair. The constant friction of hair versus surfaces (pillow, leather headrests on both his wheelchair and shower chair, upholstery fabrics of the lift chair and truck seat) resulted in a most unruly phenomenon: eight or twelve or fifteen stubborn hairs—standing straight up. No matter what.

All her family and the caregivers knew of Carol's anxiety about Paul's hair and tried to help. Heather often took styling-wax from her mother's bathroom cabinet, working each stray hair delicately between her fingers before they left the house. One day, as Carol searched her purse for the truck keys, she spied—out of the corner of her eye—Rosa frantically trying to flatten Paul's hair with spittle, just as they entered the elevator. Useless.

Carol once took drastic action: when they visited the barber, she told him to give Paul a shorter than usual haircut.

"Oh, you want a summer cut, eh?" the barber said.

It didn't work. Paul looked at his reflection in the mirror next day, shaking his head. "I look like I've been conscripted into the army."

Besides, in just days, the delinquent hairs reappeared.

Her hair anxiety pales in the face of blood count worries. What she wouldn't give to have those days back.

Today is blood transfusion number three. They get home before Paul is energized, exhaustion from the four-hour ordeal making it hard for him to hold his head up.

What must that be like? she wonders.

Paul tells her what it's like. "I'm like a baby," he says to her, a theme he expresses more and more frequently.

But today, the comment escalates.

"I'm like a goddamn baby." It's *that* he curses. Paul never curses.

"Don't say that... you're not a baby," Carol boomerangs back at him, her mind trying to drown out the music playing under his curse words.

"What can I do... tell me honestly one thing I can still do on my own?" Surprisingly, his weak voice rises in volume to match Carol's. "Name one thing... one."

Oddly enough, it reminds Carol of the list she'd made at Paul's request years before, of things he could still do. And truth be told, there is not one thing on that list he *can* still do.

The entire rest of the day, Paul is sullen. Jessie is even quieter than usual, obviously having overheard the couple's outburst. She looks like she wants to vanish into thin air.

Join the club, is all Carol can think.

Chapter 30: The Empty Bag
2001

In late August, Carol and Heather sit in Dr. Sneider's office.

The family doctor begins slowly. "I have some good news. Paul's hemoglobin seems to be holding at around ninety since his last transfusion." The doctor continues. "Trouble is, it's taken three transfusions to get him stabilized." He looks at the screen in front of him as if for confirmation or inspiration, Carol's not sure which.

"Unfortunately, the meds he's on may be a contributing factor... Coumadin is a blood thinner." The doctor shifts in his chair.

"Does he still need to take it, then?" asks Carol.

"Tricky," Dr. Sneider explains. "He takes it to avoid blood clots, which he's certainly in constant danger of."

After a moment he admits, "But the Coumadin may be contributing to some blood loss... we have to stop it... it's the lesser of two evils, really."

Heather voices another concern: "For how long can my dad continue the blood transfusions? To bring up his hemoglobin numbers?"

"No problem there," the doctor answers. "It's more a question of how long they'll be effective." He pauses. "Let's wait and see."

And that's what they learn on that fateful day in late August: they must wait and see.

"What kind of an answer is wait and see?" Carol says to her daughter, upon leaving the doctor's office. "It's like doing nothing."

In the car, Heather cries. Carol hyperventilates. *Breathe*, she reminds herself, *breathe*.

"Just tell us what to do," Carol says, as if the doctor and not her daughter were seated beside her.

Keep putting one foot in front of the other, mother and daughter decide that fateful day.

Carol remembers reading something the first woman ever to reach the summit of Mount Everest had explained in her book: looking up from your feet during a daunting climb could result in the paralyzing effect of having the entire journey laid out before you.

Carol does not dare look up, unless she is forced to.

Today she is forced to, by Jessie. "I'm just letting you know that Paul hasn't had a bowel movement for a couple of days." She continues in a dejected voice, as if it's her fault. "I'm spending more and more time putting him in the sling to hoist him over the commode because he has the urge but can't go."

Carol phones Dr. Sneider early Tuesday morning to talk bowel movements as if they were discussing the weather. The doctor says, without hesitation, that the stool softener he's on must not be doing the trick. He'll send out a registered nurse from Health Link to give Paul an enema.

"Could be dangerous. Good you called," the doctor says, confirming Carol's concerns.

The next weekend Carol jumps out of the shower only to find Rosa outside her bathroom door—waiting for her, looking alarmed. She's holding Paul's urinal bag in her hand.

"It's empty," she says, holding up the bag in her rubber-gloved hand, stating the obvious.

"So, he hasn't gone all night?" Carol asks.

"Nothing at all," replies Rosa.

Carol calls Heather first; her second call is to Dr. Sneider's office. His answering machine directs her to the Health Link hotline. In minutes, she's talking to a registered nurse.

After a few pertinent questions and answers back and forth, the nurse instructs Carol. "Press your husband's lower abdomen, but not too hard. Check for pain. I'll hold on."

By this time, Heather and her family have arrived. She and Carol watch Rosa kneel in front of Paul. Bruce escorts Ann out of the bedroom. Rosa gently presses his stomach. Paul wakes and winces simultaneously. "Does this hurt?" Rosa asks, knowing full well by his reaction that it does.

"A little," he acknowledges.

"His abdomen sure feels tight," notes Rosa.

And so that is how they come to have a registered nurse in their home on a Sunday evening instead of the family dinner party they had anticipated. The professional leans over Paul in his bed, telling him that she will replace his temporary condom catheter with an indwelling permanent one called a Foley catheter. "But first, I will empty your bladder."

Paul nods—his chief job in life now, it seems, is to agree with what's going on around him. "You'll feel better after I'm done," the nurse assures him.

"We have to drain the urine from his bladder slowly," she explains to Armand—who has now replaced Rosa from her day shift, "so that the intra-abdominal pressure does not change too abruptly. That might cause dizziness and a sudden drop in blood pressure."

Carol hears Heather on the phone in the sitting room. Probably calling her two brothers—explaining what's going on. Except, who can say exactly what is going on?

"His abdominal pressure should subside within the hour," the health link nurse says before leaving. "And your husband's urinary retention should be checked out with your own doctor, ASAP."

Finally, everyone is gone, off to their rightful places. Carol crawls into bed beside Paul rather than in her futon, even though Paul is sound asleep. Her emotions are raw and her thoughts racing. The nurse explained that much of Paul's pain may be masked, MS likely having destroyed some of his pain sensations. Carol also wonders what an indwelling Foley catheter looks like compared to a condom one. It sounds painful; she's too rattled to look.

She cannot turn her mind off.

She remembers a day a couple of years earlier when she'd been driving to work and espied out of her little eye some man walking, arms swinging in time to his brisk gait. She felt like pulling her car over to scream curses at this guy because he could walk. Or at least shake her fist at him. Or something. Instead, she had wept all the way to school.

Today, she's not so much angry as overwhelmed. She's read Harold Kushner and wants to believe that when bad things happen to good people, God is sad with them. That's the Jewish way to make sense of it all, and after years and years of attending Mass, Carol is well steeped in Christian theology too. She's been taught that God does not give us more than we can handle. That He stands close to the broken hearted. But today, she does not feel consoled.

She lies by Paul's side for a long time.

He does not rouse. She just hopes he's peeing, her delicate sensibilities about bodily functions having fully slipped away, as she fears that her husband is doing more and more often these days. Slipping away, that is.

Carol slides out of bed, tiptoes over to the other side where the catheter bag is suspended from the chrome bars. She bends to check it, as a hunter of long ago might carefully check his traps. Eureka. Carol sees yellow urine dripping. She watches a moment to be sure she's not mistaken, before sneaking over to her futon bed.

Paul is due a blood transfusion the following Wednesday. She can't believe what their lives are reduced to: blood, dripping from a plastic bag into Paul's veins every few weeks, and urine, dripping into another plastic bag, daily, if he's lucky.

***

Paul doesn't make it to the fourth transfusion. Instead, Carol finds herself phoning Dr. Sneider. "I have to talk to him as soon as possible," she tells the receptionist who by now recognizes her early morning jittery voice. "A nurse came to drain his bladder and insert a Foley catheter."

She calls Heather immediately thereafter. "I know it's the first week of school, but can you come with me to Dr. Sneider's office tomorrow?" Carol is afraid to convey the rest. "The doctor wants to talk to us. Alone." She hears Heather's sharp intake of breath even over the phone.

Next day, Carol's mind goes blank the moment she and Heather sit down in Dr. Sneider's office. The doctor begins.

"Remember Paul's early swallowing difficulties? I think… well, those were probably the first tell-tale signs of muscle degradation due to MS." He shifts in his chair. "Now, unfortunately, it's his bowel and bladder muscles that are being compromised."

It's the through line that Dr. Sneider seems to be suggesting that's unnerving Carol.

"His increasing sleep apnea may be signaling something bigger too... like the respiratory muscles in his chest... the ones that control breathing." He pauses. "Their impairment would spell big trouble."

It's Heather who finally speaks, asking if anything can stop the muscles from weakening, or, at least, slow them down.

"Unfortunately not. I wish I had a different answer for you." He looks down at his desk before saying, "And Paul's losing blood. Ordinarily we'd order a colonoscopy or gastroscopy but... to be honest, those procedures are far too intrusive given the circumstances."

Then Dr. Sneider veers off topic, or so it seems. "Ordinarily, I wouldn't broach this topic without Paul here, but because I know how difficult it is for him to get into the office... I was wondering... if you folks know... if you realize... that you are doing a kind of end-of-life care at home. Is that what you—what Paul—what all of you want?"

Neither Carol nor Heather answer. Heather reaches to hold her mother's hand.

"Of course, we'll try again for another blood transfusion." The doctor gauges the situation correctly, and gives them some positives to offset their fear: "Paul's mental confusion has lessened, from what you're telling me, so oxygen must be getting to the brain. The enema worked for now, and the Foley catheter is doing the trick for his bladder... and it can stay in place... well, indefinitely."

Carol gets up. She needs to leave. She must talk to Paul. And her sons.

Heather follows her lead.

The Uninvited Guest

This time Carol joins Heather in a crying jag in the car. And it's ugly.

Later, much later, Carol will try to remember if they'd even said goodbye to Dr. Sneider before leaving his office.

Eventually, Carol talks to Paul. But not to tell him what the doctor said; she just can't find the words. She tells her husband instead that the indwelling catheter he received is working well and can stay in as long as necessary.

Before Carol knows it, Glen drives in from Calgary, and Nate flies in from Vancouver.

They talk endlessly of how and what exactly to tell Paul about the muscle deterioration in his chest and the implication this has for his breathing and the internal bleeding and his declining hemoglobin numbers.

They wait too long. On September 11 every life in the universe is put on hold, including the Fletchers'.

Glen happens to be in the bedroom with Paul when the initial plane hits the North Tower in New York.

"How the hell could a plane be that far off course?" he utters to his dad.

Jessie is sponge bathing Paul. She stops. All eyes are glued to the television.

Over the next four days, the entire family—and the world—are connected to the TV, as if by umbilical cord.

They discuss names they've never heard before, including Osama bin Laden. Repeatedly. Heart-stopping audio of frantic last phone calls made from offices high in the sky fill the air waves. Death tolls rise daily. First responders appear, as if from the old grainy black and white movie era, the dust from the towers making them look like WWI soldiers emerging from European trenches.

Heather cries as she watches people hurtling themselves out of windows in the sky,

221

Bruce holds her close.

But Paul cannot hold onto the facts. He watches the news with them, even asks some pointed questions, but in the end, it's like he's seeing the planes hit the Twin Towers for the first time—every time. They bring him back to what's happening, but it keeps slipping away from him.

Carol's fear drives her to call Dr. Sneider again, telling him about Paul's confusion. The doctor is not surprised.

"He's probably not getting enough oxygen to his brain. Let's push up the date of his next blood transfusion."

But Paul is too weak even for that.

The Fletchers are in lockstep with the traumatized Americans across the border.

When their sons head home, listlessly, needing to return to work, Paul does not even ask where everyone has gone. The children telephone constantly so that their dad can hear their voices, but he seems disconnected from the sound over the speaker phone. His voice is lost to them too, too weak for them to hear.

The Fletcher world is becoming silent.

Chapter 31: "Are We There Yet?"
2001

Carol feels like she's on a path littered with threatening signposts—*slow down, steep curve, danger ahead,* or scariest of all—*dead end.* She spends much of her time looking down at the urine catheter bag hanging on the rail of Paul's bed. She keeps checking and rechecking the stats sheets for Paul's hemoglobin numbers. She does mental checks on Paul too, asking what he ate for lunch—then confirming with Rosa or Jessie, to check if enough oxygen is getting to his brain. Watching. Waiting. Wondering.

For some strange reason this harkens back to an earlier phase in their lives, when strangers seemed to be wondering about Paul's life too. She called that time the *Still Phase.*

She and Paul would be out and about in the community, and someone would ask, "Are you still driving, Paul?" Another day, another person. "Can you still cut the grass?"

What she wouldn't give for someone to come up to her and ask her if Paul is still going to restaurants. Or to church, or out in his truck. She would answer civilly, something she had not always pulled off, in the days of yesteryear.

The ultimate *Still Question* brought them to their knees one day, just outside their bank: do you still live at home, Paul?

Yes, Paul still lives at home and today a special home delivery is being made by the Aids to Daily Living people. An IV pole and bags of solution filled with fluid and electrolytes are being dropped off, as well as butterfly needles. Dr. Sneider had recommended the administering of this solution as a way of keeping Paul comfortable—hydration meaning comfortable, Carol learned that day. The practice is known as *clysis* and is done subcutaneously; that is, just under the surface of the skin rather than in a vein, as the doctor had explained the day he ordered it.

And that's what this September Sunday brings to their lives: Jessie slipping a butterfly needle just under Paul's skin— subcutaneously—to keep Paul hydrated. Comfortable.

"Not one morsel of food," Rosa says on Monday evening to Carol. "All he managed to get down was enough thickened water for his pills, but that's it."

The ringing phone interrupts Rosa's concerned voice. It's Heather.

"I just talked to Glen and Nate, and they're relieved that I can take time off again to be with Dad," Heather tells her mom. "Glen and Tracy will be here Friday. Nate and Kim are thinking the same."

Silence. Then finally, "And, Mom, the immediate family must be told." Heather ends the call explaining that she is off to her parish council meeting at the church.

Heather must have phoned someone in the family though because the visits of charity begin within the hour: John and his wife Barb are first to arrive. Paul's eyes flutter open momentarily at the sound of his big brother's booming voice. Carol wonders if Paul notices the inconsolable look on his brother's face. Angie and Sarah arrive soon after, taking turns hugging Carol or holding Paul's hand incessantly. Even George shows up.

The Uninvited Guest

Heather is happy to find her dad a wee bit better on Tuesday morning—even saying a few words to Jessie upon her arrival, something he had not done at all on Monday. Carol leaves Heather in charge, going into work to prepare for the time she's taking off.

At the end of the day, Heather tells her mother that things did not go well. "I skipped out around noon to buy some swabs to moisten Dad's dry lips. The pharmacy is across from the McDonald's." Heather is on the verge of tears. "On a whim, I decided to pick up a fast food lunch. Rosa and Armand had dropped in on Jessie's shift to see how Dad was doing so I bought food for them all."

Carol reaches for Heather's hands, holding them tightly.

"Of course, Dad smelled the fries and asked for a few... I knew he would have trouble swallowing, but I couldn't say no." Now her tears flow. "And of course, he started coughing, well, choking really, the minute he tried to swallow one." All three caregivers ran down the hall into the bedroom, Carol learns from her daughter. Armand flopped Paul over his arm, pounded his back and out popped the culprit french fry.

Carol and Heather sit in silence for a moment.

"Can you imagine if Dad had choked to death on a fry?" Heather says to her mom as they bring the long and difficult Tuesday to its end. "On my watch."

Wednesday is a scene. They are like people in a painting, imitating the tableaux Carol's seen in art galleries. The weird ones with children dressed like miniature adults, a dog lurking in the background, Elizabethan times.

Heather is draped over one side of her dad's bed with Ann and their dog Grape sitting on the other side. Grape is licking one of Paul's hands. *Does Grape know what's happening?* thinks Carol, the cockles of her heart warmed, for the first time ever, by a dog.

All this tableau needs now is a member of the clergy standing by the sickbed. Two hours later the doorbell rings, and there he stands, Father Francis.

Grape growls softly as if not wanting to be taken from Paul. Bruce picks her up and takes her to their home minutes away; Ann slinks away with them. Heather stays as do Sarah and Angie. Barb arrives moments after the priest and joins the growing semicircle forming around Paul's bed.

When Father Francis puts his hand on Paul's shoulder, he opens his eyes. Father reminds Paul that he hasn't seen him in church for a while so... well, here he is. Carol suspects that Heather had mentioned something to him at the parish council meeting on Monday evening. Father Francis says, "I'd like to give you a blessing for the sick, if it's okay with you, Paul." Paul blinks his eyes, as if in consent.

He certainly qualifies, thinks Carol.

The family is hushed as they watch Father Francis administer the sacrament to Paul. Father Francis drapes a sacred church cloth around his neck, makes the sign of the cross, and begins. Chanting. Administering oils. Administering blessings.

Father begins the Lord's Prayer. Paul—who had essentially uttered no words that day—becomes fully animated in the only place still possible: his eyes. They become two bright coals.

Paul even tries to keep up with a few words of the universal "Our Father," the most appropriate leave-taking words possible, Carol realizes at this very moment, after half-heartedly reciting the words by rote for years.

"Thy Kingdom come...."

The bedside-group mouth the words so that the only audible sounds are of Paul's shadowy voice and Father Francis' priestly one.

And then Paul does what he's been doing all of his life. "Thank you, Father," he says, almost inaudibly.

The Uninvited Guest

It hits Carol like a ton of bricks: *Did Father Francis just walk Paul home?*

***

Thursday is Carol's watch. She'd insisted that Heather stay home and rest for at least part of the day. But Paul does not wake. Not even in fits and starts. Jessie keeps a close eye on him, going about her duties, first emptying his catheter bag (little urine in it). Next, she sponge baths him, which he sleeps through. Soundly. No one turns the television on; their world shrinks to the size of the mechanical bed, waiting for Paul's eyes to open.

Carol sits in the rocker beside Paul, reading the newspaper for a long time, not one word registering. The only thing that stays are the pictures staring out at her, from the obituaries—*those* she cannot get out of her mind. She flips the obit page quickly to try to erase the images. It strikes Carol as odd that one small column in a newspaper is meant to capture an entire lifetime; in the end, our lives are reduced to two hundred words or less, it seems.

Suddenly, she has the urge to write.

She has no idea why, but she does know *what* she must write. A letter. To Paul. She settles in the chair. Pen in hand, she begins. Jessie's eyebrows rise slightly at the sight of Carol writing as she wrings a facecloth over a basin by the side of the bed.

> *Dear Paul,*
>
> *I'm trying to recall whether I've ever written you a full letter, but I don't think so, because we were never apart for more than a week... maybe during one of my short jaunts with Barb or when you were*

227

on a business trip. I do remember sending you a postcard when I went to Hawaii with Mom and Angie. Afterward you said it made you sad that the Fletcher family never made it to Hawaii together. I'm sorry I sent the postcard.

I'm sorry too for signing you up for Tai Chi after your diagnosis. Your balance was so bad. No wonder you hated it.

And I'm so sorry I signed us up for the support group meetings. The sight of people with later stage MS—a terrifying preview of what our future was going to look like. Which you seemed to intuit, but I totally missed. I wish we would have gone to a movie or a walk around the park instead.

I'm sorry that I did not place the cedar chest you built in high school shop class in the sitting room, once you were held captive in that room. You would have loved being reminded of the things you had made with your hands. You had a natural talent with wood. So glad Nate inherited your wood-genes.

Sorry I never learned to blab less. Or refrain from gossiping. You led by sterling example, every chance you got. But it didn't stick.

I'm so sorry I never kept my promise about giving you more showers. When we first got the shower chair, I promised myself I would. But I failed. Often when I was saying goodbye to you in the morning, you would ask me to scratch your itchy scalp as, of course, you could not reach up to do it. How could

I have not worked in an extra shower during the week, no matter what?

That brings me to one of my darkest secrets: the day I scratched you. Not your scalp. You. On purpose. In anger. I do not remember what set me off that morning–but I couldn't control myself. I yelled at you first. Then I tore at the bedclothes around you, venting my anger. Then I tore into you. Your skin. Scratched your forearm. Only for a second, but long enough to leave marks. As quickly as it had begun, it was over. I cannot tell you how many times shame settles around my heart–squeezing and squeezing–to this day. You were so vulnerable and had hours and hours on your hands to relive that grotesque event.

I'm sorry that I was bored by many of the things that fascinated you like dams and bridges; bears and alligators; trees and flowers; cars and trucks; and the weather. I didn't try hard enough.

Sorry I never agreed to every single side trip you ever suggested when we were on holidays back in the day, no matter how many bodies of water we had to cross or how many hours it added to our journey.

Sorry I read all those Shakespeare passages aloud to you. You were always such a good sport, patiently listening. Remember when Barb pointed out that you were at my mercy–a captive audience–was how she described it. We had a good laugh then but I'm still sorry.

I'm so sorry that we never got to the Queen Charlotte Islands, a trip I had planned as a thank you for supporting me through university as an adult student; we had to forgo that trip because I got my job right after graduation. Just so you know, whenever my spirit sagged while waging our battle against MS–and it did–I had only to recall your sacrifice of the chance to see the aurora borealis to put all else into perspective.

I am sorry I called the Hoyer Lift the beast. It was the instrument of your resurrection. But, as usual, it took me time to get it. You got it even as TJ explained it in hospital, introducing it into our lives. I needed more time. Sorry.

I wish we could have gotten you to Glen and Tracy's house in Calgary. We ran out of time. It's not fair.

I have a memory that brings some balance to the universe: you carried all three of our children for a long time–in your arms as babes, on your shoulders as toddlers, on your back when they were eight and nine-years-old–it was one of your pleasures in life, visible to all who bore witness to it. What does it say about a man who considers it a joy to carry around his brood for as long as possible?

 She sits for a long time before scribbling "Love, Carol" below the letter. Her attention turns to Jessie as she tries to rouse Paul for some lunch, to no avail.

 By late afternoon Carol knows she needs to talk to Glen and Nate. "Good you're coming," she tells both boys.

 Jessie is now doing leg and arm exercise on Paul as he sleeps. She ends her shift with their ritual foot massage but seems reluctant to leave. She leans over and kisses Paul on the cheek before going. It startles Carol. She imagines Paul being startled to waking. She's wrong. He sleeps right through this first-ever kiss from Jessie.

Carol crawls into the bed, as she routinely does this time every weekday. She wonders why she hasn't asked Paul how he's kept on going, especially when things got rough. And how he's kept us going too?

Carol remembers reading about a prisoner of war, the Vietnam War, in fact, who said that it was necessary to acknowledge the brutal reality of one's situation while keeping a kind of hope alive; resiliency is how she thinks he described it. Paul must have figured that out too. When he needed it, he drew from a deep reservoir of resiliency. And he hadn't even read the article about the soldier.

Carol squeezes Paul's hand. *Thank you for not going away that Christmas in the hospital. We weren't ready.*

She must have dozed off because suddenly she hears Rosa at the back door. She and Heather and Bruce and Ann arriving on her heels, probably with the dinner they promised to bring.

She considers commanding Paul to open his eyes. Just open your eyes so that things can go back to normal.

She does no commanding. Rather she silently and carefully rises from their bed, planting her feet on the cold floor.

"Papa's sleeping," Ann says, reminding Carol of the young child she was when she first came into their lives.

After a subdued dinner, Bruce hauls Carol's futon from the shower stall behind the green curtain in Paul's bathroom, where it stands, rolled up. Carol thinks back to about a year ago, on an evening when Paul's words were coming out more garbled than usual and Rosa was having difficulty deciphering what he was saying. His persistent repeating of anything that they could not understand—which frustrated Carol—now sends her heart into delirium. Paul was worried that Rosa would forget to bring the futon from his bathroom before she left, to place on the floor for Carol's use.

His wish to execute what he saw as his husbandly duty—his life's task—was in danger of being left undone. It's what they had promised each other at nineteen and twenty-three years of age. Paul had not forgotten.

This Thursday evening is fast coming to an end.

"If anything happens," Heather insists as they are leaving, "and I mean anything... call immediately."

"Of course," Carol says. "I will. I promise."

Chapter 32: Was it Thursday or Friday?
2001

The next thing Carol hears is a ringing phone, sounding way too loud. She jumps up, runs to the sitting room and answers it. She glances at the clock: 6:14.

"Yes, he slept, Heather... no snoring... not even any sleep apnea. He's sleeping."

"Okay, Mom, we're on our way over."

Carol walks back to the bedroom and stands suspended in the doorway—the same doorway the two young boys who broke into their house had stood over eight years ago now—and looks at Paul. She draws a breath. She's almost certain that he's gone. Death does have its own stillness.

She lied to Heather. Again. Her dad did not have a good sleep. She goes over to the bed, leans over Paul, waiting for him to breathe and prove her wrong. But no breath. She hears her heart beating frightfully loud, like it's outside her body.

She kisses Paul on his forehead and ruffles his wavy hair, his beautiful hair. She lifts his heavy hand to her cheek, holding it between her own. His eyes are closed and she tries to will some movement into his eyelids. But he looks so peaceful that she cannot wish him back.

She kisses his wedding ring, carefully laying his heavy hand at his side, unfurling his swollen fingers.

"Oh, Paul... Paul... oh, Paul," she hears someone in the room say. It takes a few seconds for her to realize that it's her own tearful voice she hears.

When she unlocks the back door, she does not have to say any words to her family. Her face gives it away. Glen and Tracy arrive from Calgary minutes after Heather and her family, having driven through the night.

From the moment of Paul's death, Carol experiences the identical out-of-body phenomenon she'd felt during Paul's hospitalization: becoming a spectator to her own life.

Carol watches as the five members of her family drape themselves over Paul; Glen keeps repeating how cold Paul is as he grasps his hand. His wife Tracy nods in agreement; Heather and Bruce have their arms around Ann, who tips forward slightly leaning on her Papa's bed.

Carol, as a rational spectator, thinks, *Paul's not cold. His body *is* cold.*

Carol hears Heather call an ambulance. But the conversation is too long. She watches as her daughter jots down a phone number. "The dispatcher said that if Dad's... if his body is cold, we should call the coroner."

Glen makes *that* call. Someone at the other end of the phone asks a few questions. Glen hangs up and tells the family that a coroner should arrive at the house within a couple of hours. Eventually, Bruce thinks it best that he and Ann leave; Carol thinks he wants Ann to remember her Papa in his bed, not being removed by some coroner.

Heather, Glen, and Tracy continue to lean over Paul, stroking his face and his hair and his hands. The trio is like one giant octopus, arms like tentacles, intermingling with Paul's still and cold body.

The Uninvited Guest

Words pour out. "You're the best dad ever." "I wish you didn't have to go." "What are we going to do without you, Dad?"

The words morph into stories of how much their dad loved boating with them. Teaching them to swim. Diving off the pier. Teaching them to drive. Planting flowers together. Trimming the hedge.

Heather glances up at her dad and says, "He looks so peaceful."

At these words Carol's spectator façade falls in heaps around her and she hyperventilates. "I didn't wake when your dad needed me... he died alone."

Heather insists otherwise. "You were here, Mom. You were beside him. Dad wouldn't have wanted to upset you. And remember when we left last night, how sound asleep he was?"

"But what if he woke up, looking for me over on the futon?" Then she's more alarmed. "What if he was calling me and I didn't hear him?" Carol opens her eyes wide. "And we'll never really know whether he died on the 20th or the 21st."

Heather and Glen both hang on to their mom for dear life, straight through to the end of her tears of lamentation, her feeling of having abandoned her husband at the very moment of his death spilling all over them.

"I'm sure he slipped away in his sleep," Glen says finally, tears sliding down his cheeks. He turns to his sister and says, "Do you think it's possible Dad was in a coma when you left last night?"

"Now that you say it," she hesitates. "He probably was."

"Doctors tell families to talk to their relatives, even in a coma," Carol sobs, louder still at her children's exchange of words. "And we didn't even talk to him. He would have heard us," Carol adds after her moment of realization.

Glen interjects. "I hope Nate and Kim make it here before the coroner. They should be picking up their rental at the airport about now."

Moments later, a panicky thought materializes in Carol's head as she glances at her watch. "Jessie will be here any minute to begin her shift."

"It's okay," Heather says. "It's okay."

And it is. Jessie hugs Carol. She crosses the room, bends over Paul, sadness but not surprise spread across her face.

She rubs Paul's cold hands, in circles. Clockwise. Using first her fingers. Then her palm. Counterclockwise too. She's silent. She does the same to his cheeks. Small respectful circular motions, ritualistically. To his forehead. To the top of his head. Carol half expects her to begin on Paul's arms and his legs, replacing the exercises she'd done with Paul every weekday morning for almost two years now.

Jessie turns to Carol after a few minutes and says, "If there's anything I can do, please let me know... anything." She leaves, giving a doleful nod in the direction of the family.

Glen answers the front door thirty minutes later, leading two official looking men where they need to be. The coroners walk over to Paul, inspect his body, and confirm his death.

And then it begins. Name of the deceased? Born when? Where? Who found him? At what time? Time last seen alive? By whom? Any known diseases? When was the deceased last hospitalized? Why no ambulance? The last questions sound accusatory, bringing Carol back to a horrible flashback: not bringing Paul to the hospital quickly enough when he'd aspirated and had pneumonia. Carol glances from one child to the other.

Heather takes over.

"Sir, my dad has had multiple sclerosis for more than a decade... we've been in touch with his neurologist and our family doctor all along."

"Doctors' names?" the coroner asks briskly, then writes through Heather's responses, not looking up.

"And... two weeks ago, a Health Link nurse drained his bladder." The men both look up at Heather when she says, "My dad's been having blood transfusions, up until two weeks ago too."

Finally, the questions stop, except for one. "Do you folks want his ring?"

"Yes... we couldn't get it off," Carol replies. "His hands were swollen... and numb."

"Could you please wait in the next room while we prepare the body?" The coroner is already trying to twist the ring on Paul's finger. "We'll call for you when we're done."

The family moves *en masse* to the sitting room where they all stare at the fish in the aquarium. No one sits down. Paul's lift chair sits conspicuously empty. Carol is wondering aloud who they should call first, knowing that one call will put in motion the funeral pilgrimage they're about to embark on.

And where, oh where, are Nate and Kim?

There seems to be some confusion in the bedroom. Heather and Glen hurry in to find one coroner holding Paul's arm in the air at an awkward angle. The other man pulling on Paul's ring. Hard.

"You'll break his finger," Carol hears her son say sharply to the coroner.

Carol runs to the bedroom just as the man drops Paul's arm, as if stung by a bee.

"That's my dad," sobs Heather. "Be respectful... Please."

Glen and Heather stand their ground—guarding their dad as he'd done so many times in their lives, on bike rides down the back alley, or dives into a swimming pool, or walks to school across a busy intersection.

One of the coroners timidly asks if they have soap. Carol retrieves a bar of Palmolive from Paul's bathroom, and a saturated face cloth, the one Jessie probably used on him just yesterday. The green suds are generously slathered over Paul's finger, dripping on the bedding. The ring is off with a couple of twists. As it's placed in the palm of Carol's hand, she closes her fingers tightly around it.

Soon, the gurney with Paul's body now covered from head to toe is ready to be wheeled out.

This is nothing like going to the hospital and coming back home, thinks Carol. *And Paul doesn't even get a last elevator ride,* Carol suddenly realizes. *The gurney won't fit in the elevator.* The coroners walk purposefully down the front steps of the house.

She joins them at the waiting vehicle—the first of Paul's last rides. Official last rides with an honour guard of his family.

Nate and Kim miss him, that is, miss Paul's body. They pull up in the back driveway fifteen minutes after the coroner's departure. Glen, Tracy, and Heather rush out to meet them.

Carol is bending, struggling to put on her shoes at the screen door. As she straightens up, she looks through the door and sees Nate roll down the window of his rental. Carol never hears what words are spoken.

The silent movie begins. Nate's head drops, landing on the steering wheel. She watches as he raises a hand—hitting the steering wheel with his closed fist, three times. Kim covers her mouth with one hand while the other moves to rest on Nate's shoulder.

If I go through this back door to comfort my children out on the driveway, then it will be true, and our lives will never be the same. If I skip into our kitchen to whip up an impromptu lunch… everything will be normal… if I just make lunch. My family will come into the house together, gather round the table as if this were an ordinary visit, and we could all make-believe that Paul is napping in his bed with Jessie hovering over him. Then he'd still be alive. Marvellously alive.

Chapter 33: Straight and Spruce

The funeral planners are seated at their kitchen table, the scent of strong morning coffee permeating the air. In teacher-like fashion, Heather is getting it all down in a notebook. She looks at her brothers. "You and Glen, and Uncle John representing Dad's family... that's three pallbearers."

Glen continues, "And, of course, Bruce will be the fourth."

Carol's heart races but she says what she's thinking anyway. "I think your dad would want Darryl to be a pallbearer." No one objects. Is she doing this to assuage her guilt at having been so angry at Darryl for leaving them, or is she doing this because it's what Paul would want? *A bit of both*, she hopes.

Next Nate speaks in a hushed tone: "Okay, that's five, and the sixth should be George. Dad spent almost as much time with him at the dealership as he spent with us." He adds, almost as an afterthought, "and he was Dad's faithful visitor to the end."

The doorbell rings, offering a much-needed respite from the oddest Saturday morning the family have ever had.

It's a neighbour, with her hands full, the first to get the funeral-food-train started. "Thought you folks could use some lunch."

Carol is reminded of the neighbourhood's reaction to Paul's disease when he was first diagnosed. Their subdivision had all the usual squabbles over fence lines and one-upmanship.

Add to that, the *othering* of the one visible immigrant family on the block—deliberate or not.

Nevertheless, the neighbourhood became their brother's keeper, uniting to shovel the Fletchers' walks in winter, trim the hedge and trees in spring, cut the grass in summer, and pile wood near the garage for their fireplace in fall. It made all the difference.

But Carol believes in her heart of hearts that the neighbours' reaction to Paul's illness went deeper: they knew that if some *uninvited guest* had snuck into one of their homes in the dead of night—Paul would have shown up to help.

The funeral planners get up to leave but Nate stops them with one more story. "Do you remember when the hydraulic fluid in the Hoyer Lift froze? Mom thought Dad was going to be stranded at Uncle John and Aunt Barb's."

"It was thirty degrees below zero that day," Glen adds. "Everyone was trying to figure out what to do, then Dad told us to get a hairdryer."

Nate chuckles. "Sure enough, it worked... and only took a few minutes."

"You were like pioneers at the mercy of a Canadian winter," says Carol.

Stories told, and guests gone home, the house is *oh so quiet*.

Carol must call Darryl, Rosa, Jessie, and Armand. She invites each of them to join the family viewing of Paul the next day: it's what he would want.

And now, Carol has one of her last wifely duties to perform: choosing Paul's funeral clothes. She was the one who had coordinated Paul's business attire in his working days. Paul relied on her to tell him which tie matched which suit. Cherished minutes of intimacy that began their day—she realizes at this moment—so ordinary that she'd completely missed them.

It takes Carol a long time to pick out Paul's tie. She ultimately chooses the midnight-black one they bought on a trip to Australia years before, the one with miniature red *Sydney Opera Houses* popping out.

She knows it's silly, but Paul cannot be barefoot for his last appearance on earth. He needs his shoes. Truth be told, he hasn't really needed his shoes in a long, long time.

As she leaves the house, she holds the clothes hanger with Paul's dark suit, white shirt, and tie close to her body. She slips the letter she wrote to Paul on the day before he died into his suit pocket. As an afterthought, she adds a business card to his jacket pocket too.

The next time she sees Paul's clothes, he's wearing them for the private family viewing. She checks his pocket to be sure her letter and his business card are there.

Carol was expecting to view the remains of a very sick man. Over the years of his illness, Paul's body had become an albatross around his neck, a heavy burden indeed. But as she gazes into the coffin, the broken-bodied man is gone. And in his stead, lies her transformed husband. Not misshapen by chronic disease or distorted by unnatural weight gain caused by sitting in a wheelchair for years or any evidence of bed head.

Paul is straight and spruce. And his beautiful hair in place, exactly the way he had once combed it himself. Carol imagines Paul having taken *high flight* as in the poem of the same name. He has *slipped the surly bonds of Earth and danced the skies on laughter-silvered wings.*

Carol is beside herself. She grabs Glen's arm saying, "Your dad looks so good. He looks so good."

The Uninvited Guest

Her children are alarmed, their mother sounding more gleeful by the minute. Is glee even allowed in a funeral home?

"He looks so handsome," she keeps repeating to all three of her children, grasping at their arms. "Not sick... not sick at all." She mentions his hair, his glorious hair, more than once.

What her family cannot possibly realize is that Carol had lost her *handsome* husband so long ago that she'd forgotten he was there at all. Death has brought him back to her.

Paul's immediate family and his four careworkers stand in that tiny room for a long time, their grief as individual as the people themselves. Sounds of soft crying and gulping noises into Kleenex. No wailing. No gnashing of teeth. But whispers. Sighing. Breathing. The hushed hurting sounds of love.

Much later that evening, Carol will say that it seems a kind of justice that Paul is free of the albatross, returned to his own body—for his last journey. She hears her mother's distinct "for sure" above murmuring voices in their crowded living room.

Eventually, Paul's three children sequester themselves in the downstairs rec room, the one with the fireplace where Nate had offered to *walk his father home* just before his wedding.

Carol's children *should have* said goodbye to their dad when he was old. Shriveled up, silver-haired or bald. That's the deal, isn't it? The natural order of death has been broken but tonight is not the time to reconcile that.

Tonight is the night that three pens scratch into the night. Long, long into the night.

Paul's children write their hearts out, a eulogy, to be delivered at their father's funeral in two days' time.

***

Since the funeral three things have stayed with Carol: one is funny, one is cruel, and the last is beautiful.

The funeral started out as one might expect: the Knights of Columbus, the fraternity to which Paul belonged, led the procession into the church. Once the casket was in place on the bier in front of the altar, the men marched forward, donning their purple plumed showy hats, suit jackets adorned with copious medals, and ceremonial swords dangling at their sides—creating a dramatic sight all its own, harkening back to a forgotten era.

The Knights came to attention and unsheathed their long straight swords, held in pristine white-gloved hands, and formed a sword-canopy over the coffin. They stood in solemn formation for a few minutes.

This was when the moment turned funny, comical-tragical even. Many of the Knights were senior citizens so to hold the tips of their swords perfectly still for any length of time was challenging. The tips of the swords were in perpetual motion, collapsing on and off the tip of the corresponding sword across the way, the metal tinkling sounds breaking the eerie silence in the church. Carol has no idea why she found the sight and sound of the tinkling swords humorous.

As for what was cruel, it was when Carol realized that their two dearest friends—April and Marcel—could not join them at the funeral lunch downstairs after Mass because of an unexpected twist of fate: the church elevator was out of order that day. Their two friends in wheelchairs were left at the church doors waiting for DATS, as Carol and her family celebrated Paul's life in the downstairs parish hall. April and Marcel could probably hear the clatter of plates and soft conversations in the room below them.

As for the beautiful, it was the eulogy, the parting words Paul's three children said to their father and to a church full of family and friends.

The Uninvited Guest

From Heather: "In a family filled with teachers, my dad, without ever stepping up to a classroom blackboard, was one of the best teachers of all."

From Nate: "I don't ever remember Dad telling me that returning a borrowed car with a full gas tank was the right thing to do, but I knew that it was. My father taught by example."

And the final words from Glen: "As Dad's disease advanced, we knew he was still playing catch with us, as in days of old in our backyard. He would straighten up, smack his fist into his glove—ready for whatever life might hurl at him—and tell us to watch this."

And we did.

We certainly did, Carol thinks.

Chapter 34: Walking the Streets of Paradise

One week after the funeral, everyone having gone their separate ways, a phone call nearly does Carol in. It's the funeral home asking to speak to Paul Fletcher's widow.

The funeral director prattles on about sympathy cards needing to be picked up and something about a few extra funeral charges incurred before finally getting to his point. "When will you be in to pick up Paul's urn?" he says, so matter-of-factly that it sounds like he's talking about a suit that has been altered and needs picking up. *Don't they train these people?*

The day does not improve. The phone rings again. She's hoping it's one of the kids. It's not. Someone from Aids to Daily Living is calling to arrange a pick-up time. At first Carol thinks it's a wrong number. But the speaker at the other end of the phone reminds her that there is a hospital bed, a commode chair, a Hoyer Lift, and an IV pole with any leftover solution that need picking up. The caller reads Carol the number of each item. He also mentions that there is a note in the file saying that they are donating a wheelchair to the agency as well. He's calling to confirm the address.

The handicapped life the family had carved out for themselves over years is disappearing at every turn, as surely as did Paul. No more homecare workers with keys to their back door. No more Monday morning emergency calls to Dr. Sneider or nurses dashing in to take Paul's blood. The wheelchair sits idle. The elevator silent. They will even have to turn in the handicapped placard dangling from the mirror in the red truck.

By the time Heather arrives later that afternoon, the Fletchers' accessible home has basically been dismantled. And Carol is beside herself.

"The guy who picked up the Hoyer Lift," Carol explains to her daughter, "was throwing it around like it was a beat-up lawnmower headed for the garbage dump." Carol could not have predicted how strange and upsetting this dismantling would feel. "I couldn't see what he did with the sling," Carol continues, "but I'm sure it's lost by now." Heather listens with concern. "The two men stuffed the mattress from the hospital bed on top of other things, then shoved the rails of the bed on opposite sides of the vehicle." Carol squeezes her eyes shut, as if to erase the image. "But the worst was your dad's wheelchair because the van was already overflowing." Carol is pointing to where the van was parked. "The guy stuffed the chair in the back of the van, slamming the door to keep it in."

"All that after the way Dad looked after things," Heather says ever so softly.

Carol wrings her hands. "Heather, I'm going to miss pushing your dad in that chair, so much... remember how we would sometimes forget to release the brake before starting?" Carol hesitates only briefly. "That man just shoved the chair into his van, Heather. We should never have donated it to those people."

Heather rubs Carol's back doing her best rendition of a mother's love, saying "There, there. Someone will still be able to use that chair, Mom."

"But your dad would be so upset that it's scratched up."

The rest of Carol's week is taken out of her hands. She does not see behind the curtain to know exactly how it comes about, but before she knows it her children, sans their spouses, have descended on the home they grew up in—again. And they have a plan. They're going to paint the bedroom, accessible bathroom, and sitting room.

It gives Carol time. And she needs the time to read the sympathy cards that keep filling the mailbox. She adds them to the huge cache of sympathy cards that the funeral director handed her along with Paul's urn. She keeps a running tally: two hundred and seven cards to date. The trouble is that the numbers annoy Carol. She tells her children as much as they paint away. They are perplexed by their mother's reaction, especially her decision to count the cards in the first place.

Until she explains further: Carol does the math, figuring that if even one quarter of those same people who obviously held Paul in high enough esteem to attend his funeral or send a card, if only that number had visited Paul just once at home while he was handicapped, he would have had a rich social life, despite being housebound.

"Which was not the case," Carol states emphatically to her children at dinner one evening after their backbreaking day of painting.

"But Dad had his regular visitors, Mom... and his family was around... even his caregivers kept him company," Glen pleads.

"But the visiting was piecemeal," Carol retorts. "A person here, a person there... and it was mostly George."

For some reason this discussion harkens back to a TV show all three of her children had watched growing up, and the question its host, Mr. Rogers, would pose daily: *Won't you be my neighbour?*

Maybe if you're sick for a short time I can be your neighbour, but not if you're disabled for a long time and scare me and I don't understand you when you talk and I don't know what to say...

Carol cringes at the thought, as she must admit, that before Paul was struck with MS, she too, would probably have never been friends with April or Marcel.

In the end, it's Carol's children who bring her over from the sympathy-card-dark-side. "Mom, the number of cards is incredible. We even got a card from our family doctor," Glen reminds his mother.

"Think of the beautiful comments people made about Dad," Heather says to her mom.

"Things we might never have known otherwise," Nate adds.

In fact, one of the cards lives up to Nate's explanation. Carol knew nothing of the incident that had occurred some twenty years previous: Paul's former employee outlined in his sympathy card that when he'd first started working at the dealership as an apprentice mechanic, his father had died unexpectedly in Saskatchewan. The squat, unevenly formed handwriting went on to say that he regretted never properly thanking Paul for his kindness. *Not only did Paul give me the time off to attend the funeral*, the man wrote, *but he also gave me money for a bus ticket*. The card was signed, *Luke*.

Carol's favourite card, though, comes from her elderly aunt. She'd inscribed these words in her curlicue one-room-schoolhouse handwriting: *Paul is now walking the streets of Paradise, with Jesus.* This woman knew that Paul had not walked anywhere in a long time.

"No, no, no," Carol says to her children. "Aunt Mary is wrong. Paul is *driving* the streets of Paradise. Driving here, there. Driving, everywhere."

"With Jesus?" Glen quips.

Carol places Luke and Aunt Mary's cards in prominent view on the sideboard that is overflowing with fading funeral flowers.

***

It feels so good to be back working out speech problems with her students. Being near young bodies and young minds seems to offer Carol a future.

"The minute you feel up to book club, just let me know," Barb says one Saturday evening.

"I will but I'm not ready yet," says Carol honestly.

Carol is unsure how to begin the next discussion but knows she's done stuffing her fears. "I need to tell you something, Barb." Barb stops pouring coffee into her cup and looks up. "About the funeral."

"What about it?" Barb asks.

"Well, everyone at the funeral was saying how sorry they were, how great Paul was… all the things that people say at funerals." Carol inhales and exhales slowly. "But I couldn't be a proper widow, except for the black dress I was wearing, because all I was thinking about was how relieved I felt. Relieved that I didn't have to put Paul in an extended care facility like April and Marcel."

Barb puts down her coffee.

Carol is just getting started. "No one wanted to hear how grateful I was that Paul would never have to suffer the humiliation of dangling over the commode chair again, or how he would never have to experience another choking episode, or feel frustrated that he couldn't shake someone's hand or reach up to scratch his itchy scalp."

Tears spill down Barb's cheeks.

Carol continues, "No one attending that funeral wanted to hear that I was happy that Paul would not have to give up one more thing. Ever again. And you know what I am most proud of?"

Barb's eyebrows go up as far as they can go. "What?"

"Paul never got a bedsore. Not even one. After all the doctors, and physio people, and nurses who warned us about them, over, and over again... well, we did it. Paul never got a bedsore. Hours and hours of sitting, and laying in bed too, and, in the end, Paul never got a bedsore."

Two pots of coffee later, Carol brings her confession full circle.

"The one thing I know for sure," she says, "is that our decision to buy the truck was exactly the right one at exactly the right moment."

"Why do you think that was?" asks Barb.

"Well, partly because it was Paul's idea, of course. But it felt like it was one of the few times in all this mess that we were able to give Paul back a bit of the life he had lost... I think that's what it was. Those moments in that truck with Paul, were some of the sweetest I have ever known."

Carol surprises even herself with her next words. "In my whole life."

Chapter 35: Hidden Treasure

Carol's newly painted bedroom (without one scratch caused by a wheelchair pedal not quite navigating a turn) reminds her of something one might come across in a decorating magazine. And there are too many pillows on the bed.

She puts her wedding picture on the bureau below where the TV unit once hung, to give the room some history. 1971, to be exact. Next to it, she places the photo of Paul in the helicopter during the city tour they took on his last birthday, his 51st.

Paul's name is removed from the title of the house. Funny, because in the era in which they married, Carol was too young to even have her name on the mortgage, and now, she owns the house outright. She leaves Paul's name on the utility bills as no one seems to mind, as long as the bills get paid on time. It comforts Carol, somehow, to see envelopes bearing Paul's name arriving in the mailbox.

She does not have to look at the clock to know that 4 p.m. has arrived. She experiences a physical desire akin to what she imagines an alcoholic must face. It does not send her scouring the house for hidden bottles of alcohol, though; instead, she longs for the hospital bed, longing even more to crawl into it beside Paul, amazed at how much she misses the years of ritual hospital bed chats that grounded their lives living with MS.

The Uninvited Guest

Of course, both the hospital bed and Paul have come to an inauspicious end.

Carol begins to pace, rubbing the back of her neck, needing to fill the void. She wanders from her bedroom to the sitting room to her study. She's about to return to her bedroom when the books stacked in formidable piles on the floor beside her desk catch her eye. That's it. She'll organize. It'll impress her children the next time they visit to see the books neatly lined up where the aquarium once sat; she plops herself in her office chair so that she can more adroitly roll from pile to pile of books. Even as a child she was not one to sit on the floor, as do the students in her school hallways. She turns to begin with the books to her left: sitting atop the pile is Paul's small coiled flip calendar.

For years it sat to the right of his lift chair. Her zealous house painters must have set the thing here for safekeeping. It has no year affixed to it, just days and months with a quotation featured on each small page. Carol never noticed its title before: A Daily Calendar. *Using the same calendar year after year would certainly have appealed to Paul's sense of frugality, and I'm sure he's the only one who added entries to the calendar over many years, probably not the intent of the creators.* Carol has no idea if Paul got the desk calendar as a gift or purchased it himself.

Carol flips to today's date: September 29. Two entries above the month, date, and quotation are in Paul's handwriting—so it goes back a while.

She begins at the top of the page reading Paul's handwriting, already showing signs of deterioration: *John felled 2 trees in his front yard, 1991.*

The next entry is an out-of-control scrawl dipping into the words of the quotation that sit on the page. Despite his hands obviously giving out on him, he managed to write: *Temperature today -4 Celsius, 1993.*

Carol reads the entry below the quotation that is in Darryl's handwriting: *Heather learns to make butter tarts, 1994.*

Then Rosa's neat printing beneath that: *Carol dyed her hair, 1995.*

What a wide range of events on that particular day, Carol thinks. She flips through the calendar for the next hour, reading entry after entry. Many are about their three children, documenting when and where they got jobs or who they were dating or a new apartment address. Entry after entry are birthdays, anniversaries, promotion dates, as well as many times and dates of the death of friends or neighbours or church members. Many holiday entries include who went where and when. There are vehicle purchases aplenty, of various folks—always, always noting the make, model, and year of the vehicle. And the colour too.

Some entries are so mundane as to make Carol chuckle, like the one on March 26 that says, *Dishwasher repaired* or the one on April 5 that gives a nod to Daylight Saving Time*: Moved clock ahead one hour.*

Some entries, or lack thereof, confound her. Paul never documented the day that he retired.

Another way to keep his faint hope clause alive, Carol muses.

She must call Heather.

"It's so sad. And funny. And happy," Carol says, clutching the phone as if it's a life raft in the middle of a roiling river.

"I never paid attention to his day calendar." Carol talks right over Heather, who is trying to make sense of this call and her mom's gibberish. "I didn't realize what he was doing. And how detailed it was. Or what it all meant."

It takes Heather another moment to figure out what her mother is talking about.

The Uninvited Guest

"Oh yeah, the calendar... Dad had me write in it a few times too. I remember when he asked me to add my first day of teaching."

"That doesn't surprise me," Carol continues, bemused, "but would you believe your dad asked Rosa to add that Charles Schutz retired in December of 1999? And he documented Rosa's first day in Canada as July 20, 1992."

After fifteen minutes of reading entry after entry aloud, it's the one on February 16, 1997 that is her daughter's undoing: *Ann loses a front tooth.* Carol hears nothing, then realizes that Heather is crying.

Both women in Paul's life come to the consensus that he was giving them a front seat view of the Fletcher history that included all he cared about, all that mattered: his family, the weather, his neighbourhood, commerce, pets, concerts, natural disasters, sports, the government, vehicles, the heavens, the trees and flowers... always the tulips, especially the red ones.

By the next weekend when Carol talks to Glen, she can barely contain herself as she shares the hidden treasure she's unearthed in their home.

"On March 5 your dad had one of the homecare workers write that you and Tracy put a deposit down on a lot." Glen explains that he remembers that calendar sitting next to the globe, but he never really looked at it.

"He also recorded when you and Tracy met, and the address of your first apartment. And I bet you didn't know that one year on April third—Calgary got 45 centimetres of snow whereas Edmonton got none," teases Carol, trying to convey the scope of his father's recordings.

"No, I don't remember that," Glen teases back.

"Does he document any details about his MS?" asks Glen.

"Only two that I noticed," Carol informs her son. "The day he got diagnosed, September 2, 1992, and the day he came back from the University Hospital, January 8, 1999." Carol thinks a moment more before adding, "Oh, I guess it's four if you count the entry about Darryl starting NAIT and when Rosa came to Canada."

"That's so Dad," says Glen.

The minute Carol's off the phone, she realizes she forgot to tell Glen that Paul documented the date the kids had come down from Calgary to install the aquarium in the sitting room. *Next time*, she thinks. *I'll tell them next time.*

Carol's call to Nate goes in a different direction. First off, Nate has no recollection whatsoever of the calendar.

"You must have seen it. It was always in plain view next to his lift chair."

Carol shares mostly the sports and politics entries with Nate, things he's interested in too.

"Dad had Armand write this on October 1. *Gretzky's No. 99 retired by Oilers, 1999.*"

"That is a date to remember," says Nate.

"He also had someone document Pierre Trudeau's death on September 28, 2000. And he noted the time as 3 p.m."

"Wow," Nate says. "That's almost exactly a year before Dad died."

Both mother and son are quiet for a few moments, trying to digest the marvel of Paul. Finally, Carol shares an entry to lighten the mood, "And did you know that you went golfing with Jerry and Max on September 26 in 1992?"

Nate wonders aloud about what might have become of his two high-school buddies.

Knowing how much Nate shares his father's love of nature, Carol reads many of the notations on when this or that was

The Uninvited Guest

planted or bloomed: *crocuses, roses, mayday tree, plum tree, tulips... always the tulips.*

"Gee, I knew Dad loved plants," Nate says, sounding reverent, "but I had no idea how much attention he paid to them."

Carol hangs up the phone, her son's words ringing in her ears. She immediately remembers a phrase—*attention must be paid*—from her favourite play, *Death of a Salesman. Attention must be paid.*

That's what Paul was doing: paying attention to his life. Paying attention to *their* lives too. And to *all* of life. Plowing through all the mire and mud of things, as well as the joy. She mustn't forget the joy.

Carol spends a few minutes searching for an entry about buying the F-150, her heart pounding as she flips though the calendar. She finds it. *Purchased a red Ford today instead of a Chevy. Works with the Hoyer Lift. Bought the floor model from a nice young salesman.*

The entry was longer than usual. It was written by Rosa in March of 2000.

It was there all along. And she missed it. Paul was narrating his story. Their story, all along. Best storyteller ever. Paul. Paul Fletcher.

In the end, Carol leaves her books piled high on the floor of her study.

She places Paul's calendar on her bedside table where the evening shadows dance with the light of the lamp, illuminating Paul's story.

Acknowledgments

Thanks to my high school teacher—Sister Margaret Rose—who made me fall in love with the play Hamlet in her English 30 class. I have never looked back.

Thanks to the Literary Writing Club at Archbishop MacDonald High School that I oversaw with my beloved friend and colleague Lynn Weinlos. I learned a lot from both her and the writing students we taught. Our English Department Head, Wayne Stelter, deserves a thanks too as he attended our *long* evening Lit Nights *faithfully*, providing the writers with an invaluable experience: having their words heard.

Thanks to Eunice Scarfe whose writing classes I attended over the years: some of the very writing prompts she used in class are the impetus for a few chapters in this novel.

Thanks to my friend and colleague Chris Klein who convinced me to take time off school to complete the first iteration of this book, good advice which I am glad I heeded.

My time at The Banff Centre of Arts and Creativity where I was immersed in a community of writers was an exhilarating experience. Thanks to all I met there.

Thanks to Linda Klem who wrote a short story for an ARTA magazine contest: she documented an incident from her own life as fiction. When I read it, a lightbulb went on: I was determined to convert my memoir into fiction.

Thanks to Beryl Forbes who was a fresh set of eyes for my work. Despite never having met Len, she felt that the novel brought him to life.

Thanks to Robert Rice. When he highlighted my character Paul's habit of recording events in his daily calendar, a seed was planted: the novel should end with Paul's words from that calendar.

Thanks to Elaine Merrick who suggested my manuscript could be instructive for people living through a chronic medical condition.

Thanks to the editor, Katie Bickell, whose best advice was, "When the story is big, write small." She also instructed me in ways that I might cut an unwieldy 144,000 word manuscript in half.

Thanks also to an anonymous editor from the Writer's Guild of Alberta who suggested I might focus my novel by cutting some of Carol's meandering stories.

Thanks to Matthew Alba who brought me across the finish line: his comprehensive line-editing, pertinent questions, and word choice queries resulted in a more polished manuscript. His biggest practical contribution though: the tracking of my narrative timeline, *what happened and when.*

Thanks to Gordon Filewych whose artwork graces the cover of this book. The tulip and daily calendar are lovely images that come to symbolize the character of Paul.

Thanks to my sons Kevin and Kenneth whose own creative endeavors in music and film respectively have informed the way I think about the artistic process.

Thanks to my daughter Karen. She has read and reread and read again more iterations of this manuscript than I can count. She never seemed to tire of her mother's drafts, ideas, images, and her crazy need to put words to paper, although being a writer herself has probably helped. Karen put happy and sad faces in the margins of my writing when she was moved. She wrote, "Really, mom?" when I had gone *over the top* and "Yikes!" when I had gone altogether *too far*. An apt word choice or an effective image warranted a "Nice." in the margin. Karen's greatest contribution: allowing me to find my voice to tell this story. I thank her from the bottom of my heart for all her love, help, and support, including this last segment of the journey—self-publishing—which I could not have managed without her!

Many thanks to my husband, Albaro Barrios. His help with the medical information in this novel was crucial, especially the lingo and dialogue doctors and nurses might use to express their ideas. But most importantly, I appreciate his persistence in asking when I was going to do something with my writing. In 2011, he found and framed a magazine ad for a printing company. It said: "Every story needs a book. Make yours." I glanced at it often, feeling Albaro's love and encouragement throughout this lengthy process. He is exactly the kind of cheerleader a writer-wife needs, convincing me that I had a story worth telling.

Thanks to Jamie Ollivier and Rory Dickinson of FriesenPress who made my first foray into the world of publishing less daunting and pleasantly accessible, even for a luddite like me.

And, of course, I must acknowledge my readers because everyone who reads this novel is perhaps in some small way keeping Len Filewych's legacy alive. Thank you. Thank you. Thank you.

Afterword

I have been asked why I write. The answer: my love of fiction has drawn me to great writers—Margaret Atwood, Margaret Laurence, Alice Munro, Grahame Green, Mordecai Richler, Frank McCourt, Miriam Toews, Robertson Davies, F. Scott Fitzgerald, Barbara Kingsolver, W. O. Mitchell, Henrick Ibsen, Jane Austen, Seamus Heaney (whom I knew personally), e. e. cummings, Langston Hughes, William Wordsworth, Shel Silverstein, Robert Frost, William Blake, J. D. Salinger, Leo Tolstoy, Ann Tyler, Eudora Welty, John Steinbeck, Arthur Miller, Tennessee Williams, Anton Chekhov, Toni Morrison, Jonathan Swift—and, of course William Shakespeare.

These writers and so many more made me want to try my hand at their *superb craft*. It's a humbling task, indeed! But it is the *trying* that I so love.

Printed in the USA
CPSIA information can be obtained
at www.ICGtesting.com
JSHW081245290224
57928JS00008B/104